"Mary Fisher has inspired millions of people with the quiet power of her art and her words. In **Uneasy Silence**, she does it again, bearing eloquent witness to cries for justice and compassion."

Darren Walker
President, the Ford Foundation

"Our troubled world desperately needs its renowned elders to share their wisdom, their accumulated experiences, their carefully gained knowledge. They cannot stay silent. I have known Mary Fisher for decades. She exemplifies extraordinary courage, compassion, grace and wisdom. Her brilliant new book, **Uneasy Silence** demonstrates all this and more as it leads you to find your path of courage, your own true voice."

Brian Weiss, M.D.
Best-Selling Author of
Many Lives, Many Masters

"To read Mary Fisher's **Uneasy Silence** is to take an unforgettable journey with a beloved friend."

Raashan Ahmad
Artistic & Executive Director, Vital Spaces

"Through Mary's practice of awareness, we are gifted with a way of being in the world. She has taken wounds in life and danced with them. Her creative acts travel a spiritual path within her. In **Uneasy Silence**, words pass through her extraordinary heart."

Kathleen Glynn
Producer of Oscar and Emmy
Award-winning Film & Television

"Mary Fisher is a one-of-a-kind powerhouse. She has been morally consistent, which we need now more than ever. Her drive comes from being grounded in ethics, not popularity. She has always been willing to challenge economic, health, and educational systems of power and help bring about positive change.

It is a gift to call her a teacher and a dear friend. Her words in this book will inspire all who read it."

David Kessler
Author and Grief Specialist

"To read Mary Fisher's **Uneasy Silence** is to be shown, again, why she tops my list of unique, interesting, authentic, creative and courageous friends."

Keb' Mo' (Kevin Moore)
5-Time Grammy Winning Blues Musician

"Mary Fisher is quite simply an American treasure. She came into my life when my greatest pursuit was finding my own authentic voice. "To be free and be heard" is the lesson Mary is offering all of us in the pages of **Uneasy Silence**, her 7th powerful contribution to American discourse.

For decades, Mary has been lending her voice to those thought to be voiceless while all the while inspiring people over the world to find their own. Funny, fun, honest, and sharp, Mary's **Uneasy Silence** will challenge even the loudest among us to listen, learn, and lead differently."

Laphonza Butler
United States Senator
President Emeritus, EMILYs List

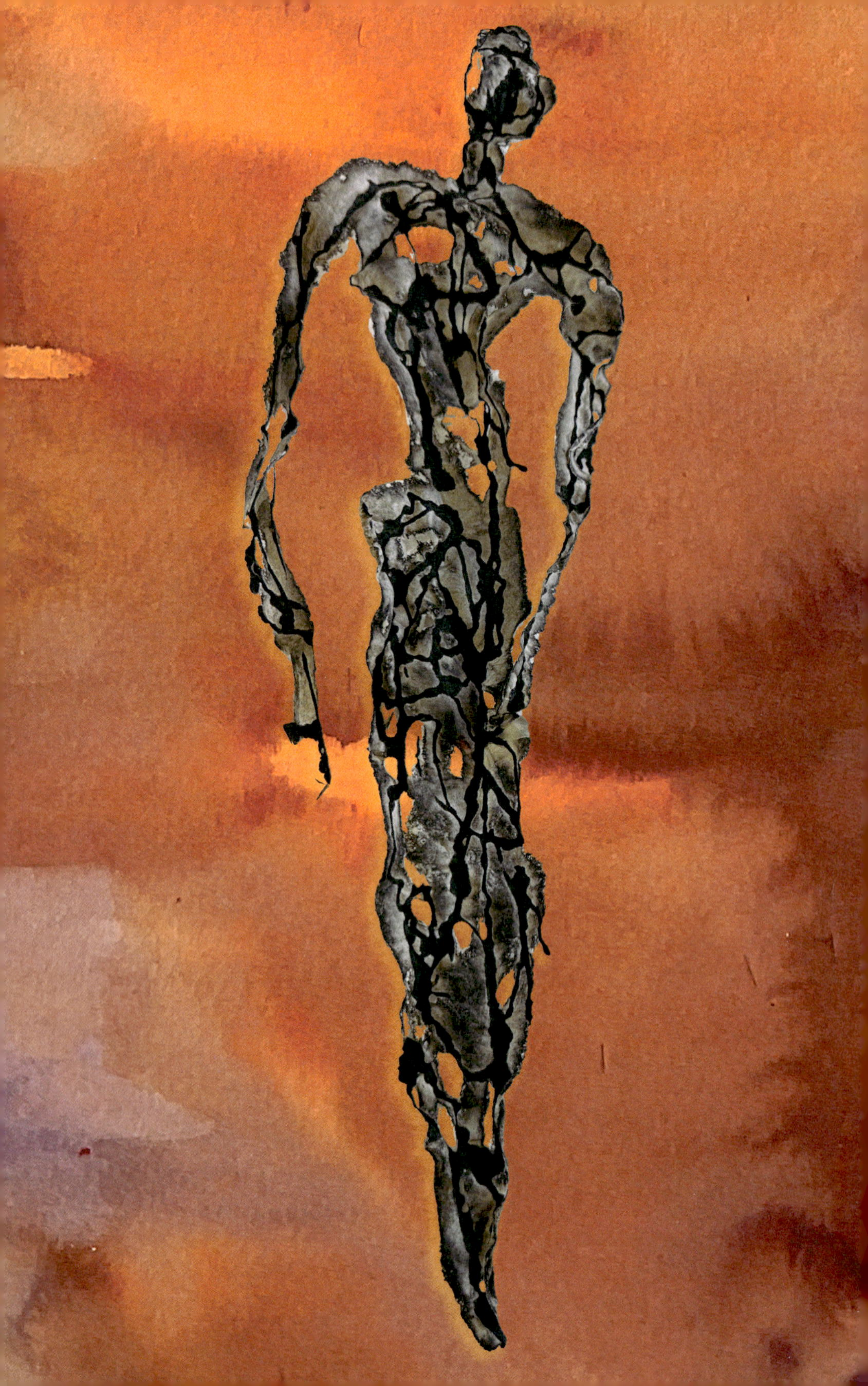

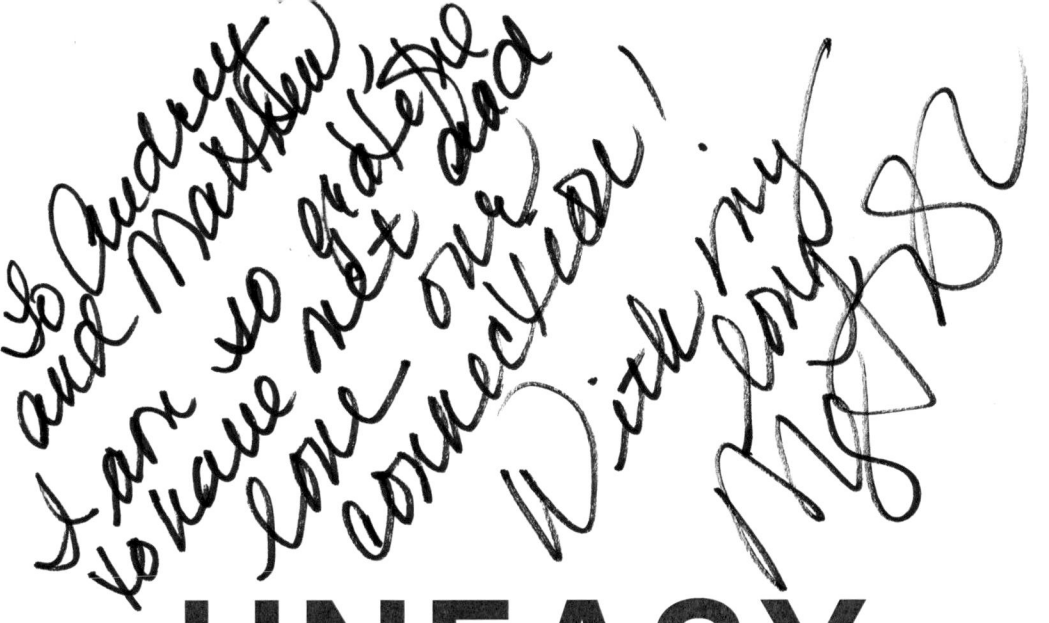

To Audrey and Matthew,
I am so grateful to have met dad our love connection!
With my love,
Mary

UNEASY SILENCE

MARY FISHER

An activist seeks justice and courage
over a lifetime of change

Published by RTM Books
Santa Fe, NM

www.maryfisher.com

Copyright © 2025 Mary D. Fisher

All rights reserved

No part of this book may be reproduced, stored in a retrieval system or transmitted by any means, electronic, mechanical, photocopying, recording, or otherwise, without written permission from the copyright holder.

Cover and interior artwork by Mary Fisher
Cover design by Juliana Um
Author photo by José Picayo

Fisher, Mary, 1948 -
Uneasy Silence, An Activist Seeks Justice and Courage over a Lifetime of Change:

    Also issued as an ebook
    Also issued as an audiobook read by the author

    ISBN: 979-8-218-51656-7

Printed in the United States of America

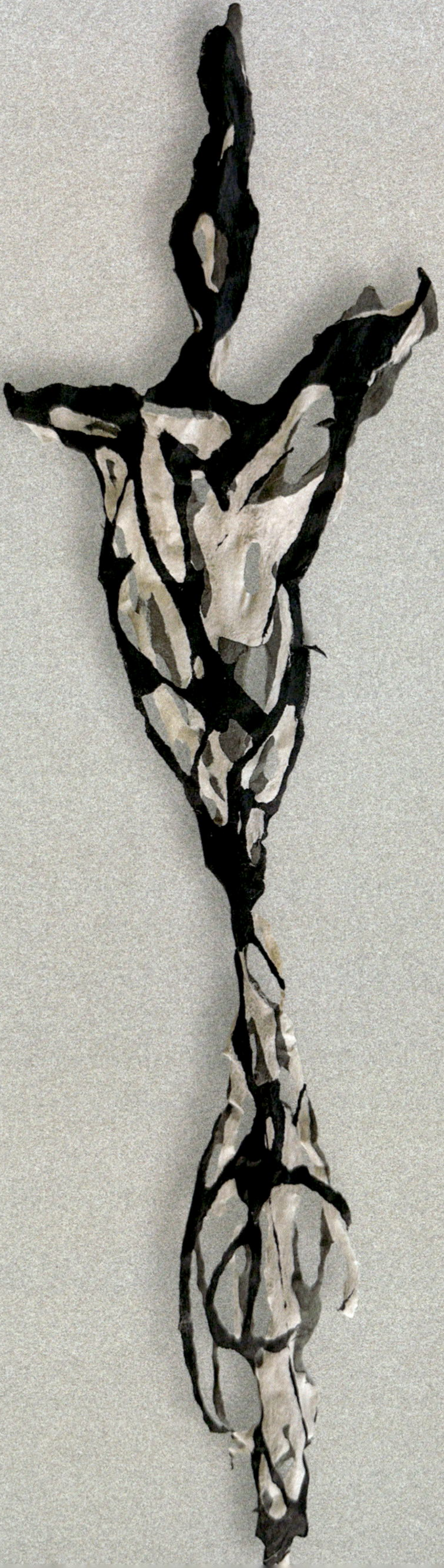

Other Books by This Author

Sleep with the Angels

I'll Not Go Quietly

My Name is Mary

Angels In Our Midst: A Caregiver's Diary In Words and Photographs 1993-1995

Abataka: A Collection of Quilts, Sculpture and Textiles

Messenger: A Self-Portrait

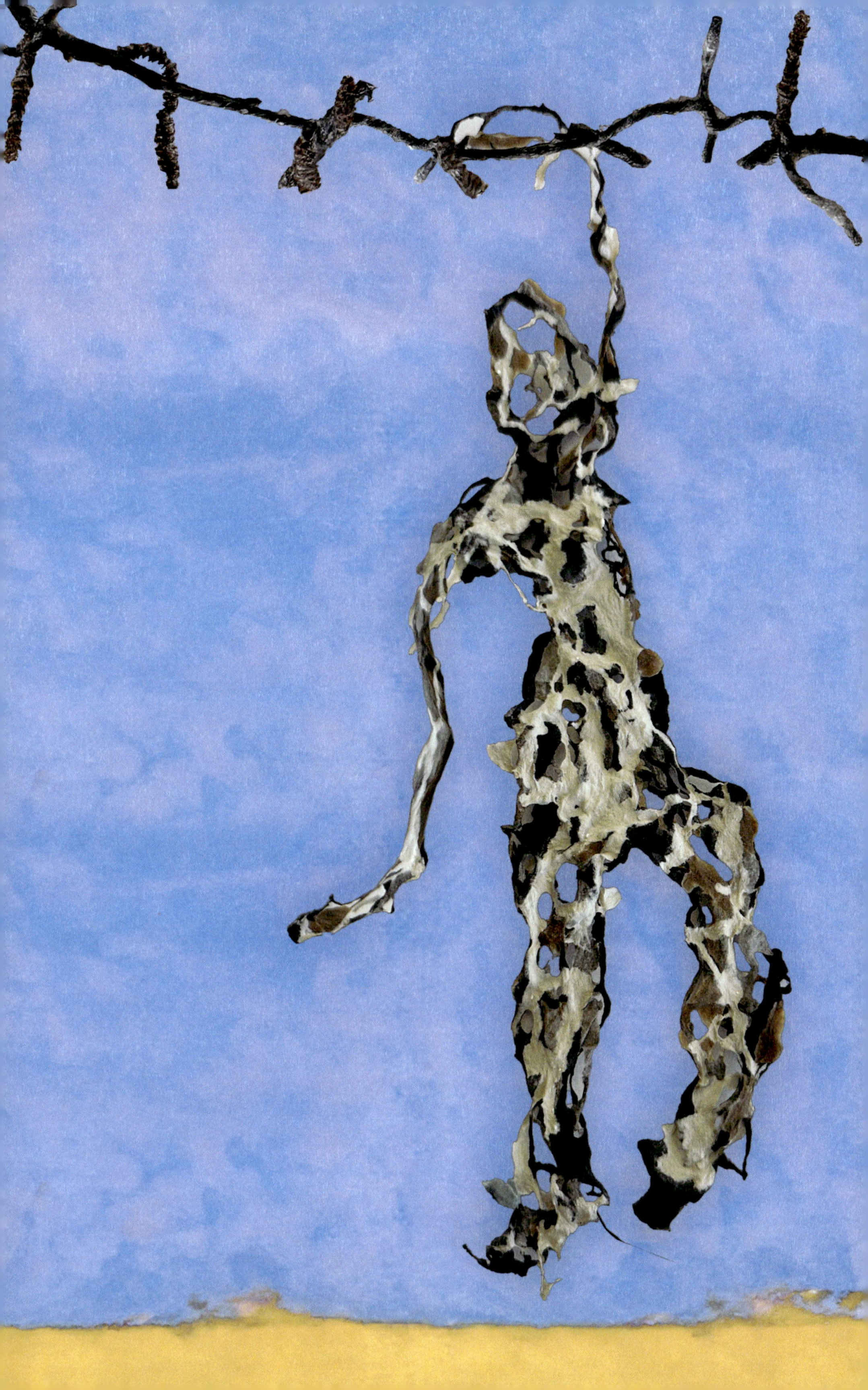

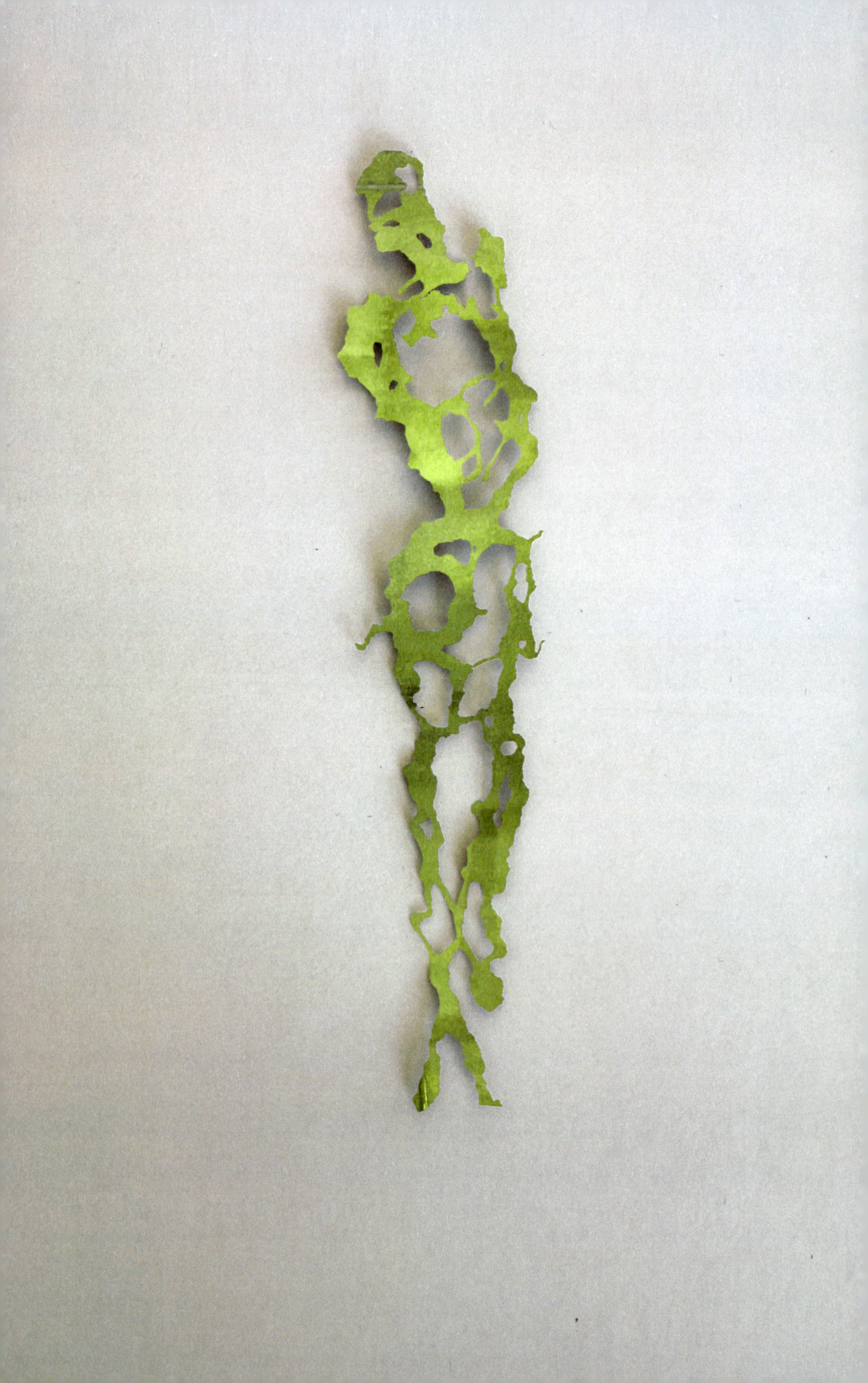

MARY FISHER

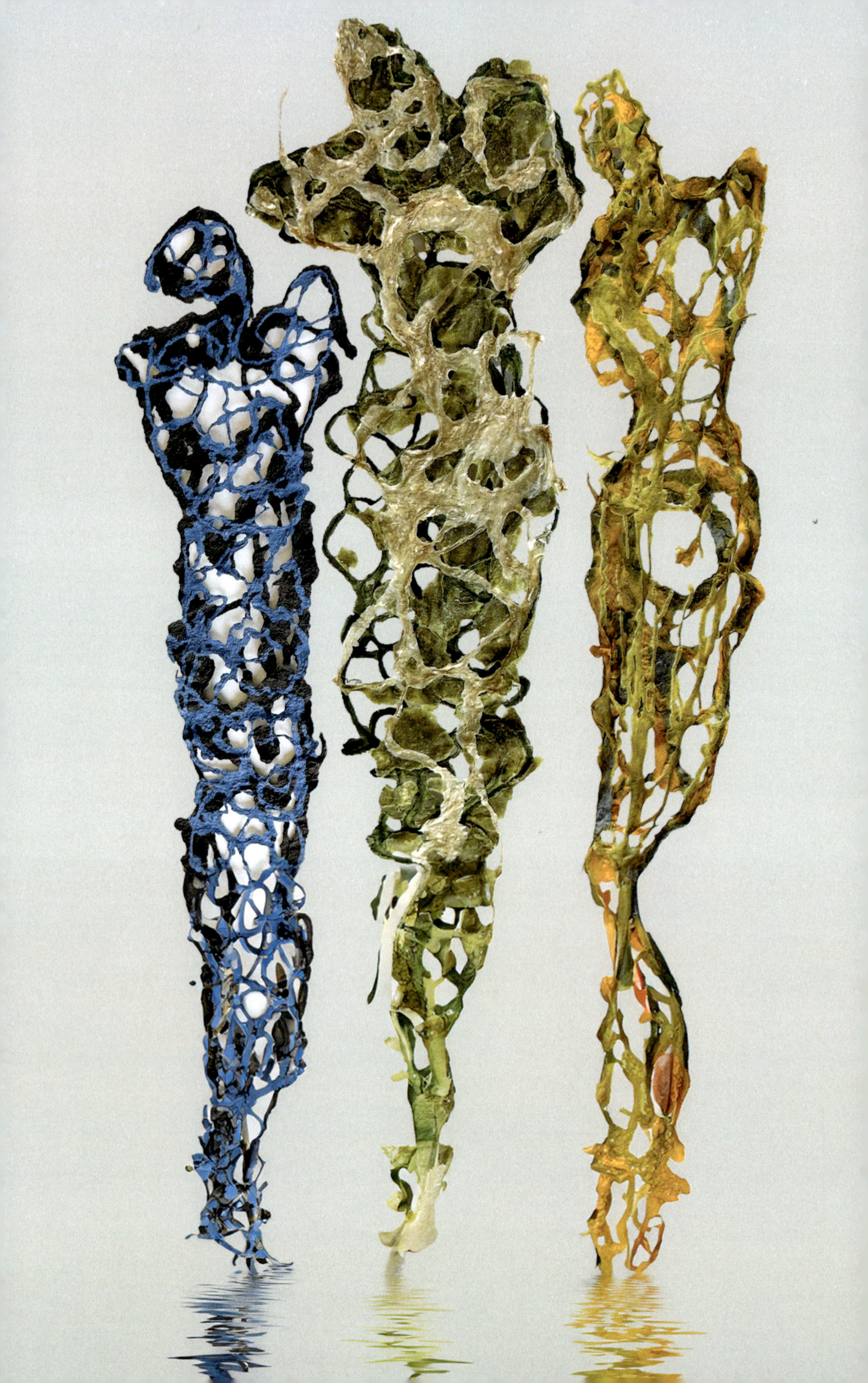

DEDICATION

For my Grandchildren Sloane, Silas and Lenny:

I never imagined living long enough to experience the miracle of you, to thrill to your laughter and to know that there is a future. But I have.

So these stories are for you.

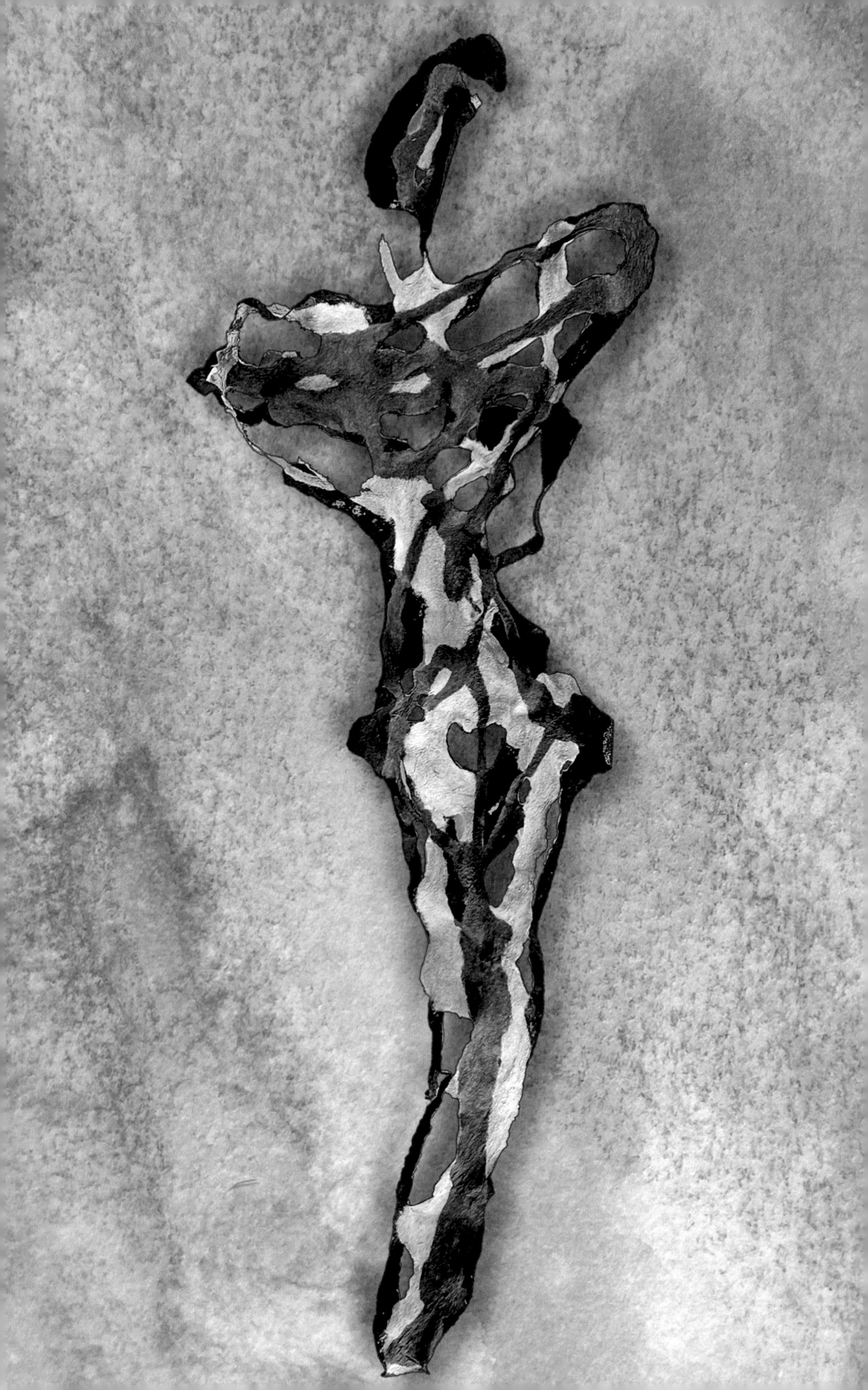

TABLE OF CONTENTS

GUEST FOREWORD by JUDITH LIGHT	1
AUTHOR'S PREFACE	5
EPIGRAPH	11
Chapter 1: SILENCE	13
Chapter 2: WHAT'S TRUTH?	21
Chapter 3: WORDS HAVE POWER	31
Chapter 4: CHOICE	43
Chapter 5: COMING OUT	55
Chapter 6: WHISPERING LOUDLY	69
Chapter 7: WITNESS	79
Chapter 8: SPEAKING WITHOUT WORDS	91
Chapter 9: VOICES AND VIOLENCE	101
Chapter 10: NOT GOING QUIETLY	113
Chapter 11: THE MEASURE OF LOVE	125
Chapter 12: ALTERNATIVE FACTS	135
Chapter 13: POVERTY NEXT DOOR	145
Chapter 14: HARVEST OF HUNGER	155
Chapter 15: THE OTHER	165
Chapter 16: FAMILY OF CHOICE	177
Chapter 17: JOY	187
Chapter 18: STAND UP!	201
AFTERWORD	211
ACKNOWLEDGMENTS	215
BIBLIOGRAPHY	219

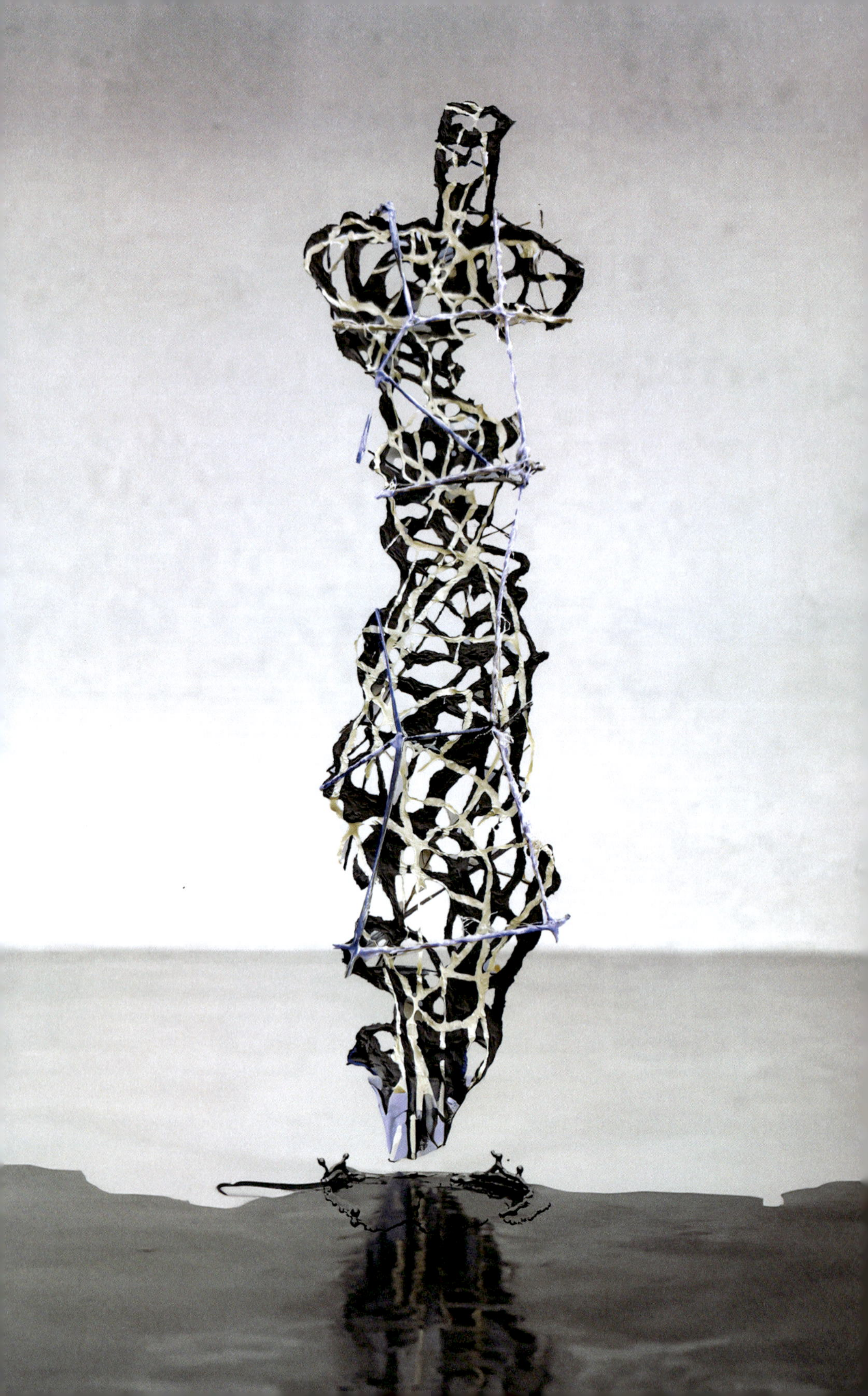

Guest Foreword

By Judith Light

When I put down *Uneasy Silence*, I realized that I'd known Mary Fisher for lifetimes and, in this lifetime, I've known her for decades.

If you've not met her before, you're in for a powerful experience. *Uneasy Silence* is a moving and vulnerable telling of a well-lived life, surprising in its length of years. She was diagnosed with HIV/AIDS in 1991 when it was a death sentence. However, rather than retreat into self-pity, Mary went public with her diagnosis and mounted a one-woman campaign against the bias and cruelty faced by others with the disease.

Many who remember Mary picture her when we first met her, at the 1992 Republican National Convention. This once advance person for President Gerald Ford was wearing a black dress with a Peter Pan white collar offset by a sparkling red AIDS ribbon. The beautiful mother of two preschoolers, in her quiet and steady voice, told the world and *showed* the world she was now the new face of AIDS, struggling along with her LGBTQIA+ brothers and sisters.

"I would never have asked to be HIV-positive," she said that evening. "But I believe that in all things there is good purpose, and so I stand before you, and before the nation, gladly…."

For most of us, that one speech would have been enough; for Mary, it was just a warmup. Since the first time we met, more than 30 years ago, Mary and I have shared a deep commitment to advocacy for those who cannot advocate for themselves. We've swapped late-night calls and introduced each other at public events. We've worked side-by-side to make a difference in the lives of others. In her life with AIDS and, later, her struggle with cancer, she's proven to be a most remarkable advocate: honest, humble, funny, unstoppable, inspiring.

Mary has written six other books, two of them memoirs; however, **Uneasy Silence** is different. It's Mary's reporting in a new voice: a voice that came out of the isolation of the Covid Pandemic; a voice that longs for community and calls us to find it with her; a voice familiar to all who've experienced inexplicable pain and grief. In fast-paced stories and stunning examples, she urges us to answer brutal politics by being kinder and gentler, and truly listening to one another.

The voice of **Uneasy Silence** is unmistakably that of my sister in advocacy, Mary. A familiar voice, seasoned by the knowledge that we are not alone. A self-aware voice, modest but bold. An advocate's voice now layered with age and ripened with wisdom. If she's outspoken it's because she's fearless, focused on what's true not necessarily what's comfortable. She brings a connectedness, grounded in courage, in spirituality and in the certainty that we are here for a purpose: service to others.

Mary has been a gift in my life. You'll also know her as a gift when you finish this book. You'll want to pass along the gift of Mary to friends and family.

Tell the world that Mary Fisher did not die. She's here, full of life and grace, inviting us to stand with her, bearing witness to truth with a new clarity and a stunningly fresh voice: so loud, so proud, even within an uneasy silence.

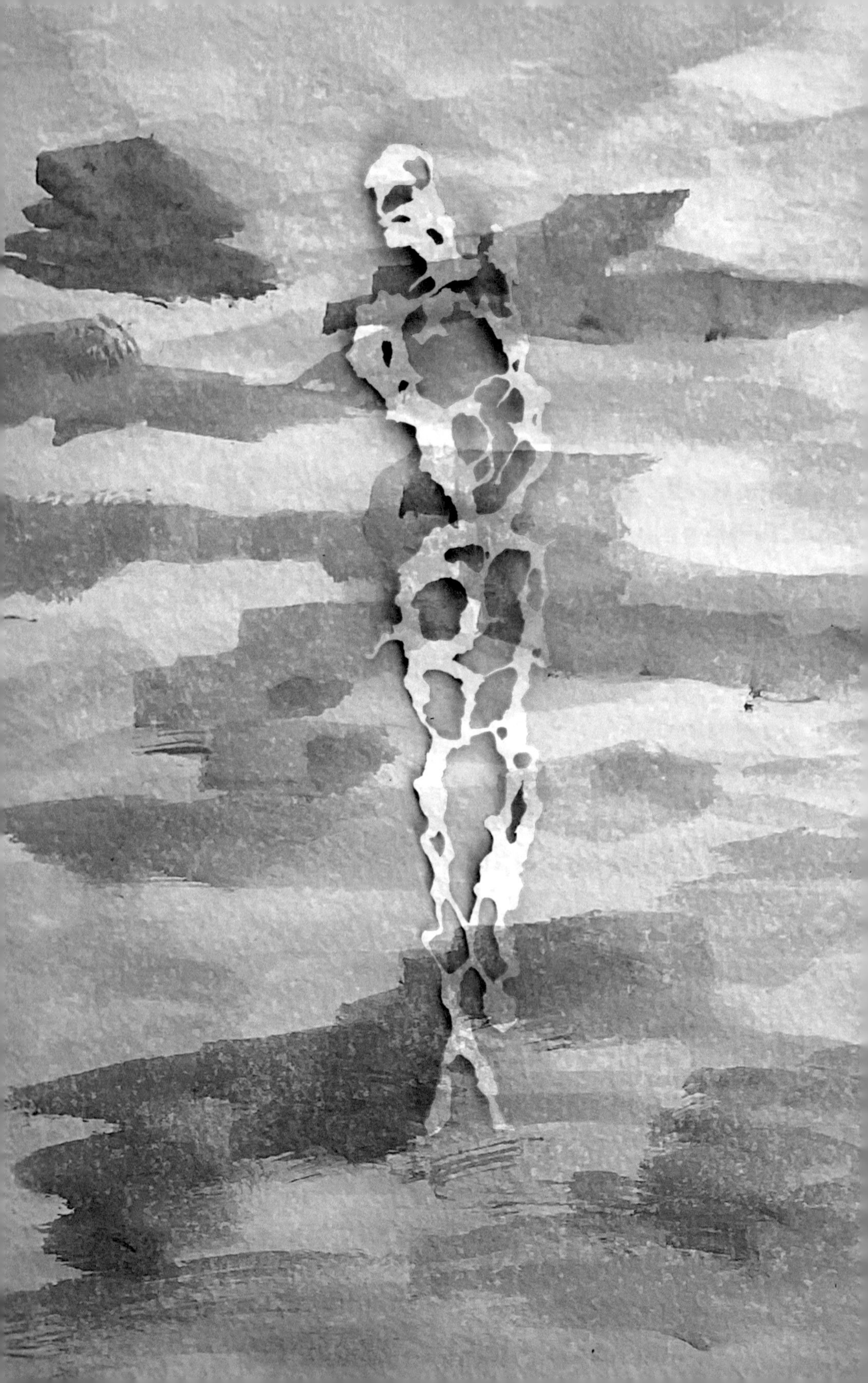

PREFACE

It's been a decade-and-a-half since we published my second memoir, *Messenger: A Self Portrait*. Since then the world has changed in ways that were, fifteen years ago, unimagined and often unimaginable. So have I.

I suppose having three memoirs could be embarrassing, as if I couldn't quite make up my mind the first time. But that's not how I got to three of these. The first — *My Name Is Mary* — was the story of my life as a young mother dying of AIDS. It was current in 1995 but outdated when antiretroviral drugs converted AIDS from a lethal to a mostly chronic disease in the late '90s.

My second memoir — *Messenger: A Self Portrait* — was written in 2012 while I was suffering the aftermath of breast cancer and related surgeries. Life was no longer just about dying; it was focused on living. Even so, I never expected to stay well enough, long enough, to justify another book more than a decade later. But here we are, and so much for expectations.

If any single event triggered my desire to create a third memoir, my seventh book, it was the COVID-19 Pandemic that found America in early 2020 and is not erased yet.

Reconsidering My Story.

In July of 1991 my diagnosis as an HIV-positive woman was confirmed. In August 1992 I gave a somewhat famous speech at the Republican National Convention in Houston. When I left Texas to go home with my two toddlers, I had become "the AIDS lady," "the blonde who gave that speech" and "the only Republican with AIDS." In the thirty-plus years since then I've given countless interviews and speeches, mostly about life with AIDS. My books have tracked my progress from dying to living (and to occasionally dying again), from being a mother to being a grandmother. My life has proven much longer, vastly better and brutally harder than I had imagined possible the day I was told "I'm sorry, Mary, your test was positive."

The COVID-19 Pandemic changed me. My life is a collection of stories of change, and this was a Big One. I had extended stretches of time alone to remember my own past. The alone times brought a spiritual depth to how I see this life, its preciousness and its purpose. For the first time in decades, I was no longer traveling and giving speeches, no longer being self-defined by AIDS or illness. Instead, I was homebound with hundreds of millions of others, masked and terrified, imagining myself on a ventilator as life was sucked from my body.

Constant news broadcasts counted the sick and dying. New York City ran out of body bags. To slow the pace of infections, nursing homes prevented families from holding the hands of dying parents, mates from touching their fading spouses. As the numbers of the infected rocketed upward, self-promoters laid down a blanket of incompetence and lies.

Within days of the quarantine that put us at home, George Floyd was murdered and Black Lives Matter roared to life. I watched and listened and realized more clearly than ever the brutalities Black men (and women) have endured throughout my lifetime. I saw myself — small, white and privileged — in a world of Black trouble.

Television became my window to the world. What I saw was the poor, the hungry, the homeless on nearly every broadcast channel. I couldn't escape the reality that those with the least were suffering the most. I could order food delivered to my apartment but nearby the poor became disproportionately infected, and then poorer, and always hungrier. The weight of injustice grew heavy.

Books and broadcasts made me wonder how the richest nation on earth did not feed its own children, would not embrace its own elderly, and left its professional healthcare heroes too financially drained and too physically exhausted to go on. I began to ask what part I play in sustaining the injustice and the inequity. Was it true that neighbors needed to become strangers? Was it really the case that all compassion for The Other had evaporated in our isolation, in our dread of the virus and our fear of death? Is it true that our nation is divided by castes and that I, by birth and adoption and the undeniable benefits of injustice, have lived three-quarters of a century as a member of the ruling caste — and never knew?

Dying Again.

When the Pandemic's spread slowed, I was slated to have a relatively common surgical procedure on my eyes. While it may have been routine in the big scheme of things, it proved to be nearly lethal when I was over-anesthetized with fentanyl. Someone wasn't paying attention. The surgeon finally noticed that my breathing had stopped; if he had looked closely, he'd have noticed that my heart had also stopped beating. By ordinary standards, I was dead.

I came to in a nearby hospital's emergency room after an ambulance ride I still do not remember. Since I'd apparently been kept alive by chest-pounding, quick-thinking medics, I was brought back to life where I could wonder, "Why am I still alive?!?" My belief is that if we have life, we have purpose. But I couldn't shake the notion that I'd lived long enough and that I really didn't need some new purpose. Honestly, I was ready to go.

The effects of the botched surgery slowly wore off. Given a few months of quiet reflection and a series of conversations with thoughtful advisors and friends, I concluded that if I have one more life in me, already at an age I never expected to see, I may also have one more look at the narrative of my life, the stories that now stretch over three-quarters of a century.

I'd gone into surgery hoping to improve my eyesight. I suppose we achieved that in ways I'd not anticipated: I was enabled to see life differently, my life and the lives of others around me. More than ever I see a nation full of troubles and triumphs, desperate poverty and unparalleled wealth, miracles in science and hopelessness in prisons. It's all been here for a very long time, but I'm experiencing it in new, sometimes hilarious and sometimes painful ways. I want to stand up, reach out and speak out. So…a third memoir.

Others.

I'm not the only one who has changed during the days of the Pandemic. As my friend Elise Loehnen reported in her recent treatise *On Our Best Behavior: The Seven Deadly Sins and the Price Women Pay to be Good*:

> *I've been writing this book amid a pandemic, a racial reckoning, climate instability, and war. It's scary out there, but it also feels like a hopeful, albeit strange, time. I think of the past several years of disruption as the turmoil required for the change we need: We were woken up, startled out of complacence, and made to look at what we didn't want to see, at what festers beneath the surface. ...And while we must still contend with gross injustice, inequity, and an increasingly unstable, overtaxed, and angry planet, it seems that increasing numbers of us recognize it's time to push toward and fight for a more balanced future. Hopefully, the hurdles that bar our progress will continue to fall. [pp. xxv-xxvi]*

The chapters in this book are stories of discovery. Some were subtle with gigantic consequences. Others were trivial, or embarrassing, or outrageous. All taught me something, often when I had zero interest in learning. Strung together, the chapters make up a life narrative of an accidental activist. I'm in my eighth decade. Having made it this far, telling the truth is easier, climbing stairs is harder, and worry about what others say or think of me has nearly disappeared.

I'm still changing because I'm still breathing — despite the eye surgeon's anesthesiologist.

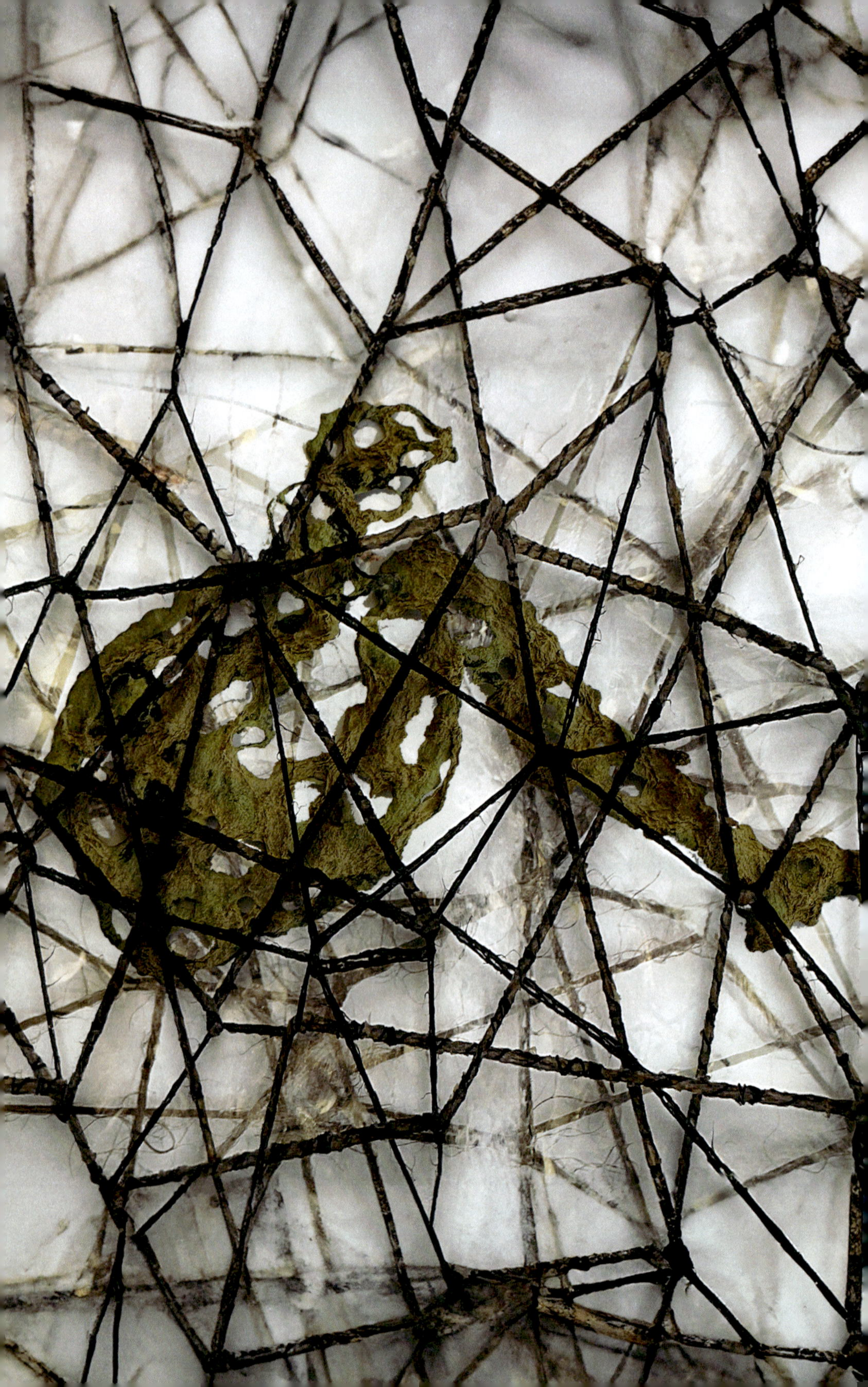

Our lives begin to end the day we become silent about things that matter.

Martin Luther King, Jr.[1]

Note to Epigraph

1. We presume this quotation originated with the Rev. Dr. Martin Luther King, Jr., but we do not know. Certainly it echoes his March 8, 1965, sermon in Selma (AL) where the blood of civil rights marchers streamed over the planks of the Edmund Pettus Bridge on "Bloody Sunday." (For a detailed description of this event, see the Pulitzer rewarded biography of the late Congressman John Lewis, *His Truth is Marching On: John Lewis and the Power of Hope* by Jon Meacham.)

   "Deep down in our non-violent creed," said King in his sermon, "is the conviction there are some things so dear, some things so precious, some things so eternally true, that they're worth dying for."

   Then he sharpened his point: "A man of 36 might be afraid his home will get bombed, or he's afraid that he will lose his job, or he's afraid that he will get shot, or beat down by state troopers — and he may go on and live until he's 80. But he's just as dead at 36 as he would be at 80. Because a man dies when he refuses to stand up for that which is right. A man dies when he refuses to stand up for justice. A man dies when he refuses to take a stand for that which is true."

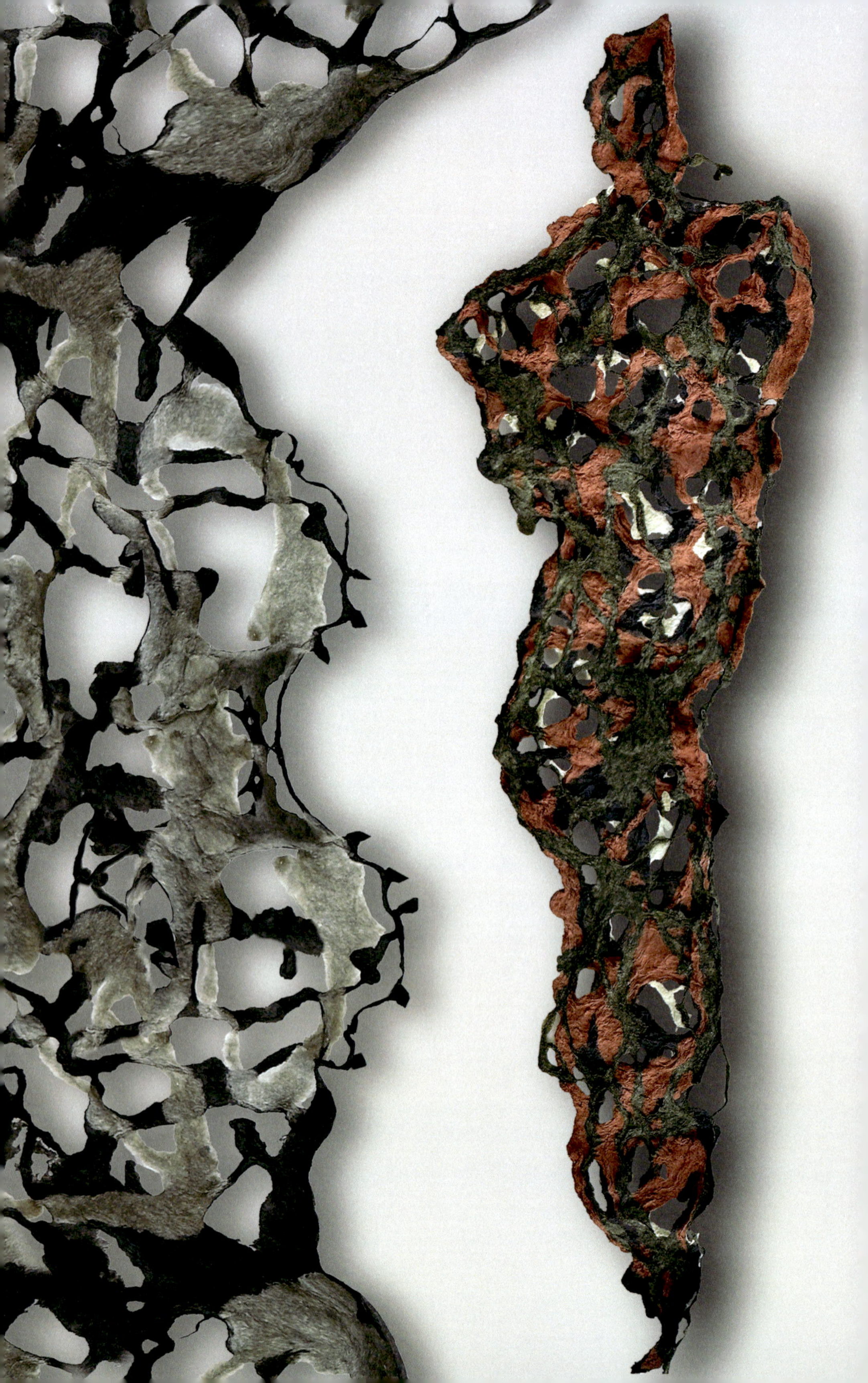

CHAPTER ONE

Silence

The voice of conscience is so delicate that it is easy to stifle it; but it is also so clear that it is impossible to mistake it.

Germaine de Staël[1]

In 2015 I had moved to Palm Beach to care for my ailing mother. After her passing, I relocated to Los Angeles to be nearer children and grandchildren. I arrived in Los Angeles in 2020, just as the Pandemic was also moving in. I took that personally. From the first reports of COVID-19 through all the months of isolation, masks, 6-foot gaps in the grocery store line — through it all, I felt as if it was a deadly, coiled enemy that was just waiting to strike me as I came by.

The global horror started quietly enough, with reports of a virulent virus that might have escaped a research laboratory — a "lab leak" — in Wuhan, China. China denied it. Scientists affirmed it. I sort of believed it. By March 2020, the Pandemic was the lead story across the US and around the globe on every news source, every day, and, for those of us who don't sleep well, every night.

As the initial weeks ground on and the horrors of death and dying became almost commonplace, I pulled increasingly inward. I was doing more than following the rules, which were especially strict in California. I was actively, excessively isolating. Most of my life has been full of people: sons, friends, neighbors, fellow artists, studio colleagues, women's groups, women with AIDS, public appearances. But as the Pandemic grew ever more threatening, so did my withdrawal. I stayed away from people I knew well. I "tested" obsessively. The virus wasn't just something "out there." It was knocking on my door, threatening my life, bringing fear in ways both rational and irrational. I lived a life of terror. And I became profoundly, almost indescribably, quiet. Even whispered words caught in my throat.

Born of the Forties.

I arrived in this world in the fading shadow of World War Two (1948) and spent my earliest years in Bluefield, West Virginia, a stone's throw from Louisville, Kentucky, where my mother's parents, Harry and Florence Switow — Papaharry and Flohoney — doted on their first grandchild: me. As I've said elsewhere, "There was no doubt that I belonged here. They fussed over me as a toddler and I paid for their attention with Shirley Temple curls and curtsies, dancing and singing on cue when the adults were gathered."[2]

My mother was the quintessential Southern Belle. She had good taste and fine style in design, in dress, and in polite behavior. She outfitted me in all things "girlish" from shiny shoes to the ribbons in my hair. It was fine for my brother, two years my junior, to jump in springtime mud puddles and come home dripping with slop. I was to be above such miscreant doings. Boys could roughhouse; girls dressed their dolls. Boys could be aggressive and fight; girls were meant to be genteel and modest, sugar and spice and all things nice. You know the ditty that shaped our lives:

> *What are little boys made of?*
> *What are little boys made of?*
> *Snips and snails*
> *And puppy-dogs' tails*
> *That's what little boys are made of.*
> *And what are little girls made of?*
>
> *What are little girls made of?*
> *Sugar and spice*
> *And everything nice*
> *That's what little girls are made of.*

Dr. Robin Harwick reminds us that adults have used the rhyme as a "way of saying, 'stop it,' the way you are behaving is not lady-like." The poem, she says, was used to "put me in my place and to silence me. It also sent the clear message that what was allowable for boys, was not allowable for girls."[3]

The grandmother in me will fight to the death to enable my grandchildren to escape the biased stereotypes of gender. I'll teach any granddaughter that she may jump in mud puddles and match her brother blow-for-blow. I may love their curls and cuteness, but I do not want them to be defined by sugar and spice.

In the 1940s, in Louisville, Kentucky, girls were girls and boys were boys and never the twain were confused. Gender was divided and frozen in place. The culture had its expectations and we learned them well. I was a girl…sugar and spice and everything nice.

Raised to Be Good.

My first memoir nearly thirty years ago opened with an 8-word truth: "All my life I've wanted to be good."

I've admittedly redefined what it means to "be good" and, in the process, I've come to see how profoundly I've been shaped by the belief that to be good is to be quiet. I'm a living illustration of Yollanda Zhang's 2018 article whose title tells the story: "'Good Girls Are Quiet': How Society Tells Our Daughters to Self-Silence." Nicole Thaxton could have had me in mind when she wrote "good girls don't learn relational skills like voicing their needs, placing boundaries, or conflict resolution. It's best to be polite, stay quiet, please others, hide our feelings, and never be rude."[4] Mind you, I'm well into my seventies and the echoes of that tradition still haunt me. I hear it all these years later: "Good girls are quiet girls."

I now know that when keeping our thoughts to ourselves, it's only our speech that has stopped, not our brains. A century ago courageous women risked reputations and lives in pursuit of the vote. The term "suffragette" was intended to slander and diminish them. They marched then, and we march today, because even our occasional silence never stopped our thinking. We are proud to be suffragettes. We were silent, after all, not stupid. Unexpressed thoughts are silence, that's all. We internalize but don't necessarily vocalize. We maintain our quiet even, or perhaps especially, when chaos and contradictions appear all around us. In ways sometimes amusing and sometimes deadly, women of my generation were taught to keep silent. Even when violated in grotesque ways, we were warned that breaking the silence would cause us even more harm. We were not only silent. We were silenced.

Take my earliest memories with George, for example, my biological father. I loved George, my mother's first husband. He was my daddy with a great smile and an infectious laugh.

The day my parents' marriage was crashing into its unhappy end I had noticed that George was loading things from the house into his car. Something told me that this was no ordinary car-loading; something was going on that three-year-old me could sense but not understand.

So I asked, "What are you doing?" No response.

"Why are you loading your car?" Silence. "Where are you going?" "Ask your mother."

George never said goodbye. No hugs. No reassurances. No explanations. Nothing but a deeply uneasy silence. When I asked my mother what was happening, she said "Daddy's leaving."

"Why?"

"Well, because he likes football and I don't, and you need to be a big girl now."

Being a big girl was code for "don't ask any more questions." It was clear to me, even at three years of age, that something was terribly wrong and that, to be good, I couldn't ask any more about it. To be good was to be quiet. I could think but not speak, worry but not talk. When in doubt or facing what was unanswered, proper behavior was, in a word, silence.

What I could not have understood in 1951 was that there had never been the embarrassment of a divorce in the Switow family. I doubt that I knew what the word "divorce" meant. I imagine my mother also took refuge in the silence of private shame. She knew the stain she was bringing to her family. No one needed to hear her confess it. I suppose it was easier to blame football than experience the agony of heartbreak.

I somehow knew that this event, this car-loaded abandonment by George, was a private matter. I was not to report outside the family. What was expected of me then and for years to follow was clear: Be good and live quietly in that uneasy silence that answers none of your heart's questions. What's in the family stays in the family. It's private. We don't discuss it in public. In fact, we don't discuss it at all.

In the absence of an explanation, I was left to assume, as children do, that I had done something terribly wrong, that I was the cause of whatever drove George off. It must have been my fault.

I had truly wanted to be a good girl. I wanted my daddy back. But what I knew was the silent home of guilt and shame.

Notes to Chapter One

1. Anne Louise Germaine de Staël-Holstein, née Necker, 1766-1817, commonly known as Madame de Staël. She was a prominent woman of letters and politics in both Paris and Geneva. The daughter of a banker father and salon hostess mother, she was outspoken in both literary and wealthy circles. She was a severe and persistent critic of Napoleon, writing vigorously against his "tyrannical nature and ambitions," which eventually cost her her freedom. Napoleon had her exiled and, according to generally reliable witnesses, persecuted before she died, four years prior to Napoleon's passing.

2. Mary Fisher, *My Name Is Mary: A Memoir*, p. 36; Scribner, NY, NY, 1995.

3. Robin Harwick, PhD, Medium, February 22, 2020.

4. Yollanda Zhang, Archives of HuffPost Canada, June 6, 2018. Ms. Zhang describes the ways in which her parents were teaching her six-year-old daughter not simply to be a listener, or to speak wisely, but to remain silent. Her parents, she wrote, "have placed a premium on behaviours that are submissive: being quiet, being seen but not heard and being a good listener. My daughter is internalizing these values.... It takes away some of my daughter's voice and tells her that, in order to be a 'good girl,' she needs to be quiet."

   Dr. Nicole Thaxton is a board-certified, Licensed Professional Counselor. She founded the Atlanta Wellness Collective and is widely regarded as a go-to source on high functioning anxiety and mental health. In reviewing her own life, she says she was born a high achiever, writing "Let No One Outwork You Today" on her bedroom wall, when she was eight.

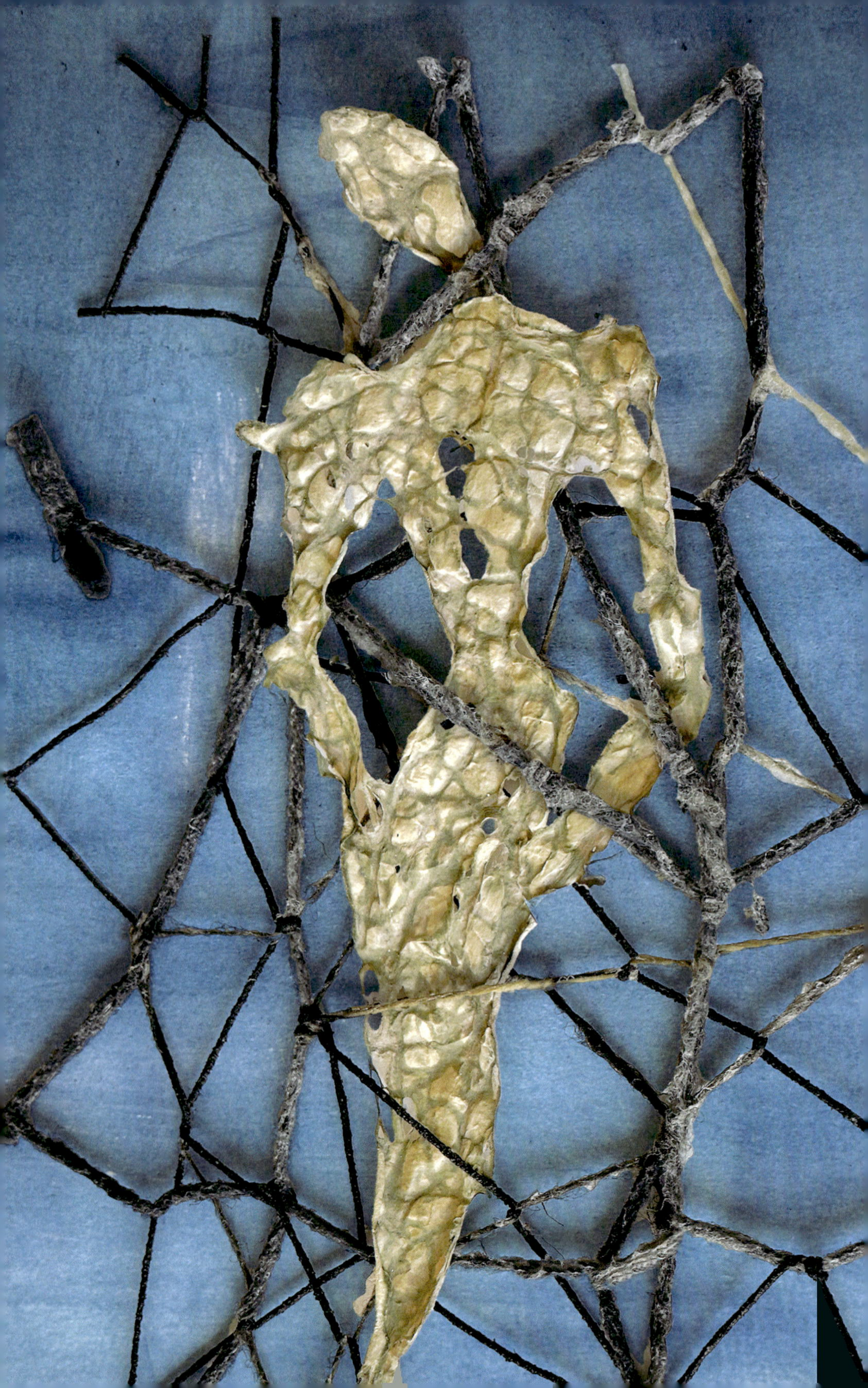

CHAPTER TWO

What's Truth?

Before there was a United States of America, there was enslavement. Theirs was a living death passed down for twelve generations.

Isabel Wilkerson[1]

I've known a score of therapists who believe the most causative realities in our lives are often the quiet secrets we squirrel away. We try to dismiss even from our memories things too painful to be accepted. The past quarter century has brought us new understanding of the impact of trauma from a Marine's post-traumatic stress disorder (PTSD) to my own memories of how, as a child on an airplane, I was fondled by a stranger.

We lock some memories into our past. We don't want to visit them, admit them, allow them to define us. If they begin to seep out, they fill our reservoir of secret guilt, too agonizing to be admitted even decades later. Although we may have been at an age of total innocence, we feel a sense of shame that scars our sense of ourselves. We promise ourselves that we'll take these incidents to our graves. We hide these realities as valiantly as we can, certain that silence somehow equals safety. But it doesn't. In the strained silence of my memories, that stranger's hands are still exploring my body.

I had known periods of quiet long before the recent Pandemic and I was well-acquainted with silence. While still a grade school student, I had learned pointed lessons in keeping safe by keeping silent while at home. When my (second) father, Max Fisher, appeared at the dinner table after a day of work, we children shrank into glances and whispers. I can still hear the silverware clinking on an empty plate. If we did nothing that broke the silence, we wouldn't get in trouble.

The rule in the Michigan house where I grew up was clear: Stay quiet when asked about what you did with your childhood friends. Say nothing when asked about your mother's drinking or hidden behaviors. Don't talk. Don't draw attention to yourself. Silence was the safest territory.

But safety isn't resolution, and silence can be nothing more than hiding. As children and adolescents, it offers us no answers to the hard and haunting questions. It leaves us to wonder, and often to dread, what realities are afoot in our world. We don't quite know and therefore we guess.

Over time, we learn to become the source of our own explanations, right or wrong, but ours. As adulthood dawns, so does judgment about what sources can be believed and accepted. We trust this report because it comes from a reliable source; we reject that story because we know it comes from an unreliable or questionable person. Eventually we become adults, and we say to ourselves that there can't really be "alternative facts." Can there?[2]

It isn't an entirely rational process. Much of this growing awareness of the truth is a feeling, a sensibility, a comfort or discomfort. Something is being described in ways that don't feel real or true to us — and the key is they don't *seem* right. We're being told something that doesn't jibe with what we believe. Someone is feeding us data they want us to accept but it doesn't settle next to what we believe is reality. Something, even if we don't know quite what, is wrong. We have an itch, a hunch, a notion that the stuff coming our way doesn't square with our experience. It leaves us no more educated, no more certain, living in an uneasy silence.

Despite all the contradictions and violations — from misinformation generated by Artificial Intelligence to spouses who wander from their vows — with time and experience we earn a sense of knowing confidence. We think, mostly correctly, that we can recognize truth when we see it.

Learning to Please Others.

If we're sandwiched between a warring husband and wife at the family's Thanksgiving table, we may go looking for silence. It's both a choice and a strategy. Anything we say may be interpreted as the first volley in a fight they're waiting to start. We bite our tongue until it bleeds. We try to spare the idiot to keep the peace. It's an uneasy and irritating silence but one we prefer to open warfare.

Years ago, it was easy to be with my teenage friends away from our homes. We liked each other, and we weren't troublemakers. We knew nothing of riots and rebellions, of urban anger and racial profiling. "Our indiscretions involved beer, not LSD. Economically, we were pampered. Culturally, we were indulged. Politically, we were Republican."[3] And with only rare exception, we were white.

Then came Detroit's riots, five days in July of 1967 filled with smoke, bloodshed, and rage. My friends and I watched from a safe distance as flames shot up from the city and clouds of fury rolled across the Canadian border. We stayed in our well-protected suburbs while Detroit burned and we wondered why.

"It doesn't concern you," was my father's response when I asked what was happening, or maybe why. He wasn't mean, just dismissive. "It doesn't concern you" was the end of it as far as he thought. He might as well have said "because they like football and I don't."

A half-century passed before I realized that I had been carrying the burden of Detroit's riots all my life. I was uneasy, deeply uneasy. When Isabel Wilkerson introduced me to the truth in her stunning *Caste: The Origins of Our Discontents*, I immediately recognized the truth that the smoke and blood did absolutely concern me. The riots were, in fact, all about me and the legacy I've inherited as a privileged white woman in America.

Centuries of racial injustice were feeding the flames that came to life in Detroit and other cities in the late '60s. The riots came at the end of a very long fuse lit by Federal housing policies, employment discrimination, estate protections for the wealthy, mortgage funds available only to whites, police brutality and lynchings, lots of lynchings, "one a day for decades," and above all — way, way above all — the indelible remnants of slavery.[4] Fifty years after Detroit burned I read Wilkerson's profoundly researched and reasoned account of America's caste system, a system so effective at destroying whole populations that it became the model for Jewish eradication in the Holocaust.

Suddenly I knew why my silence was so uneasy and my soul, watching George Floyd die, cried out to be heard.

Hiding in Discretion.

Thirty-some years ago I had one husband and two very small boys. I adored them all and loved being a mother. Being a wife was less comfortable because there were too many uneasy silences, times I felt that something was wrong but I couldn't put my finger on it. There were the outbursts that came at unexpected times and over imagined offenses. If there were explanations for inappropriate expressions of seething anger, I did not know them. If there were rumors about another lifestyle or other relationships, I chose not to explore them. I preferred the uneasy silence that followed each argument. I was discreet to the point of blindness.

Then came the day I heard a doctor give my diagnosis as an HIV-positive woman, infected by her husband. One of my sons, Max, had come to us through birth; the other, Zachary, had arrived by adoption. Given Max's history as my biological child, my heart stopped beating when I imagined his future. It took days to have Max tested and only when the results were in — "he's negative, Mary" — did I start breathing again.

Following my diagnosis, I knew I needed to do something; it was my *modus operandi* when facing any challenge. My soul cried out, "Do something!" and I didn't know what to do. It was an era in which AIDS and shame traveled together. If I were to speak out, what would my children suffer? And what about my parents and siblings: What would my diagnosis do to their reputations?

Three decades later, as the COVID-19 Pandemic flooded the nation, I was enduring my fear of the virus sealed off from the world in near-perfect isolation. I wasn't giving speeches. I wasn't hosting dinners. I wasn't having any human contact that I could avoid. The world existed only on the other side of my laptop or television; everything I heard or saw was, literally, screened. I watched as body bags piled up. I saw elderly people dying alone, trapped in nursing homes that could admit no family members. I listened to obvious fabrications that flowed from the White House. Silently, I imagined that — somehow — truth about science and medicine would win the day when pitted against noisy political theatrics. Day after day things seemed to be dissolving into dishonesty and chaos. But apart from expressing myself in a few essays online, I watched and waited in isolation and silence.

Some of my silence resulted from disbelief. Since the days I served President Gerald Ford as one of his "advancemen," I've viewed the presidency with awe. The Oval Office is sacred ground for me. From carpets to windows to that desk where the president works, this is a temple to democracy, a shrine that must not be contaminated with dishonor and dishonesty. What I was witnessing contradicted my experience and beliefs. I was too shocked to believe what I was seeing and hearing; I was stunned into silence.

Thirty years after her passing, I still treasure hearing the powerful voice of the late Congresswoman Barbara Jordan. Sixteen years before I spoke to the Republicans in Houston, she was the first African-American and the first woman to deliver a keynote address at a Democratic National Convention (1976). What I saw through my television window on the Pandemic in the 2020s was her warning that "the great danger America faces [is] that we will cease to be one nation and become instead a collection of interest groups: city against suburb, region against region, individual against individual, each seeking to satisfy private wants." Fifty-some years after her warning, she's been proven right. We've allowed loud, angry, deceitful voices to divide us against ourselves.

But who am I to say these things? Good girls are quiet girls. We don't speak too boldly, too loudly, too brashly. We're discreet (read: silent). That said, my soul has become unhappy in my silence. The truth is not that hard to discern. Silence is troubling in the face of bloody wars, the threat of global environmental collapse, the certainty that there will be another virus, and the uncertainty of the democracy that I previously assumed to be immortal.

I'm convinced that it's time to move out of my uneasy silence and into a public expression of my soul's desire. If this comes with risk, let the risks be built on truth. I don't need more than that.

I don't want to embarrass my children or, at some future reading, trouble my grandchildren. But the reasons not to speak out have faded. I long to speak the truth as nearly as I can understand it. I've arrived at the point where my silence isn't discretion. It's complicity.

Notes to Chapter Two

1. Isabel Wilkerson, *Caste: The Origins of Our Discontents*, p. 45; Random House (US), 2020. Dr. Wilkerson's first major book, *The Warmth of Other Suns: The Epic Story of America's Great Migration*, was first published in 2011 by Vintage Books, a division of Penguin Random House. It told, in exquisite and moving detail, the story of the Great Black Migration from south to north from 1915-1970. "[T]hey did not dream the American dream," she wrote in her epilogue (p.538), "they willed it into being by a definition of their own choosing. They did not ask to be accepted but declared themselves the Americans that perhaps few others recognized but that they had always been deep within their hearts."

2. Kellyanne Conway, advisor to Donald Trump, used the euphemism "alternative facts" when she appeared on NBC's *Meet the Press* on January 22, 2017, in a dialogue with the show's moderator, Chuck Todd. Todd challenged her use of "alternative facts" with this retort: "'Alternative facts' are not facts. They're falsehoods." But the term had come to life as a symbol of Trump's disregard for truth. Years later the possibility of alternative facts is still alive and well.

3. Mary Fisher, *My Name is Mary*, p. 48

4. Isabel Wilkerson, *Caste: The Origins of Our Discontents*, p. 45; (Random House (US) 2020).

   While her brilliant arguments span some 400 pages, in a single page she set the stage for the truth about America's racial inequalities. We live in a time when Florida textbooks claim the legacy of slavery to be "learned skills by which to achieve income and independence." Against that shroud of dishonor, Dr. Wilkerson explains the truth of what slavery truly was:

The institution of slavery was, for a quarter millennium, the conversion of human beings into currency, into machines who existed solely for the profit of their owners, to be worked as long as the owners desired, who had no rights over their bodies or loved ones, who could be mortgaged, bred, won in a bet, given as wedding presents, bequeathed to heirs, sold away from spouses or children to cover an owner's debt or to spite a rival or to settle an estate. They were regularly whipped, raped, and branded, subjected to any whim or distemper of the people who owned them. Some were castrated or endured other tortures too grisly for these pages.... Before there was a United States of America, there was enslavement. Theirs was a living death passed down for twelve generations.

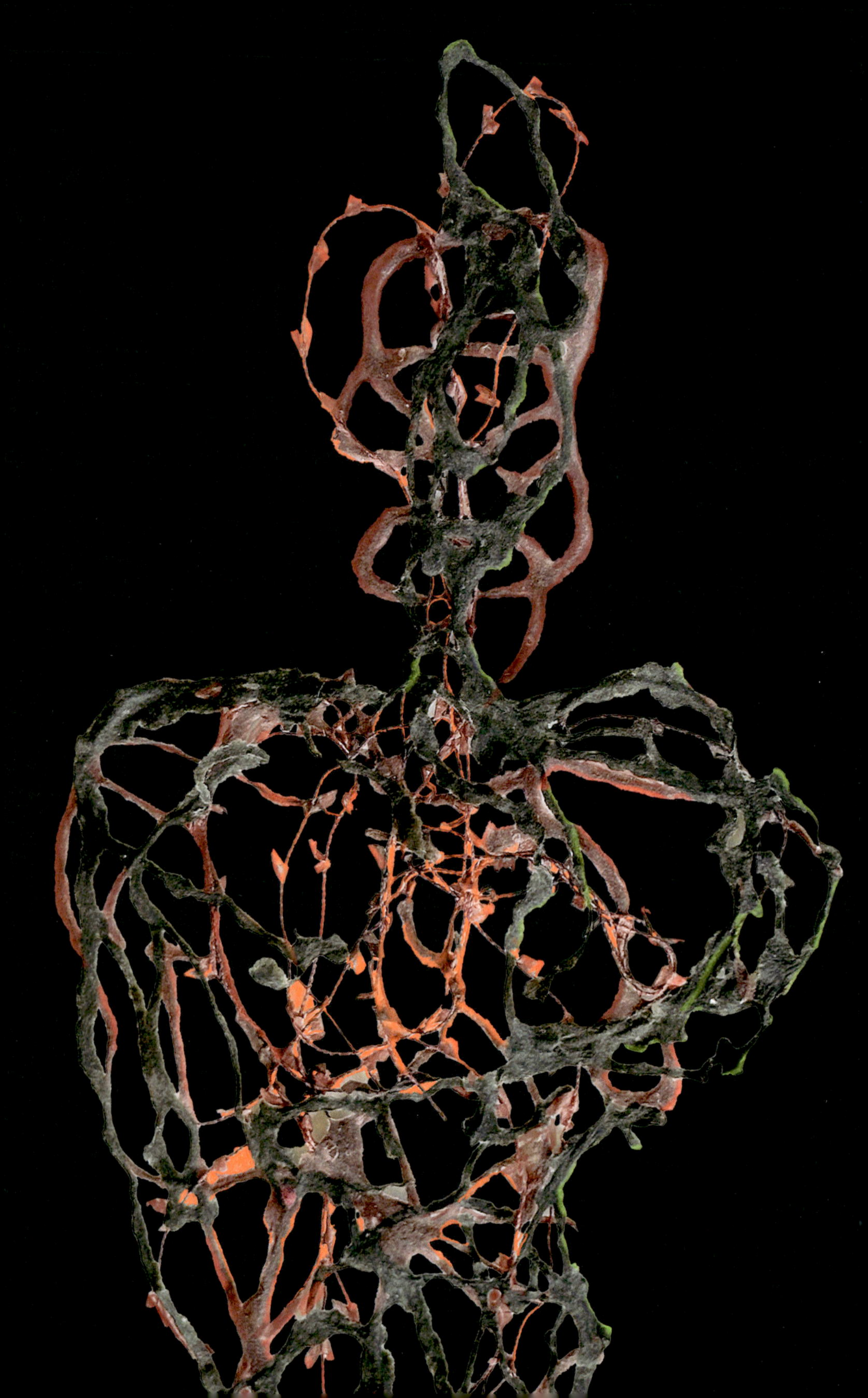

CHAPTER THREE

Words Have Power

*Better to remain silent and be thought a fool than
to speak and to remove all doubt.*[1]

W e communicate in countless ways: writing, art, tears, email, touch, speech, hugs, frowns, giggles, and more. Typically, the instrument we use most is *words*. Written words. Spoken words. Intentional or accidental words. Words loud and soft. Words affectionate and brutish. Profanity. Shopping lists. Screams. Poems. Plans. Whispers. Prayers. We live with, and sometimes by, our words.

The same power that's vested in words can be vested in silence. Imagine that we've had an argument and I'm now enduring "the silent treatment." Because words have such power, so does the absence of words. To communicate is human, and both words and silence communicate.

About Meaning.

I've always agreed with writer and historian Garry Wills, who told us, "The problem with words is, they have meaning." He had a point. We can't use words indiscriminately to make them mean what we want them to mean. They already have meaning even before I get to them.

So, if words already have meaning, I can't (just for example) dilute the violence of an assault on our nation's Capitol by changing the words. Rioters and thugs cannot become "tourists visiting the Capitol" and mobs breaking through doors and windows cannot become "a group of law-abiding Americans expressing themselves." Why not? Because words have meaning.

Words serve an important role in our relationships with others and with our world: They are the billboards of our souls. They are how we introduce ourselves to strangers and identify ourselves in groups. We show ourselves and what we value, or don't, in the words we choose. Once upon a time when Republicans and Democrats debated each other, they would refer to their counterparts as their "distinguished opponent." More recently, a candidate called those he disliked "vermin" and labeled all migrants "rapists," telling us more about the candidate than his critics. "Speak clearly," said the ever-articulate Oliver Wendell Holmes, "if you speak at all; carve every word before you let it fall." Why? Because what I say is who I am.

Words do more than describe. They exude force. An innocent "I love you" from a three-year-old may carry enough strength to convince two battling parents to tone it down. Words have launched wars and been the negotiator's only instrument of peace. Because they have such power, we're wise to use them with some care. In a casual conversation with friends, we can be largely candid and unguarded. In an interview with *The New York Times*, I've learned to exercise some discipline because all the reader will get is the words I use. I choose my words with care.

Power of Silence.

Because the urge and ability to communicate is natural to most human beings, and because words have muscles of meaning, we can also communicate powerfully by *not* using words, by *not* speaking. In some settings, our silence may speak more loudly than words. Think of the slammed bedroom door that ended the argument; the silence that follows is inexpressibly clear. Think of the silence which is a cold man's only response to his estranged daughter's "but I love you, Dad."

The sources and reasons for silence are limitless. When a conversation has droned on for too long; when I've heard my teenager explain my many faults once again; when my neighbor upstairs passes judgment on my neighbor downstairs; when I really have nothing to say, silence is not only reasonable. It's preferable.

On the other hand, I may take refuge in silence for less noble reasons. I may feel unworthy to express an idea or opinion. I may worry that saying something — saying anything — will get me in trouble. I'm intimidated, frightened, uncertain. I've been told to, in vernacular terms, "sit down and shut up." I have no right to speak. I cower under the assault of a critic's judgment. I'm whipped into silence by the messages I'm receiving.

All this sounds like theory but, in fact, it's the stuff that shaped me as a child and young adult. During adolescence and early adulthood I was known as "the quiet one" in our home. There was a reason I kept still.

> *The family messages I read most clearly about myself…had a steady theme: I was unsatisfactory. I was too short. The problem: thyroid. The solution: pills. I was too heavy. The problem: diet. The solution: pills. The pills made me hyperactive, so I couldn't sleep. The solution: sleeping pills. When these pills left me drowsy in the morning, a new prescription cured me almost back to hyperactivity. By the time I graduated from high school, I was a walking pharmacy.[2]*

Power of Words.

Behind every prescription was a conversation in which words conveyed their intended meanings. I wasn't petite; I was short. Not curvaceous; plump. As I've said elsewhere, with a "growing sense of self-loathing," I wondered "if everyone felt like I did and, if not, what were they taking?" I went into a shell of silence, passively acquiescing to parents and doctors. And the words kept echoing through days and nights of self-flagellation. I was unacceptable.

"Sticks and stones may break my bones, but words will never hurt me." Bullshit. Talk to a quiet thirteen-year-old boy who is poor at sports, reluctant in groups, and small for his age. See if he'll break out of silence long enough to describe how the bully taunts him. Try a fourteen-year-old girl whose family can't afford this year's fashions. Or a fifteen-year-old whose every walk down the school hallway is a march through a gauntlet to hell. It isn't sticks and stones that account for suicide as the leading cause of death for 13- and 14-year-olds in the United States. It's words. Words that leave someone not yet mature to dive into an ageless world of anxiety, depression, and hopelessness over a bleak future and the conclusion that life isn't worth living.[3]

Words are not the only cause of emotional withdrawal and fear. Actual physical violence and political torture don't need to be expressed in words. But for most of us, most of the time, the messages we receive about our world, our lives and our value arrive in a package of words. We are judged and then told. When the messages are overwhelmingly negative, we shrink into silence.

Facebook's one-time Chief Operating Officer Sheryl Sandberg observed that girls are called "bossy" simply because they voice an opinion. "Between elementary and high school, girls' self-esteem drops 3.5 times more than boys'. Girls are twice as likely as boys to worry that leadership roles will make them seem 'bossy.' Girls get less airtime in class. They are called on less and interrupted more."[4]

The fact that I was socially successful at school redeemed my teen years. Being elected class president all four years of high school signaled that I was competent and even popular. But long after leaving high school, I was still hearing the messages of my unworthiness. I failed to measure up to expectations. In a family where "money talks," I would never get a job paying high wages. To be a volunteer always felt as though I was not quite worthy to be hired. I didn't graduate college. In discussions of world affairs, I was careful not to say too much, even about Israel — and this was after I had spent nearly a year there. I was bent toward silence.

In my silence, I leaned hard toward the sense that I was not and never would be "enough." Never would I amount to much. It was three easy steps from there to a profound sense of inadequacy. Lacking confidence, my courage failed; and lacking courage, silence replaced my voice.

I know that modesty sometimes recommends silence. So does awe. A sunset over the desert may silence us with its beauty. Mozart's *Requiem* can leave us breathless and silent.

Pain can outstrip any words. A friend's spouse dies after a cruel and lingering illness. Although words have power, they are no match for silence as we hold her quietly and she sobs.

To the extent that words have power, so does silence. To see children dying during war and simply shrug is inhumane. To watch a political party self-destruct without comment is a waste of the power of truth. Silence in the face of such assaults on truth may be widely interpreted as consent.

Words and Conscience.

By the time we have entered adulthood, the vast majority of us have a basic sense of right and wrong. It's a moral gyroscope known as "conscience," and when the voice of our conscience speaks to us, we hear it. We may want to ignore it, or silence it, or deny it. But it refuses our efforts to dismiss it. It leaves us in our silence, listening to ourselves as we worry. It creates a mood that says we're not comfortable, we're not okay. Something is seriously amiss. I'm living in a terribly uneasy silence.

I was moved when Pete Dominick, a writer for several late-night television shows, observed America's political challenges and wrote, "We need to call out the lying, the grifting, the violence." We need, he said, to speak boldly against authoritarians and the words they use. "They try to convince people that" the route to safety and comfort is found by "keeping your head down, seeing little, and saying even less."[5] They hope we'll be silent even while they broadcast abuse and slander.

"Saying even less" soon becomes a pattern of silence. The strongman wants to exile all critics to a state of silence. End the protests. Shut down the opponents. Musician Elena Higgins penned a protest song whose troubling refrain is "by our silence we gave our consent." She is telling us, again, what Martin Luther King told us a half-century ago: "In the end, we will remember not the words of our enemies but the silence of our friends."[6] Message received.

We all have reasons to hide. After all, we may think, Who am I to protest? What qualifies me to speak out? And what difference could I possibly make? The message I've internalized over the years is that I am incapable of changing evil into good. More intelligent, more experienced, more newsworthy people need to take the podium and take the lead. They can speak to power. I'll be content to listen. Maybe I'll send a dollar or two. But I have my hands full with life as it is. It won't help anybody, including me, to rock the boat. I have reasons to avoid going public. And so I remain in my uneasy silence.

Then I hear again the words of Nobel laureate Elie Wiesel. He narrowly survived the Holocaust, assigned first to Auschwitz's concentration camp and then to Buchenwald's. "We must always take sides," he wrote. "Neutrality helps the oppressor, never the victim. Silence encourages the tormentor, never the tormented. The opposite of love is not hate, it's indifference."[7]

Not caring enough to speak out is my version of indifference. My conscience may be screaming at me but I stay quiet. I spend worry-filled days and sleepless nights, knowing the injustice and suffering are calling my name.

I've become convinced that you and I can harness the power of words. We've been entrusted as human beings with language. We can assemble words into potent messages and deliver them with varying degrees of wisdom or foolishness. Given this power, we cannot afford to stay perpetually silent. Words that are not used have already lost their battle with the silence in which undemocratic "leaders" do their dirty work.

For years, I held power I truly did not know I had. It took a life-and-death crisis to bring me to a speaker's platform with an audience of hundreds of millions in 1992. I mounted the stage one evening in Houston, not yet understanding the power my own words might hold, still uncertain that I would make a difference.

I came armed with nothing more than words.

Notes to Chapter Three

1. The wording and source of this quotation are contested; either Abraham Lincoln or Mark Twain is typically credited. The version used here is usually attributed to Lincoln. The so-called Twain version is "It's better to keep your mouth shut and appear stupid than open it and remove all doubt."

2. Mary Fisher, *My Name is Mary*, p. 17

3. Stephanie Pappas, *American Psychological Association Monitor on Psychology*, Vol. 54 No. 5, p. 54; July 1, 2023,

   Between 2000 and 2018, the suicide rate among youth ages 10 to 24 rose from 6.8 per 100,000 to 10.7 per 100,000, according to death certificate data (Curtin, S. C., National Vital Statistics Report, Vol. 69, No. 11, 2020 [PDF, 477KB]). This rise pushed suicide into the second leading cause of death for people ages 10 to 14 in 2021, according to the CDC (Facts About Suicide, May 2023). The overall suicide rate declined in 2019 and 2020 before rising nearly back to the 2018 peak again in 2021 (Stone, D. M., et al. Morbidity and Mortality Weekly Report, Vol. 72, No. 6, 2023). The most alarming trend in this period was a sharp rise in suicide among Black youth ages 10 to 24. In this group, the suicide rate increased from 8.2 per 100,000 in 2018 to 11.2 per 100,000 in 2021, a rise of 36.6%. "Adolescent Black girls, compared with other demographics, have the highest increase in suicide attempts," said Meza.

   American Indian and Alaska Native youth have even higher rates of suicide, with a rate of 36.3 per 100,000 in 2021. For White youth, the rate in 2021 was 12.4 per 100,000, compared with 7.9 for Hispanic or Latino youth and 9.4 for Asian youth.

   The CDC report paints a picture of US high school students in distress. An increasing number of students reported persistent feelings of sadness or hopelessness in 2021, including 57% of girls (up from 36% in 2011), 29% of boys, and 69% of LGBTQ+ students.

4. Sheryl Sandberg requoted by Georgette Gilmore in the *Montclair Local*, March 11, 2014.

5. Pete Dominick in *Lucid*, December 8, 2023.

6. Martin Luther King, Jr., said this in his November 1967 Dexter Avenue Baptist Church (Montgomery, AL) Massey Lectures for the Canadian Broadcasting Corporation. It was subsequently published in the collection *Conscience for Change*, and republished a year later under the title *The Trumpet of Conscience*.

7. Elie Wiesel, *The Night Trilogy: Night, Dawn, The Accident*. Multiple publishers.

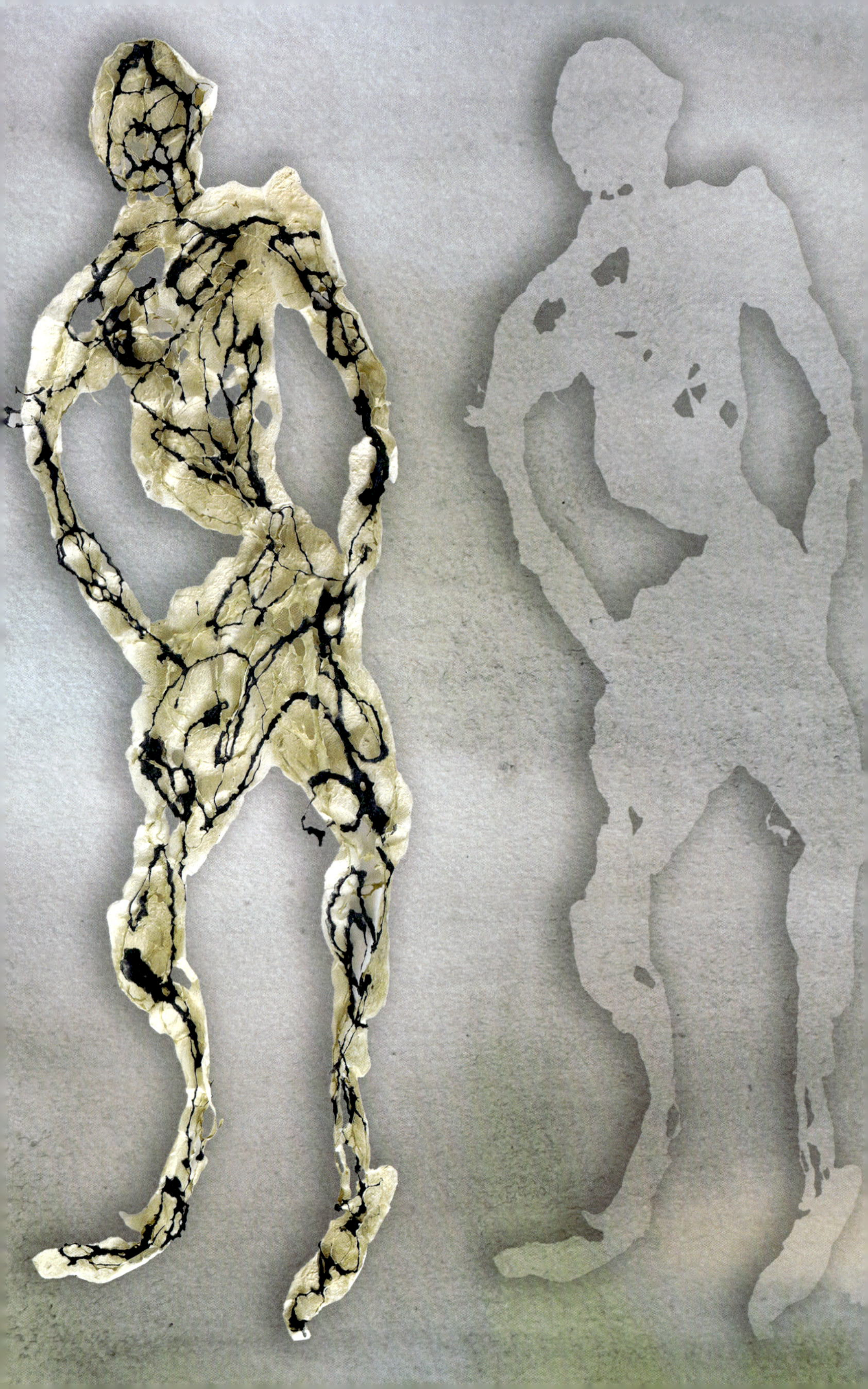

CHAPTER FOUR

Choice

We've learned that quiet isn't always peace.

Amanda Gorman[1]

I can be hounded into silence by life's uncertainties. There are moments in life, especially motherhood or politics, in which I'm simply baffled. I can't make sense out of what I think I'm seeing. I don't know what to say in such moments so it's prudent to choose silence and say nothing.

Although children and close friends tend to worry if I tell them this truth, I've sometimes wondered if I may have outlived the expiration date stamped on my birth certificate. If I've served whatever purpose I was given, would it be okay with everyone if I politely excused myself? Silence is a good place to consider such options; discussing them with loved ones hasn't proven to be such a good idea.

Then there are days when I need to slow down, dismiss the busyness charted on my calendar, and contemplate the Big Questions. Okay, if I'm going to be here for a while, why? And with that question I'm off on a search for what I haven't been able to find elsewhere: myself. Me. Mary.

Years of the Pandemic.

The COVID-19 Pandemic slipped into our neighborhoods without permission. It hasn't entirely left, and I think we've not yet calculated the damage we sustained during the virus's visit. The isolation of those months, even if self-imposed, continues to impact my feelings and behaviors. Infants struggling to breathe and elderly parents longing for a child's touch, they are the silent victims that have not yet escaped the virus. The pain inflicted on the generation of those just coming into adulthood won't be fully realized for years, perhaps for decades. It's one thing to say that we've closed schools for a year or two, that lessons will be delivered via Zoom. It's something else to deprive budding adolescents of social contact with peers. Suicide rates of people ages 14-22 rocketed up. And even now, the vacillating rates of COVID-19, RSV, and other viruses can quickly call me back into hiding.

So it's a mixed bag: Some silence is friendly and some is mean. The constant noise filling my ears can make me long to turn down the volume on life. I'll take a pass on my hearing aids today, thank you, or I'll try those new earphones that promise to block out the noise altogether. I wake to urban noise or, when visiting the countryside, am flooded by the ubiquitous river of news that answers my phone addiction. My every environment is polluted by sirens, chatter, noise. When for a moment it's interrupted by silence, I slowly exhale. I feel my blood pressure drop. What am I hearing? Is that silence? How magnificent.

No wonder silence has long been the setting for monastic life. I like the story of the young monk in a monastery where residents were allowed to speak two words every ten years. After his first decade, he comes before the head abbot to speak his two words: "Better food." The head abbot understands and assigns a new chef to the kitchen. A decade later, the monk says to the abbot, "Warmer blankets." New blankets were promptly ordered. Ten years later the monk appears once again for his two-word hearing. This time he says, "I quit." The head abbot replies, "Good! You've done nothing in 30 years but complain."

Over time, I've come to realize that silence isn't empty. It's full of memories, ideas, regrets, hopes, possibilities, even a few jokes my mother used to tell. Were I to admit that "I'm thinking," that doesn't mean you should interrupt me because you think I'm doing nothing. Nothing? I just told you: I'm thinking.

"I've begun to realize," wrote the great Chaim Potok as he introduced *The Chosen*, "that you can listen to silence and learn from it. It has a quality and a dimension all its own." He's right, and he wasn't alone. For centuries, philosophers and scientists and religions have recommended a practice of silence. "Many of us have forgotten (or even fear) quiet," wrote Vijay Eswaran in a thoughtful *Harvard Business Review* feature. "We live in a world full of noise and chatter. A world wherein our daily routines are inundated with distractions and responsibilities." As an alternative, Eswaran urges "being silent" because "it allows us to channel our energies. It gives us the clarity we need to calmly face challenges and uncertainty."[2]

There is mystery and magic to be uncovered in silence. The quiet of aloneness can get a bad rap, sometimes deservedly so. But silence is still rich with the possibility of discovery, especially of ourselves.

Choosing Silence.

When I opt for an hour or two of silence, I'm also choosing to slow down. I don't fully understand how sound impacts time, but I do know that the crazy busyness of my usual days can be stopped if I decide to spend some moments in quiet reflection, maybe meditation, maybe just quiet.

Silence isn't a guarantor of peace, exactly. It can contain monsters as well as angels. In the months after my HIV diagnosis, silence was the place I went most often to be alone and to cry. I couldn't imagine leaving my small sons, having them grow into adulthood as orphans. I knew no one else could love them as I did. But in the silence, I couldn't imagine any other future either. I would die and they would live on, perhaps remembering me. It was a time of restless quiet, uneasy silence.

With time and conversations about the choices I needed to make, the silence became less foreboding. Given the social prejudice against HIV — it was, after all, that "gay disease" in a time when "gay" meant "dirty" — I wondered if staying silent about my diagnosis was cowardice or prudence. Family members and friends voted both ways, some favoring privacy and others pressing for public disclosure. My days were filled mostly with the children but the nights were filled with silence in which the voices I'd heard, arguing for one option or another, replayed themselves over and over again.

In the silence I would remember the words of my hero and role model, Betty Ford. "Once you've said it out-loud in public, you can never take it back again." It came from her as a simple fact, one she had fully experienced with alcoholism and with breast cancer. "Once you've said it out loud…."

And I heard another voice, persistently. It belonged to Sally Fisher (no relation), a powerhouse woman then living in Santa Fe who knew the AIDS epidemic intimately. Friends had introduced us in late summer of 1991, just after my diagnosis, and we spent time together discussing what I should do. We'd had a long lunch together one afternoon and were leaving the restaurant when she said she was sorry for what I was facing. And then she added, "But I also need to tell you that we've been waiting for someone like you to come along."

Sally and her friends might have been waiting for someone but I couldn't imagine that I was the one. I didn't think about having been a live-television producer for some years as an experience that used any skill. I'd been the first woman to serve as an advanceman for a president; it never occurred to me that I might have demonstrated some competence in that role. When I thought of myself — my "self-definition" — I saw myself as a mom with two little kids, divorced, no degree, an artist who loved the studio as a place of quiet. Magic Johnson, who'd come out about his HIV status a few months after I was diagnosed, had a worldwide platform; I had none. He was the famous one; not me.

It was hard for me to accept that Sally and company really understood who I was and, more importantly, who I was not. I doubted I was the one for whom they had been waiting.

These were tough times.

The House of Stories.

Despite Marshall McLuhan's theory that "the medium is the message," I'm inclined to think that my stories are my message. I'm drawn to the late N. Scott Momaday's elegant "we live in a house made of stories."[3] As Momaday would insist, my life is a narrative, not a list; a drama or a comedy but not a post-it note. It's the stories I've accumulated from my earliest memory to yesterday's accident. What's my message? My life. I am the stories I tell you. If you accept the stories as true, I'm grateful; if you reject them as silly, it isn't my story you're rejecting. It's me.

My life really is a story. It has a main plot but tends to wander off into subplots, some entertaining and some truly forgettable. Characters who are vaguely familiar step in from another time and place. Slowly, quietly, I come to recognize some of them as a part of my story and therefore a part of me. When there is sufficient silence to calm my harried mind, when the noise that filled the day with wretched news and gasping ideals is finally shut down, these are the times, in the silence, that I remember the stories of my life. They come down the track like the cars of a desert freight train, one after another, a few of them related but others seemingly tied to nothing but a stray brain cell. They roll back in color and sometimes in black-and-white. It's where high school friends are still writing encouraging notes, where Betty Ford is still alive, where Sally Fisher is still saying "we've been waiting."

If there is a single place that I meet me and recognize myself, it's in silence.

Unordained.

One of the greatest joys I've known in the past thirty years has been preaching in churches and synagogues. Surveying the many denominations in which I've led worship in the US and Africa, we've concluded that I could be a Unitarian Baptist Presbyterian Methodist Catholic Lutheran Jew.

I preach because it's a joy, but everyone knows I'm working without a license. I've never been vested as a rabbi, priest, pastor, or imam. I've been given a few honorary doctorates but I'm still waiting for one in theology. But if given a congregation as an audience, I'm justified to tell my story as if it's part of a much larger, longer story — one that starts around Day One of creation. Somehow "Let there be light" becomes "Let there be Mary," and a sermon slips out.

I've forgotten where I was preaching when I recalled the story of Elijah on Mt. Sinai looking to have a chat with God. Elijah was hanging out at the entrance to a cave where he'd spent the night, hoping God would drop by. Then came a hurricane-like wind that whipped across the mountain's face; but, says the text, "the Lord was not in the wind." The mountain trembled in an earthquake, and the earthquake was followed by lightning. "But the Lord was not in the fire. And after the fire came a still, small voice." And, yes, it was in the still, small voice that Elijah heard the Creator of heaven and earth.[4]

As I've aged, I've had spiritual experiences of various sorts, led by spiritual leaders from a full range of religious and spiritual traditions. For decades, in the rooms of Alcoholics Anonymous, I've confessed the need for a power greater than myself if I'm to be delivered into sanity and sobriety. And always, when alone and reflecting in silence, I'm drawn to a divine reality containing the power of the universe and speaking to me in such a soft voice that the silence is hardly interrupted.

Perhaps that's why I was so moved when first I heard the story of newsman Dan Rather interviewing the late Mother Teresa. It goes like this:

> *Dan Rather, CBS anchor, once asked Mother Teresa what she says to God when she prays. She replied, "I don't say anything. I just listen." So Dan turned the question and asked what God says to her. Mother Teresa smiled with confidence and answered, "He doesn't say anything. He just listens. And if you don't understand it, I can't explain it to you."[5]*

The longer we suffer the insanity of angry politics, the more frequently some lies are told as if repetition will make them true, the more innocent blood that pours out in the wounds of war, the more I long for silence, a place where I can recover myself and refocus on my story.

If I can turn down or turn off the noise, I can embrace the silence and whatever it brings. In the silence I may grieve or giggle. I may recount the mistake I cannot undo, or discover that something I didn't plan worked out perfectly. I am not hiding in this silence. Neither am I "doing nothing." I go there on a search for my life and its meaning, to adjust the plot, remember the main theme, and sometimes to dismiss a useless character. If life in this silence is sometimes intentional and almost busy, it is also serene.

The narrative of my life winds around the bends and hillsides, beyond the noise, a river of experience that carries me into moments of silence. It's in the silence that, for better or for worse, I wade into my story. From time to time, when the spirits of the universe are aligned, I emerge, quieted, knowing me.

Notes to Chapter Four

1. Amanda Gorman, from "The Hill We Climb," a poem written for and read at the inauguration of President Joe Biden on the steps of the Capitol, Washington, D.C., January 20, 2021.

2. Vijay Eswaran, "Don't Underestimate the Power of Silence," *Harvard Business Review,* July 22, 2021.

3. Requoted in Kenny Ausubel, *Dreaming the Future: Reimagining Civilization in the Age of Nature*, Chelsea Green Publishing, August 28, 2012. The full quotation (p. 100) reads: "In the elegant words of Native American author N. Scott Momaday, 'We live in a house made of stories....'"

4. 1 Kings 19:12-13

5. The report on Rather's interview is famous and can be found in multiple settings with the same theme and elements in different words. Here I've requoted the summary published as "Short Story" as told on *YouTube*, May 10, 2022.

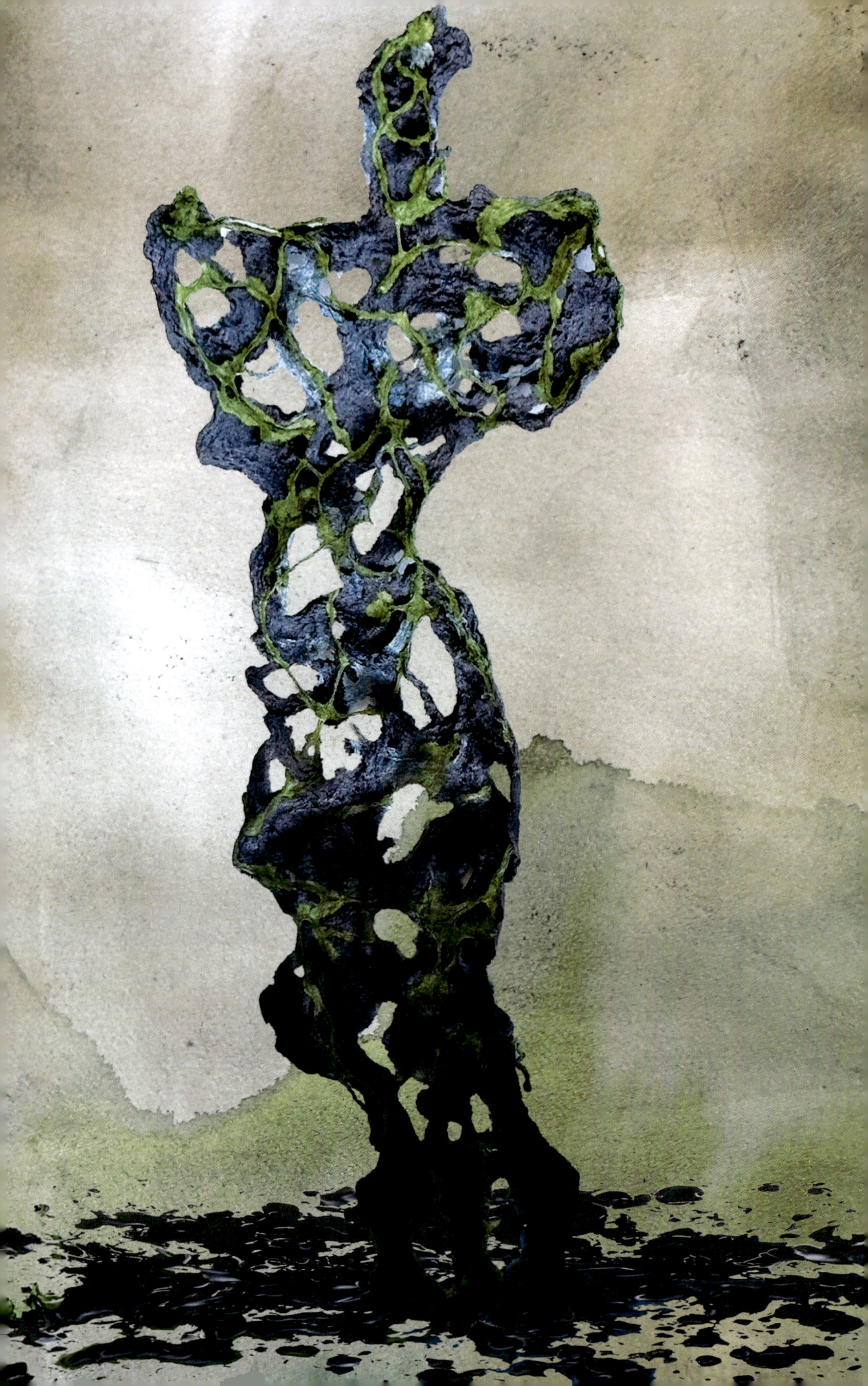

CHAPTER FIVE

Coming Out

Every generation leaves behind a legacy. What that legacy will be is determined by the people of that generation.

John Lewis[1]

If you were diagnosed HIV positive in 1991, as I was, you were on death's waiting list. I had plenty of company. Those of us who were infected knew we'd eventually have AIDS. Then we'd get sick and we'd waste and we'd die. Usually, we were given 6-8 years between diagnosis and death. Assuming I was infected in 1988 or '89, we supposed I'd last until about 1995 or '96. We also knew my last year or two wouldn't be pretty.

The AIDS crisis between 1981 and, say, 1996 was the defining moral and social issue of the time. As infections mounted, so did deaths, first measured by the hundreds, then by the thousands, and then by the tens of thousands. As the epidemic outran forecasts and expectations, faster than any public health agency had predicted, activists took to the streets. Civil protests became more and more impassioned and aggressive. With no cure, no effective treatments, and little to no evident concern from Washington, D.C., AIDS was the terror of the day, the deadly "COVID-19" of our time.

The US hemophiliac community was the first to be erased. The virus had gotten into the supply of donated blood and infected most who required transfusions. Those with hemophilia had no obvious choice and no advance warning. By the time we knew their risk, it was too late. They were dying or dead, almost to the person.

Once our hemophiliac colleagues had been taken by the virus, we soon realized that the AIDS community was composed disproportionately of men who had sex with men. We didn't know why but we saw it as part of being gay in America. In fact, we now know it struck the gay community purely as an accident of history; it could have broken out in any population where people shared bodily fluids, including the heterosexual community of which I was (and am) a part. We were learning the primary routes of transmission when intravenous drug use began claiming its victims and those who'd received blood transfusions, like Arthur Ashe, Elizabeth Glaser, and Ryan White were wasting away. There were exceptions, as there always are. But, dominantly, by the late 1980s AIDS was an epidemic of mostly gay men in their prime somewhere between 20 and 40 years of age. I was an exception.

Medicine and Prejudice.

The first report of AIDS in *The New York Times* (1981) labeled it "a gay cancer." Whatever stigma was then attached to being gay — and the stigma was broad and brutal — was immediately attached to AIDS. Tens of thousands of young men came out as gay while on their deathbeds. Shock at the death of Hollywood heartthrob Rock Hudson in 1985 was initially because he had died, but within weeks, it was because he had been gay. In a lethal jumble of fact and fear, science and bias, medicine and denial, the American AIDS community and the American gay community became nearly one.[2]

If we pull back the curtain on how research into human diseases is typically conducted, we discover that tests and trials are usually conducted on men, sometimes only white men. Why not women? Why not other races? In the case of AIDS, women weren't in the research because scientists, like others, thought the number of HIV-positive women was small and "exceptional." Why research something only a few women (like me) would ever have?

But that's not the whole story. We have to factor in money, and the cost of research. Women's bodies and physiology are more complex than men's. From hormonal cycles to the consequences of birthing, from adolescence through menopause, we're more complicated and therefore more expensive as research subjects. The simple fact is this: Doing research on women costs more than doing parallel research on men. And, therefore, this: Women are usually last to be included in research.

For a year or two in the late '80s, AZT (azidothymidine), a drug discovered and largely abandoned in the 1960s, raised hopes that AIDS could be stopped. But as *Time Magazine* reported in a look-back essay in 2017, we learned that

> *…no single drug is the answer to fighting HIV. People taking AZT soon began showing rising virus levels — but the virus was no longer the same, having mutated to resist the drug. More drugs were needed, and AIDS advocates*

> *criticized the FDA for not moving quickly enough to approve additional medications. And side effects including heart problems, weight issues and more reminded people that anything designed to battle a virus like HIV was toxic.*[3]

Hopes that had been raised by AZT's introduction were dashed by real-life experience of those relying on the drug. The AIDS community was back to dying. And I was very soon among the women who could not take AZT or, later, protease inhibitors, without life-challenging side effects.

The epidemic was four years old before then-President Ronald Reagan uttered the word "AIDS" in public (September 1985). Hospitals who refused admission to patients with AIDS out of ignorance and prejudice made a few headlines in newspapers that were soon wrapping dead fish. Morticians refusing service to those who'd died were common. The brilliant, raging playwright and my dear friend Larry Kramer organized ACT UP ("AIDS Coalition to Unleash Power") and took to the streets in screaming fury at Washington's indifference. Larry, himself infected, organized marches and protests of the sick and dying, men carrying coffins that were later put to their intended purpose, men in walkers and wheelchairs being pushed along on their (literal) deathbeds.

The year I was diagnosed, most Republican leaders were treating AIDS as a Democratic disease. The political equation was that, if people with AIDS voted at all, they would vote Democratic. It was probably correct, in fact, given the Republicans' general views of gay men and expensive epidemics.

Utah's Republican Senator, the late Orrin Hatch, joined with Democratic Senator Edward ("Ted") Kennedy to secure initial resources for AIDS prevention and treatment. At their worst, other Republican leaders responded to AIDS activists by joining right-wing religious leaders in reminding their supporters that AIDS was a punishment for gay men having gay sex. "Fund AIDS research when these deviants got sick — why? Pay for hospitals or needed hospices — that's crazy. After all, they're getting what they deserve." Such vile rhetoric was common and rarely refuted. It was, frankly, a very mean time.

Then there was me, entering stage left, a straight woman, mother of two, raised in a Republican home, exploring my artwork and life as a divorced woman being inducted as one of the newest members of America's AIDS community. As I've explained hundreds of times to millions of people: I didn't enlist in this movement. I was drafted.

The Desire to Hide.

My personal response to most things unhappy or distasteful — think a broken marriage or maybe an eviction notice — has always been the same: just move on. Moving on works for some things but if a virus you're hosting moves with you, it's a little like that old adage: Wherever you go, there you are.

So if you have a disease that's 100% certain to kill you, where do you go and what do you *do*? Days fill with shock and awe; nights bring agonizing fears — but how can you just move on when the virus is guaranteed to move with you?

One option chosen by tens of thousands of people with AIDS was, and still is, to hide. Avoid any public or even private admission of the realities. Given your symptoms, once you know them, you offer a different label: respiratory infection, perhaps. I don't know how many young gay men opted for the choice to hide, but I know by experience that their number was large. They were ashamed of their sexual orientation and didn't want their families to suffer collateral embarrassment. Infected young women like me have been especially vilified. We're dirty. Untouchables. Shall I whisper the word whores? There were good reasons why, when young men and women died, their obituaries noted "cancer" as the cause of death, or maybe pneumonia. Not AIDS.

I'd been raised as the daughter of my stepfather, Max Fisher, a successful businessman and a prominent behind-the-scenes advisor to Republican presidents, beginning with Richard Nixon. Discretion was my father's hallmark; his biography was properly titled *The Quiet Diplomat*. He was a Jew, usually the most prominent Jew in the Republican Party. He was known to be thoughtful and totally trustworthy, a good friend to Michigan's governor George Romney when he was vying for the White House and to other so-called "progressive Republicans" throughout the 1960s, '70s, '80s and '90s.

Over the initial 90 days or so after my diagnosis, I sought out the advice of experts recommended to me, people I could admire and trust. Sally Fisher claimed the epidemic had been waiting for me. She was in the tell-the-world camp. Others were more cautious. I'd been the first woman "advanceman" serving an American president, Gerald R. Ford. The President and Betty Ford were my children's godparents. The Fords offered insightful warnings.[4] Betty's battles with breast cancer and alcoholism had left both scars and lessons.

I'd worked first in public television and then as a producer for an ABC morning show in Detroit. My role as producer meant I was constantly convincing people to come on our show for interviews or performances. It was a great job and one that kept me involved without being on-camera. Similarly, working on the advance team for the White House means collaborating with the Secret Service while staying out of public view. I knew the media and the rules.

By the fall of 1991 I was getting a tour of the American AIDS epidemic. Dr. Henry Murray, Arthur Ashe's physician and my first HIV doctor, became a close friend and advisor. Dr. June Osborn, chair of the National Commission on AIDS, described the AIDS policy challenges her commission was facing. Dr. David Rogers, then president of the Robert Wood Johnson Foundation, and others introduced me to a world I had never known. In the process, they gently encouraged me not to fear telling the truth about my condition. They admitted I'd likely face some pretty ugly assaults. But their consensus was "go public."

I had a surreal experience when a New York City public relations firm was retained by someone in, or serving, our family. I met with the PR agents and, as nearly as I can recall, their only interest was in keeping my infection from becoming a public story and thereby embarrassing my family. They offered no helpful strategy based on telling the truth. In fact, they weren't that interested in the truth. They were worried about reputation.

As the winter holidays (1991) dawned, I was nearing the decision to tell whoever cared to listen that I had AIDS. I dreaded the labels and judgments that would be assigned to me but I also knew others were suffering worse. I guessed, accurately as it turned out, that I would be the object of some violent threats and public efforts at shaming me. Mostly, I worried about my family: If I came out of hiding, they would be dragged into public with me.

My most prevalent family concern was what might happen to my two sons, Max, then four, and Zachary, just two. I knew at the time that Brian, their father, and I would both die from AIDS, leaving the boys to be orphans at some fairly early age. I went into planning mode, creating documents, drafting agreements and trusts, arranging financial and social affairs with those who agreed to become their trustees and surrogate parents. It was a grief-inducing project built on the knowledge that death was waiting just beyond the horizon.

What I could not protect two preschoolers from, I soon discovered, was the impact of adults' ignorance and prejudice. I didn't know how to explain to the boys that their best friend was no longer allowed to play at our house or bring home stuffed animals that my son had touched. Parents spoke to each other and their children overheard their judgmentalism. I soon discovered that prejudice that's whispered is just as prejudicial as whatever's shouted.

By January 1992, Joe Stroud, then-editor of *The Detroit Free Press*, agreed that he would assign my story to a young journalist, Frank Bruni, who has since become a famed *New York Times* columnist. We agreed that the *Free Press* would have the first rights to publish the story in my hometown. Meanwhile, we made plans to go public nationally with friend and journalist Diane Sawyer on ABC's "Prime Time Live." When it was broadcast, Diane's feature was both kindly and direct. She didn't pull punches about the difficulty of being infected, but neither did she portray me as a pathetic victim.

Frank, who had spent nearly a week at my home doing interviews and organizing his thoughts, wrote precisely the story he'd promised. When the presses rolled and the story hit the streets of Detroit, as I said in my 1995 memoir, Frank had

> ...told my story, and told it better than I could have. It was neither exaggerated nor sensationalized; it was straightforward, gentle, beautifully written. There was more 'socialite' than I wanted but less than I'd feared.

Only later, when I saw the photographs and headlines, did I realize that it was the lead front-page story under the heading COMING OUT AGAINST AIDS: WEALTH, POWER AND LOVE DIDN'T BLOCK THE VIRUS.

"I want to help people get rid of the fear," Frank quoted me as saying. That was true to my experience. He had conveyed the critical message: "It doesn't matter how you got it. It can happen to anyone." This two-part message was all I had. That was my story.[5]

Telling the Truth.

What made my story so newsworthy wasn't fame, because I wasn't famous. Neither was it that I was a dying mother; homes and hospitals across America are full of dying mothers of all ages. My story was broadcast and published because in 1992 in America it seemed strange that an otherwise ordinary woman had AIDS. I was a novelty. I contradicted the dominant image of gay men wasting away. Nightly newscasts showed dying men following Larry Kramer to rallies at the US Capitol. Their screams of protest never stopped. But the best I could do was speak quietly about my concerns for my children and my hope that other women could see they too were at risk. It was the perception of novelty that gave Frank's story particular oomph.

I wasn't thrilled about being publicly vulnerable, about standing out in a gay man's epidemic, one *with* them but not one *of* them. I've never been happy making others dislike me; I was all about keeping others happy. Given my circumstances, I was ready to divide my remaining time between my children and my studio.

For all the wise counsel of others, my only authentic message was what I'd experienced. I wasn't an expert of some kind. When I appeared on broadcasts or in articles, I was repeatedly caricatured as "a common woman with two lovely children…oh, and she has AIDS." My message was my story and my story was me.

When Frank Bruni and Diane Sawyer finished telling the world that I had AIDS, I actually thought that would be the end of "going public." I'd have opposed the cruelty of judgmentalism with honesty and vulnerability. The novelty would wear off and I'd go back to being an artist and a mother. No one could accuse me of hiding because the truth — my truth — was out. I'd said it all.

I did not fully realize that once your story is in the public domain, it may take twists and turns you hadn't imagined. But once my story was being told, other people were able to reshape the story. The explosion of social media was just beginning, with its wealth of disinformation. But conventional media could, despite my protests, present Mary as "that innocent woman," a foil to "those dirty gay men."

I wanted a legacy of compassion. I wished Max and Zack could remember me with pride, perhaps with charity, and without shame. I was working to shape a legacy defined by integrity, not by illness. Texas Governor Ann Richards once said "I did not want my tombstone to read, 'She kept a really clean house.'" Understood.

If my tombstone was going to have a single-word inscription, I wanted it to be Courage or perhaps Compassion. I did not want it to be a memory of illness. But it felt like the world wanted to chisel in something else: "AIDS."

Notes to Chapter Five

1. Congressman John Lewis, *Across That Bridge: A Vision for Change and the Future of America*

2. At dinner with several of us one night shortly before he died, playwright and novelist Paul Monette said that the gay community didn't exist as a community before AIDS. There was nothing but stigma that was shared. Then came AIDS and, said Paul, "AIDS created the gay *community*."

3. "The Story Behind the First AIDS Drug," *Time Magazine*, March 19, 2017

4. Transcript of Mary Fisher interview with Richard Norton Smith as part of the Gerald R. Ford Oral History Project, June 3, 2009

5. Mary Fisher, *My Name is Mary*, p. 206

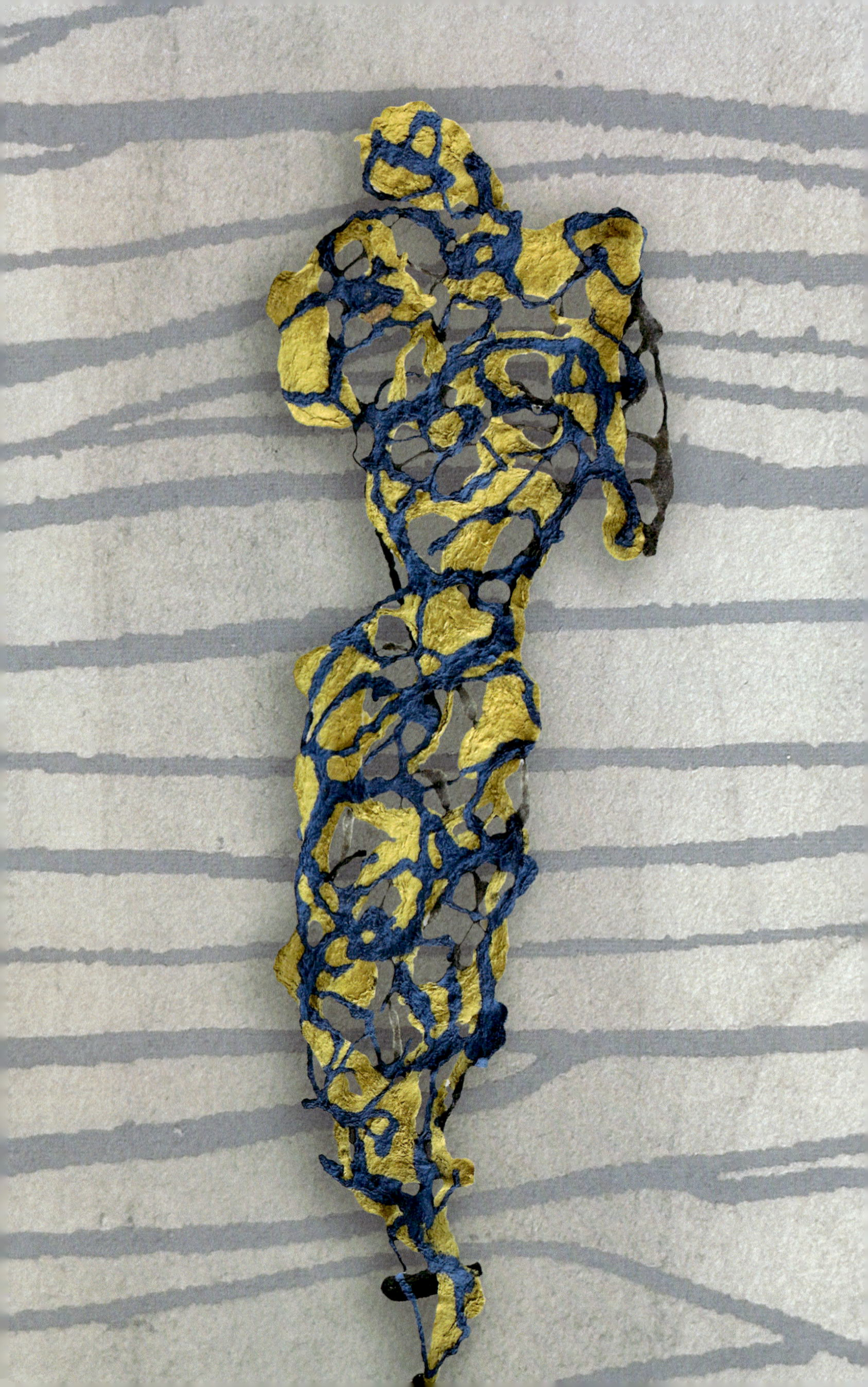

CHAPTER SIX

Whispering Loudly

In a world that wants women to whisper, I choose to yell.

Luvvie Ajayi[1]

I've never really known for sure, but I've always imagined that President George H.W. Bush wanted me to speak at the 1992 Republican National Convention because he and Barbara had lost their daughter, Robin, to an incurable disease. I don't think it was merely a political calculation especially related to AIDS. My guess is that, when he saw my father, the president knew what lay ahead and felt drawn to Dad by the agony of losing a child.[2]

Despite my expectations that my story would fade soon after it was told, the coverage by Frank Bruni and Diane Sawyer was the opening, not the closing, of my saga going public as a woman with AIDS. It led to other interviews and publications, other events and opportunities. I was invited to receive amfAR's first "Red Ribbon Award" at a glittering dinner in New York City attended by famous people. I recall feeling like I'd been invited to sit at the adult table for Thanksgiving dinner.

AIDS had, by the time I arrived, become both a scientific scourge and a deeply political issue. Additionally, 1992 was a presidential election year in which AIDS was broadly seen as a wedge issue favoring Democrats.

Judy Sherman, a friend since junior high days in Michigan, had become a prominent leader of the American Dental Association. Using her connections to congressional leaders, she convinced organizers of the Republican Platform Hearings that they should invite me to give "platform testimony" in Salt Lake City during May — testimony broadcast by a new TV network, C-Span. I got good reviews. I also offered a few remarks in Amsterdam at the International Conference on AIDS in early July, enough to keep me in the news. After weeks of will-she or won't-she be invited to speak at the Republicans' Convention in Houston, the invitation arrived. Following a bit of negotiation, I was booked for prime broadcast time Wednesday evening, August 19.

1992 may have seen the last of the truly dramatic, made-for-TV conventions. In the 1950s and '60s, conventions generated spine-tingling drama because they determined the presidential candidates for later that year. Our current system of primary elections to choose the nominee was not yet in place. In 1992, the Democratic Convention came first, in July, with Elizabeth Glaser and Bob Hattoy representing the AIDS community at the Convention podium. I was largely profiled as their counterpart four weeks later.

I was Wednesday evening's keynoter (August 19). The previous evening, Texas Senator Phil Gramm had that role. The media paid little attention to Gramm's remarks. Everyone was buzzing instead about Patrick J. Buchanan's Monday night call to war. Buchanan, who'd run his own unsuccessful presidential campaign that year, had used his time at the podium to declare "a religious war," "a cultural war for the soul of America." He claimed America was enduring a spiritual and moral collapse which could only be reversed by an assault on "radical feminism" and the erasure of those promoting "homosexual rights." His entire harangue was Nazi-enough for columnist Molly Ivins to remark that she preferred Buchanan's speech "in the original German."[3] I would have preferred silence.

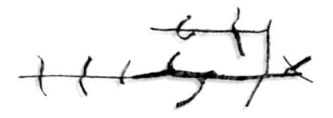

Becoming the Message.

Telling my story to journalists, and having them tell the story to their audiences, wasn't all that difficult. I did wonder if it truly made any difference, and how long it would hold the media's interest. But it didn't seem to be fading when I arrived in Houston.

I'm not trained as a speaker. I had no special credentials for telling national leaders what they should do. I didn't volunteer to have AIDS. And here I was, getting ready to speak to hundreds of millions of people worldwide, including a president and his wife, sitting with my parents in a special, camera-accessible VIP box.

"Be who you are," said a friend, "That's your power. If you simply tell the truth about your experience, unafraid of what others think, you can make an enormous impact." What he was telling me was that I only needed to be my own message. Telling my story was the message others needed to hear. That seemed simple enough.

As it developed, there was another person with AIDS who used himself as the message the evening of my speech. Steven Bradley and I had met in Amsterdam in July, and I'd been impressed with his intelligence and charm. He was youthful, handsome, funny, and deadly serious about changing the global and, especially, the American understanding of AIDS.

I was maybe three minutes into my speech when I happened to spot Steven on the convention floor beneath the podium. He was slowly unbuttoning his shirt while smiling up at me as if to say, "We're here together, babe." With a flourish, he ripped off his dress shirt to show the slogan on his T-shirt: "No one here knows I'm HIV-positive." His point, as noted at his funeral two years later, was that any human being was eligible to host the virus. He had made himself the message.

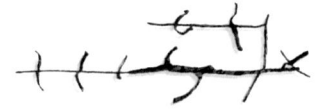

Whispering.

To be effective, I needed to represent two communities: the community of AIDS and the community of Republicans. They were not accustomed to being paired.

The Republicans were represented by some 36,000 delegates in the remodeled Astrodome. The Democrats were at home watching on TV while Larry Kramer's ACT UP crew marched and chanted along the streets of Houston. Although they differed widely, I wanted to make the Republicans my primary audience while recognizing others who'd be listening in or watching.

As soon as I could, I spoke as a Republican to those in the AIDS community who had suffered losses: "It is not you who should feel shame; it is we. We who tolerate ignorance and practice prejudice, we who have taught you to fear." I was the Republican, therefore I was one bearing shame.

Near the close of my remarks I spoke as one with AIDS, addressing my children within hearing of other Republicans:

> *I will not give in, Zachary, because I draw my courage from you. Your silly giggle gives me hope. Your gentle prayers give me strength. And you, my child, give me reason to say to America, "You are at risk." And I will not rest, Max, until I have done all I can to make your world safe. I will seek a place where intimacy is not the prelude to suffering.*

I was speaking as a Republican to Republicans, as a parent to parents, and as a bona fide member of the American AIDS community.

In the first minute of my speech I had said, "I bear a message of challenge, not self-congratulation. I want your attention, not your applause." I was speaking softly and my speech had no "applause lines" to break up the flow.

The power of speaking softly can hardly be exaggerated. We have a recent example. When President Biden, rarely ranked as one of America's great orators, delivered his first address to a joint session of Congress (2021), he spoke quietly, as veteran journalist Jeff Greenfield noted. "He kept his voice, for long stretches, at times a near-whisper of empathy or concern." And he delivered the most powerful image in his address in connection with the grotesque death of George Floyd: "We have all seen the knee of injustice on the neck of Black America." It was delivered, said Greenfield, "almost in a whisper." I know why.

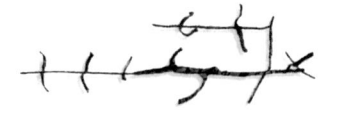

About the Whisper.

We've long known that it's not the volume of your voice that matters; it's the content.

For twenty-five years, the great AIDS spokesperson, founder, and spiritual leader of ACT UP, Larry Kramer, was one of my closest friends. I'd originally been terrified to meet him but, once introduced, we were bonded until the moment of his death at age 84. He loved the title of my convention speech, "A Whisper of AIDS."

"I need to shout," Larry would say, "so you can whisper." He said the night I spoke in Houston was "one of the best nights of my life." A playwright and dramatist, Larry understood the power of words and also the power of the pause, the silence. He was familiar with the volume of conversations in hospices and mortuaries. He knew how to use the intimacy of quiet words, the truth we tell one another in soft language that'll not be overheard. It's the level of sound we use to make people lean in and listen hard. It's modest and humble. It fits me. I don't have a shouter's voice.

The first time I used the word "whisper" in my speech was to describe our response to the death of loved ones. The last time it appeared was at the end, my call "to learn with me the lessons of history and of grace, so my children will not be afraid to say the word 'AIDS' when I am gone. Then their children, and yours, may not need to whisper it at all." Whispering seemed like the right tone for the "shroud of silence" I said the Republicans had placed over AIDS.

I've never regretted using "whisper" to shape and deliver the speech for which I'm most remembered today. Pat Robertson and Cal Thomas, then well-known and much-published ultra-conservatives, wrote stinging commentaries on me and what I'd said. The Rev. Jerry Falwell had a predictably vile set of comments about all people with AIDS. Some hate mail arrived. But most people were kind.

Brent Staples, then of *The New York Times*, wrote an editorial entitled "Teaching Mercy to Republicans." He said that "Ms. Fisher took the crusade for decency and compassion into the lion's den," and he went on to lionize me.

In October, Norman Mailer practically nominated me for sainthood in a *New Republic* essay. The man once described as "the patron saint of the curmudgeonly essay" treated me gently. The speech, he said, was "effective beyond all measure." After paragraphs of praise, he offered this finale: "When Mary Fisher spoke like an angel that night, the floor was awash in tears, and conceivably the nation as well."[4]

I'd earlier imagined that Frank Bruni's feature and Diane Sawyer's report would wrap up my public appearances as a woman with

AIDS. I imagined the same thing about the '92 Convention. I can do this and that'll be it. I'd head for home and my studio.

But that wasn't it. Rather, it was the platform from which I've launched most of my activism for more than thirty years. The speech, together with speeches that followed, opened the door for me to speak to American institutions including prisons, hospices, churches, schools, temples, and congressional committees. It propelled me to Africa as a Special Representative of UNAIDS, to Portugal and Mozambique for the US State Department, and to the Washington National Cathedral in Washington, D.C. as a guest preacher.

Because of the speech, I was introduced to women around the world who showed unquenchable courage and stunning wisdom. I was able to speak to congressional committees and encourage others with my virus to live with grace and hope.

My life was slowly sliding away under the lash of AIDS and, as I grew older and sicker, being invited to speak out gave my life purpose and meaning. I've never been thankful to have AIDS but, in ways both tender and profound, AIDS has given my life meaning in ways I could not have imagined. The speech I gave in Houston in 1992 continues to be read and still makes a difference, sometimes to my surprise. When Oxford Press selected "100 Best American Speeches of the 20th Century," they included mine.

The quiet virus was itself a whisper that has echoed through my life for decades and continues to echo today.

Notes to Chapter Six

1. Luvvie Ajayi Jones is a Nigerian-born American public speaker and four-time *New York Times* bestselling author for books including *Professional Troublemaker: The Fear-Fighter Manual* (Penguin Life, 2021).

2. Pauline Robinson Bush was the first daughter of George and Barbara Bush. She was born on December 20, 1949, and died of leukemia on October 11, 1953. She was named for Barbara's mother, who had died in a car crash just months before Robin's birth. President Bush once described his daughter as being calm and having a "sweet soul." She was "quiet and gentle, and she had lovely little blond curls." Her father would later say of Robin: "She'd fight and cry and play and make her way just like the rest, but there was about her a certain softness... Her peace made me feel strong, and so very important."

3. *American Rhetoric: Online Speech Bank.* Patrick J. Buchanan, Address to the Republican National Convention delivered August 17, 1992, Houston, Texas.

4. For a more detailed description of the lead up to the Houston convention, my speech, and the response, see *My Name is Mary*, pp. 221-248. A more recent essay entitled "The Power of a Whisper" (published on *Medium,* May 6, 2021) contained ideas about silence and speech that are replayed in this chapter.

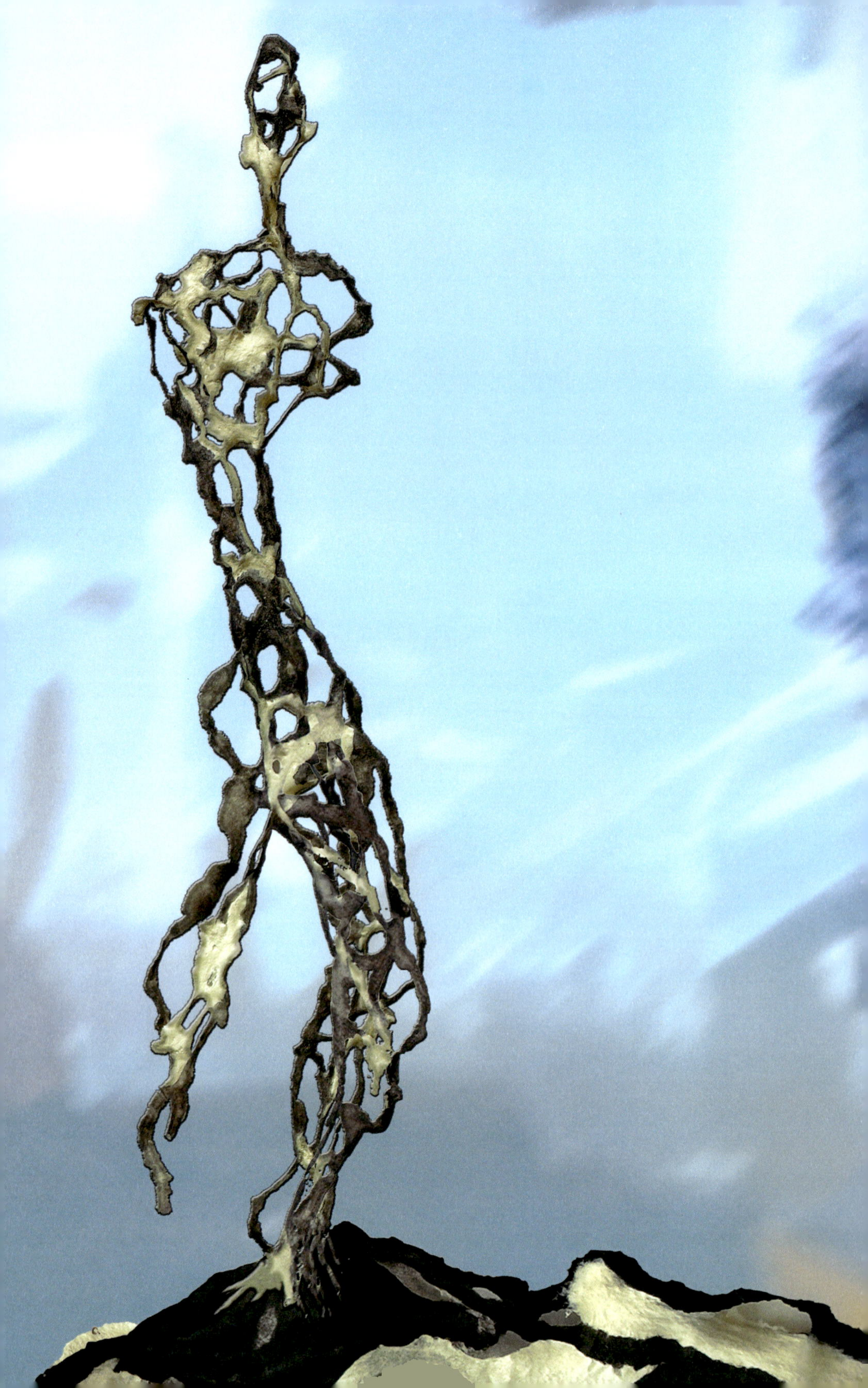

CHAPTER SEVEN

Witness

[T]here's really no such thing as the "voiceless". There are only the deliberately silenced, or the preferably unheard.

Arundhati Roy[1]

I've gained a full lifetime of learning from my experience with AIDS. Had I never been infected I'd not be who I am, for better and for worse, today.

Before I was infected and diagnosed, I had a naïve belief that most elected leaders meant to treat all Americans with dignity and respect. That belief collapsed the morning a US Senator gave me a hug on his way to the Senate floor where he equated people with AIDS to "infected fruit," neither of which — he argued — should be allowed into America. How do you retrieve a hug?

I wish I'd never been infected. I haven't enjoyed AIDS (or cancer, or other forms of suffering). But having AIDS, and having it undeniably in public, has heightened my sense of truth-telling about myself and my own experience. I do not pretend to speak for you. When I speak, I am speaking only for me. I have no right to appropriate the stories or experience of others. But being a woman with AIDS has opened me in surprising ways to other women dealing with illness and its companion problems. We know the common

79

threads woven into our lives because of illness. The patterns may vary but we understand each other's struggles.

Holding an Authentic Voice.

Before I went public with my HIV diagnosis, I thought it was expertise or brilliance that justified speaking out. My friend Dr. Tony Fauci, once the chief medical advisor to the President of the United States, could give a speech. He was the expert. Before him a stream of scholars and researchers made the news. They had something to say, something to teach us. If I had expertise, it was in making handmade paper and building sculptures — not exactly the basis for keynoting a university graduation ceremony.

My experience has taught me this: What lends authenticity to my speech, in public as in private, what gives my voice the abiding "ring of truth" that others may find persuasive, is staying with what I truly know. What I've learned about AIDS I could not have known without experiencing the unique diagnosis and the common struggle, the trembling fear of the virus's impact and the unshakeable gratitude to researchers and physicians who've translated a deadly disease into a usually sustainable illness.

I know AIDS as a woman, a mother, a widow, a person with resources and friendships; I know AIDS intimately in every cell of my body. In part, it's made me who I am today. It's also highlighted who I am *not*. I am not an intravenous drug user, although I might have been given different circumstances. I'm not a gay man, although the list of gay men I've loved and still love is very long. I'm not the grieving parent of a child who suffered the worst of AIDS and died. I'm able to listen and hear their stories with a genuine sense of identification and empathy. I don't speak for any of these, although I've been embraced by them all.

Because they knew I was a woman with AIDS, I've been invited by others who might otherwise distrust me. The virus was my "qualification" to spend time in a women's "sober house" in Harlem. The group there was young, and those with whom I was meeting were all HIV-infected. It was in the period before effective medications for AIDS, so we shared a common future: the grave. I identified with the beautiful young woman who, like me, had two children. She wished she had cancer instead of AIDS. "If I had cancer," she said wistfully, "my family would still accept me. My mother would still hug me." Yes, I understand.

When I retell the story of my visit with these women in Harlem — or report on times spent with women in prison, or in hospices, or in penthouses — I'm enriched by their experiences. Their stories lend strength to mine. By telling my stories of meeting them, listening to them, singing and dancing or crying and moaning with them, my story intersects with theirs. More than once I've met with women whose only request of me is that I "tell them what it's like. Tell them who we are. Tell them." Armed with their courage and request, I've tried to become a witness on their behalf, introducing them to any audience or congregation willing to hear me.

My most recent book (2012) was entitled *Messenger: A Self Portrait.* It's largely a collection of stories I've assimilated along the road to AIDS. Producing that work gave me an opportunity to tell my story and, in the process, remember others who share in parts of my narrative. Illustration? I was invited to speak at a luncheon of pleasant women philanthropists. The room swayed a little when I said that "babies and surgical patients are…infected through no fault of their own. They are the 'innocent victims.' But righteous gay men, street-corner hookers, or a woman like me — we're different: We're not merely infected; we're corrupted."[2] Like it or not, I am the message I bring.

Defying the Image.

If the popular image of women with AIDS in Africa were true, then all those I've met over the many years while serving the US and UNAIDS are contradictions to the stereotype.

The first time I was genuinely grateful to have AIDS — and I can qualify that statement in all sorts of ways — was in Africa, with other women who had AIDS. When they invited me into their homes and villages, and when we gathered in the communal marketplace, we told our stories to each other. Despite differences in language, culture, nationality, medical care, and life roles, we laughed at the same jokes (usually, at the expense of men). They invited me to join them in dances and songs. We embraced. We were literally "blood sisters." We were women celebrating women, refusing to yield our joy in the face of illness and death. These sisters gave me a gift I had longed to find, a strength that I have never lost.

The women who best speak for African women are African women. They include Idah Mukuka, my dear friend and colleague who's created community programs educating and empowering girls and women. Or consider Ellen Johnson Sirleaf, who led Liberia through reconciliation after a bloody civil war; Farida Charity, the brilliant young peace activist who brought calm to northern Uganda; Malala Yousafzai, the youngest-in-history Nobel Peace Prize laureate who was shot in Pakistan at age 15 for opposing Taliban restrictions on female education; Meaza Ashenafi, the first female Chief Justice of Ethiopia and the only woman graduating from her law school, who went on to revamp her nation's laws to bring justice to women; and many more. Every one of them is living proof of Geraldine Ferraro's profound claim, "Some leaders are born women."

Silencing the Oppressed.

Our stomachs sour and our souls are troubled when we see how effectively the poor or the oppressed are denied a voice. Had I never contracted AIDS I'm not sure I would have been brought face-to-face with oppression. I've now seen and heard how the oppressed are silenced by prejudice and policy and power. They are denied a voice in newsrooms and courtrooms. Our culture tends to muffle their cries and turn away, wanting not to see or hear the truth.

Some effort to silence the abused is personal, private. How shall the woman smuggled over the barbed wire border find her voice when she speaks no English? What about the woman beaten by her "lover," the child burned by the cigarettes of his "stepfather," the girl taught to stay silent by lessons of rape. One by one, these become members of the growing company of the silenced. I've met them all; they have names and special places in my memory.

In recent years, heroic women came out of Hollywood's woodwork when Harvey Weinstein was finally exposed, first by Ashley Judd; they told their utterly believable stories and thereby gained their own voice. Or consider E. Jean Carroll: She accused Donald Trump of rape and defamation. A jury found her claims convincing and awarded her $5 million in damages. After enduring further torture under Trump's vicious and profane attacks, she was awarded an additional $83.3 million in damages by a second jury. Through it all, E. Jean Carroll used her voice to demonstrate truthfulness and courage.

Among the darkest and most painful chapters of American history are those written in the blood of massacres. Some, especially against Indigenous people — the "Indians" whose land we've taken over the past centuries — were officially sanctioned efforts to slaughter men, women, and especially children. President Teddy Roosevelt left us with a magnificent legacy of national parks and the shameful belief that "the only good Indian is a dead Indian." It was an American call to the Nazis' "final solution."

Just now, a century and a half after the killings, we're coming to grips with the deception, tortures, and massacres that have scarred America's history with its indigenous peoples. From Bear River (1863) to Salt Creek (1871) to the infamous Wounded Knee (1890), the mass slaughter of innocents to eradicate entire populations was an approved official policy bolstered by lies and greed; kill the Indians and redistribute their land.

The setting of the Sand Creek Massacre (1864) in southeastern Colorado is now a National Historical Site, with a memorial where a park ranger explains how 700-some US Cavalry riders descended on peaceful Indian families who'd settled along Sand Creek for the winter. Some reports say 160 Indians were slaughtered; other estimates range up to 600. The numeric truth is uncertain but the atrocity of the slaughter is nauseatingly clear. The dead were mostly elderly, infirm, women, and especially children. Some soldiers took time after their slaughter to mutilate their victims so they could bring home body parts as trophies of their kill.

I know that American history contains accounts of heroism, decency, courage, and honor. I'm grateful to be American. But over the past few decades I've lived with an increasingly uneasy silence as a different truth of our history rises from the grave — bearing almost no resemblance to what I was taught, or not taught, in school. At first, I hoped it wasn't true. Now, I hope it isn't repeated.

Sarah Quinn tells the largely unreported story of the 1889 massacre in Leflore County, Mississippi. Black farmers, struggling to survive, organized a co-op, or "Alliance," to increase the poverty-level prices they were paid for their goods. The National Guard, called in to impose order, arrested 40 local Black men and turned them over to a local white mob. One scholar estimates that the Leflore County Massacre took the lives of 25 Black people; reports at the time actually suggested 100 people were tortured and killed, including women and children. As a strategy to take away the voice of the oppressed, Quinn notes, the killing "was purposely not recorded in the county news, and a journalist who later went to investigate found locals too terrified to speak of it."[3]

Terror works. Intimidation is a potent silencer. When Black people in Ocoee, Florida asked for the right to vote, a white mob turned Election Day 1920 into what historian Paul Ortiz has called "the single bloodiest election day in modern American history." At least sixty Black people died. Black homes were burned. Black men were castrated. The horror went largely unreported.[4] I never read about it in any history book I was assigned.

Time and again, history proves that nothing is as silent as the grave.

Voices I Don't Want to Hear.

I confess there are voices I try to avoid hearing. Some belong to charlatans pretending to be national leaders. I have no need to hear more from any of them.

The late Dr. Mathilde Krim, a founder of amfAR (American Foundation for AIDS Research), who wished I'd go public, told me this story in 1991. After she'd given a speech about women with AIDS at a regional medical conference for OB-GYNs, she asked if they had any questions they'd like to ask. "The place went dead silent," she said, "so I asked again and still got no response. Finally, one kindly doctor cleared his throat and said, 'Well, actually Dr. Krim, we don't treat women like that.' I was, as I am, a woman like that. The assembled doctors wouldn't have appreciated my voice.

WITNESS   87

In the mid-1990s, I was the keynote speaker at a Kansas City AIDS fundraiser. It had been well publicized in advance to help raise interest and funds. We shouldn't have been surprised when, as the doors opened after the event, we were greeted by the Rev. Fred Phelps and his shouting, picketing, threatening crowd. They'd come by bus to garner a little media attention and to silence those who'd spent the evening with me. Mine was a voice they didn't want to hear or have heard by others.

I'm personally uncomfortable when people I don't know approach me in public. I don't want to ask for trouble. When I'm walking to the nearby parking lot and a homeless woman suddenly appears, two children in tow, crying, "I'm hungry, please help me," I freeze. I don't want to enable begging as a strategy to get cash, I don't want to pretend not to hear, and I don't want to feel guilty if I hurry to my car. I'm not sure what's best to do but doing nothing leaves me with a troubled soul.

The voice of poverty speaks to us from every gender, every race, every age, every language, and every community. If I don't want to hear that voice it's because it makes me deeply uncomfortable.

Matthew Desmond tells me that I ought to feel something is wrong in these moments. My soul should be uneasy when I can eat and the homeless woman's children cannot.

"To understand the causes of poverty," says Desmond, "we must look beyond the poor. Those of us living lives of privilege and plenty must examine ourselves. Are we — we the secure, the insured, the housed, the college educated, the protected, the lucky — connected to all this needless suffering?"[5] He then pours out 400 pages of evidence that the answer is Yes. I'm not only connected; I'm part of what causes the poverty we don't want to see or hear. I hate this and I'd like you to hate it too.

The beggars on any street corner from India to Indianapolis can speak with enough volume and passion for us to hear them. But until we both hear and act on what we're hearing, we haven't truly listened.

The beggar with a voice is still voiceless in the arena of the powerful, the communities of people like me. They have the voice that we've learned to recognize as "the deliberately silenced, the preferably unheard."

Notes to Chapter Seven

1. Arundhati Roy, *The God of Small Things* (Random House, 1997). Written between 1992 and 1996, this was Arundhati Roy's debut novel. She is widely recognized as one of India's most revered and successful novelists. *The God of Small Things* was awarded the Booker Prize in the year of its publication.

2. Mary Fisher, *Messenger: A Self Portrait* (Greenleaf Book Group Press, 2012), pp. 32-33.

3. Sarah L. Quinn, *American Bonds: How Credit Markets Shaped a Nation* (Princeton University Press, 2019), p. 61.

4. Isabel Wilkerson, *Caste: The Origins of Our Discontents* (Random House, 2020), pp. 228-229.

5. Matthew Desmond, *Poverty, by America* (Random House, 2023), p. 8. Desmond won the Pulitzer Prize for his earlier work, *Evicted: Poverty and Profit in the American City,* and is widely recognized as a leading American "scholar of poverty."

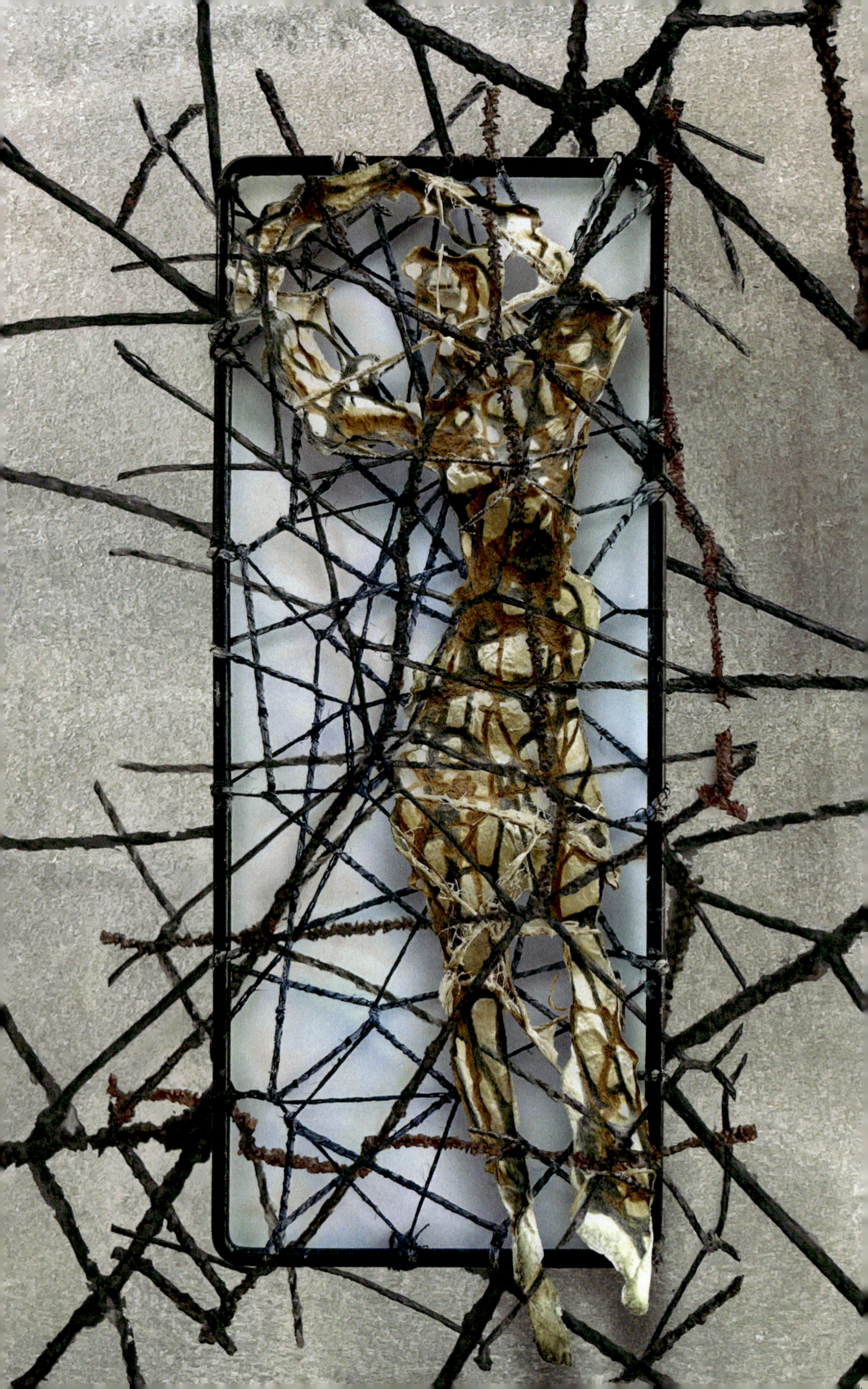

CHAPTER EIGHT

Speaking Without Words

To live a creative life, we must lose our fear of being wrong.

Joseph Chilton Pearce[1]

We communicate in so many ways. The conversation with a neighbor, cry of an infant, wail of a frustrated 2-year-old, giggles of new lovers, moans of a struggling elder, and so much more. All communicate something from us or to us, and we participate in that communication when we listen and respond. It's all about being human, I suppose.

Not all communication, of course, is by voice, or by voice alone. When I hear Andrea Bocelli hold one of those spine-tingling high Cs, it doesn't matter if the words are in Italian or English. It doesn't matter if there are any words at all. What's communicating is that voice, that impossible sound, that high C. We who are blessed to have sight may draw a deep breath when a mountain sunset appears over the western horizon; our slow exhale tells the story. Even the "voice" of the poet is more than sound: it's the arrangement of words and silences of something artfully crafted. Alvin Ailey choreographed rage and beauty. Fashion designer Tom Ford has dressed a generation in art. I once spent a day being taught tap dancing by the award-winning Gregory Hines. For more than thirty years the moving lyrics written by my dear friend Don Black have carried me through hard and fearful times.

We are communicative creatures, we humans, and we love our communication when it comes to us as art. Which is where I wanted to go in this conversation.

Beyond Speech.

I can hardly remember the details of much of my childhood and adolescence. The especially awful times have lost some of their pain, some but not all. The good times, at least in my memory, were mostly brief and rare. Except for this one event. Standing out from all other memories of those years is the moment I first walked into the room containing our school's array of looms. I was twelve years old, and I came to life when I heard my art teacher say, "It's okay, you can use it. Here, this loom is for you."

I loved the smell of the wood and the feel of the fibers, the smoothness with which the shuttle slid through the warp. I watched in wonder as threads became fabrics, and fabrics emerged with patterns. When I was troubled or sad, the loom was comfort. When I was frightened and uncertain, the loom was assurance and hope.

As the years unfolded and I graduated school, I left behind, with only occasional reunions, the room that held my reassuring loom.

What I took with me was a passion for creating beauty, a passion that's never dimmed. A friend once said he'd define art as "a way of wrapping the truth in something beautiful." My life is the truth I've always wanted to wrap in beauty.

Weaving was my first real adventure with creating art. Then came sketching, handmade paper, printing, knitting, and quilting. I've worked at art in closet-sized spaces and in spacious, welcoming studios. More than a half-century past my high school loom, I am still comforted when I walk into my studio no matter its size or locale.

Vincent van Gogh's claim that "art is to console those who are broken by life" was confirmed by his tragic end and still seems about right to me. If art can move us to tears, it can also move us to ecstasy. I've long been a supporter of Broadway Cares/Equity Fights AIDS. But I never enjoyed Broadway more than the night I had a walk-on part in Cyndi Lauper's *Kinky Boots*. I smiled for a month after my dozen minutes on stage. In fact, remembering it, I still smile.

My friends who are artists both inspire and sometimes intimidate me, but mostly they encourage me to risk being wrong, doing something that doesn't work. The late playwright Larry Kramer told me he'd rewritten his first Broadway hit, *The Normal Heart*, "at least a half-dozen times." Judith Light has won scores of awards during her half-century of acting but remains eager to take on new risks with untested roles. Don Black, who collaborated with Andrew Lloyd Webber on such hits as *Aspects of Love* and *Sunset Boulevard*, said that he approached every composition "with fear, awe and love." Actress and activist Naomi Watts showed me how exhausting it can be to work in front of the camera with a hundred million critics waiting to pass judgment. And what can I say of Keb' Mo' — Kevin Roosevelt Moore — who brings the blues to life with gentle power and visits my home "to offer a little healing" when I'm not well.

When I think of all these risk-takers, what I know I share with them is a desire to creatively expose a truth, conveying something worthwhile from one person to another. It may not be speech but it's definitely communication. And when it's absolutely, remarkably good, it may even be worthy to be called "art."

Making a Statement with Art.

Most quilters know the historic work of the Black matriarchs in the Gee's Bend community of Boykin, Alabama. These women inherited a unique technique of quilt-making with a very distinctive style. Their quilts were once said to carry messages that guided runaway slaves as they traveled the Underground Railroad. A quilt from Gee's Bend warms the body and the soul. It's a treasured piece of art and, at the same time, an enduring evidence of activism.

I was being interviewed for an article in *Architectural Digest* when I was asked how I balance my art with my activism.[2] It was a curious question because it assumed that art and activism are inherently different, as if Larry Kramer's Normal Heart (for example) wasn't both an artist's product and an activist's scream.

"For some folks," I admitted, "activism is what they've chosen to do, but that wasn't and isn't my experience."

My activism is an expression of who I am beginning as a woman and a woman with AIDS. When I've produced a book or given a speech or created a sculpture, I've always tried to make it a truthful reflection of who I am and I think most artists do [this] while they're working. Whether or not it's activism, I think it reflects who we are, what we are and how we feel.

On my best days, I'll let you know I'm thrilled to be an artist and love my opportunities as an activist. Come with me to my studio sometime and you'll see an activist artist at work.

Learning Some Hard Realities.

I still believed in the essential goodness of American leaders when, in 1995, three years after Houston's speech, I was invited by the US Senate's Committee on Rules and Administration to mount a one-woman exhibit, an historic first, in the Senate's magnificent Russell Rotunda. My art was going on display between the marble statues of the Great Hall. No female artist had ever been so honored. I was beside myself choosing pieces to go into the exhibit and preparing all the materials needed for my week of fame.

Ten days before we opened my exhibit, *The Washington Times* published a small but disparaging report on my work. The *Times* wrote on behalf of the Rev. Sun Myung Moon, its 1982 founder, who loved all things right wing. Conservative commentators and politicians were known to quote the *Times* as if it were biblical truth. No one from the paper had ever seen my art but they were certain it was "controversial" and "bizarre." I was stung by their little piece and assumed it wouldn't matter. (*Lesson One: No matter how small or unworthy, media matters.*)

The exhibit was slated to open on Monday morning, September 25. Three days earlier, as my artwork was being loaded on the truck bound for the Rotunda, I was interrupted by a call from the Senate Committee's chair. In the nicest possible terms, he told me the exhibit was off. He said one member of his committee had objected, and one was enough. My historic place in the Senate Rotunda was denied.[3]

Owing to the quick work of a few friends, including Michael Iskowitz and the late Senator Edward ("Ted") Kennedy, we mounted my artwork in the Carpenters Union Building two blocks from the Rotunda. On Monday morning, we opened the exhibit on schedule as the lead story on NBC's TODAY Show with Katie Couric broadcasting live from our space.

The disappointing flap over my exhibit actually involved only one piece, which had not yet been seen by any senator. I had sculpted a box into the look of a coffin, and around the scrolled edge I had carved a quotation from one of my speeches: "Let us unite in life rather than in death." The exhibit was all about AIDS. It was an artistic way of saying that waiting for a heavenly reunion isn't required. We could come together and achieve shared goals here and now, if we only wanted to.

I truly hadn't realized the risk I was taking when I accepted the Senate's original invitation. As an artist, I was wounded by the cancellation of the exhibit. I had wanted to stand up for every woman with AIDS. The TODAY Show was great. Katie Couric was kind. I was pleased when one presidential library and another presidential museum asked to host the exhibit. But I was bruised when, on the complaint of one senator who'd never seen my art, an honor for all women artists was withdrawn. I was pained, and I was also educated. I saw in intimate terms how the power of the patriarchy could result in decisions that impacted my life. (*Lesson Two: I'm not in control.*)

As an activist, it was an important lesson for me. I had mounted the stage in Houston in 1992, and arranged the exhibit in Washington three years later, always believing that if I could just explain the realities of AIDS to people with power, they would believe and then they would act. At the very least, I thought they would listen.

What I realized while looking toward the Capitol through the window of the Carpenters Union Building was that I'd been naïve. I was grateful for the support shown by several senators and representatives; they were kind. But they did not have the clout needed to secure more money for research. They did not have the votes to change the course of an epidemic that was then taking nearly 150,000 American lives each year with three times that number coming down the pike. They were willing to give me a hug or accept one of my red AIDS ribbons. But if I were to die, I'd be just one more casualty among the headlines of that day's deaths. *The Washington Times* wouldn't cover it.

Maybe no one in power really cared enough to stake their careers on an unpopular cause.

Remembering those days, I find myself embracing one of the glorious lines from our youthful genius poet, Amanda Gorman. She had it right. "Some days, we just need a place where we can bleed in peace."[4]

Notes to Chapter Eight

1. Source unknown.

2. See *Architectural Digest*, January 22, 2018, for the full article with photographs of some of my artwork.

3. For a full description of the flap over the Senate exhibit, see *Messenger: A Self Portrait*, pp. 146-149.

   When the exhibit's opening was planned at the Nixon Library in California, I'd been invited to deliver a keynote address. By the time the event rolled around (spring 1996) I was feeling the effects of AIDS and the side-effects of largely untested-on-women drugs. Since I was too sick to travel, the Library published my speech in a pamphlet entitled "Private Artist and Public Art."

   Many of the themes in this book are foreshadowed in that speech I never delivered:

   The language of artists is a language very much like the language of religion. Artists speak of reaching into their souls, of listening for God, of being given visions, of dreading the truth they need to show to others. The world of art echoes with the language of the ancient prophets. And I must tell you that some of the most spiritually focused and joyful moments of my life have been when God and I were making art together....

   W. H. Auden, the poet, introduced his last collection of poems with a wonderful, confessional foreword in which he publicly apologized for having earlier published some "dishonest" poetry. "A dishonest poem," he wrote, "is one which expresses, no matter how well, feelings or beliefs which the author never felt or entertained... One must be honest even about one's prejudices...."

> *Those who observe the artist's work must allow the truth to be spoken. My earlier ancestors in the tribes of Israel had the unpleasant characteristic of stoning prophets when they announced a truth the people did not like. And one wonders if such stonings are finished, even in our own day.*

4. Amanda Gorman, from her debut collection, which shares a title with one of her poems, *Call Us What We Carry: Poems*; (Viking Books, 2021).

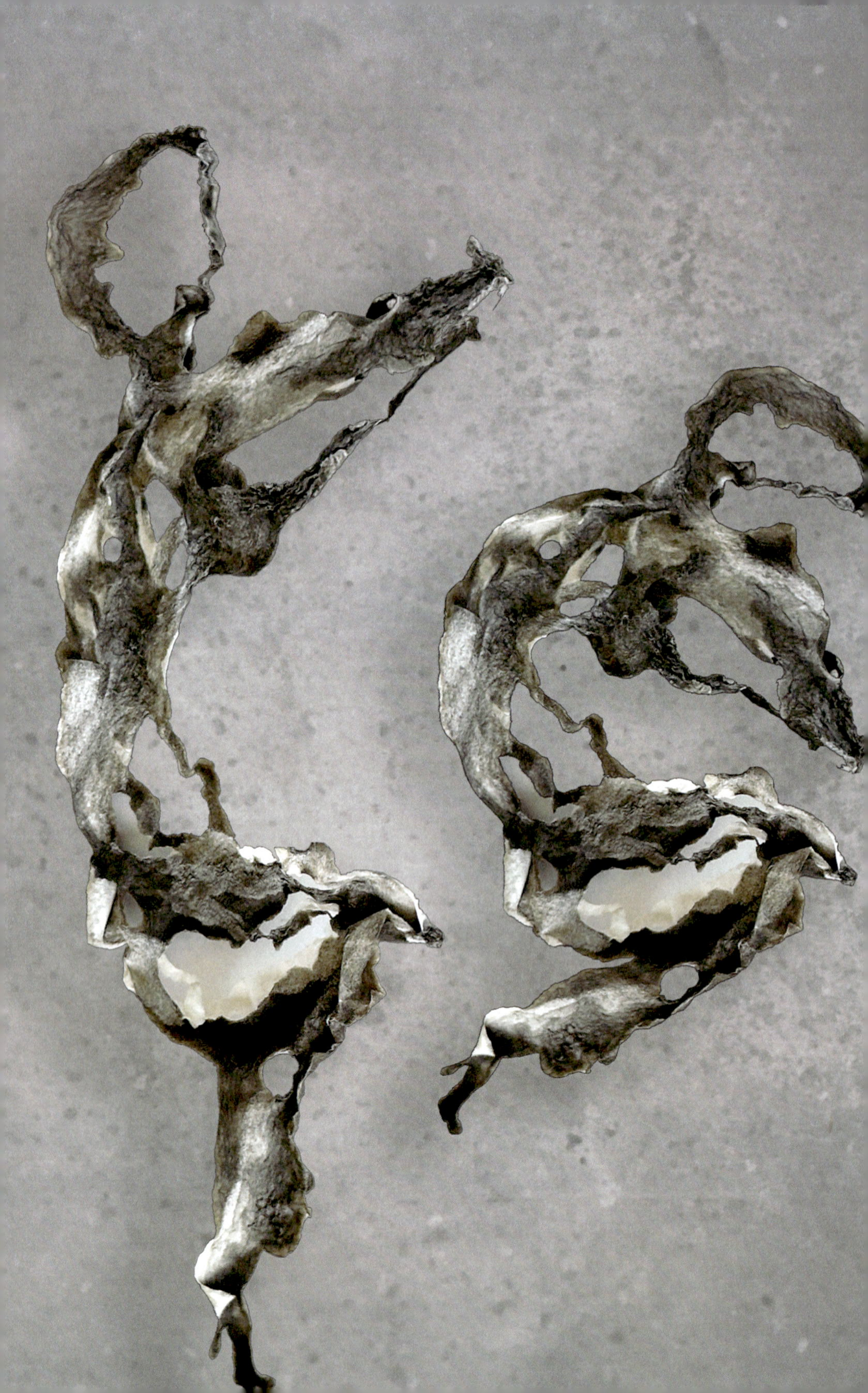

CHAPTER NINE

Voices and Violence

You have not converted a man because you have silenced him.

John Morley[1]

I hate to remind most of my friends that they scoffed at me when, in 2015, I warned that Donald Trump — known in most New York City circles as a sleazy sham — could become the next president. The media was keeping him on the national stage day after day. No matter how outrageous his speeches, they bought him free time on the daily news. And people were listening.

Since his election in 2016, Trump and those licking his boots have been hard on public truth. Lies have gained so much traction that nearly half of American voters believe them. Falsehoods packaged in rants and rages have continued to give Trump media play. Increasingly, his lies are more preposterous than they are dishonest. They're also life-threatening.

After the 2020 election, Trump (with others) went on the attack. He picked on innocent people with false claims intended to smear their integrity and crush their lives.

In Georgia, election workers Shaye Moss and her mother, Ruby Freeman, had done their jobs with distinction and gratitude. For their service to the Atlanta community, and owing to their unwillingness to bend either the rules or the truth, they were pilloried by right-wing liars led by Trump, who said Ms. Moss was "a professional vote-scammer and hustler," falsely claiming that the mother-daughter duo had cheated to help Democrats.

Giving testimony to the US Congress some months after the 2020 election, Ms. Freeman said through tears, "I've lost my name, I've lost my reputation, I've lost my sense of security." And then she added the haunting question, "Do you know what it feels like to have the president of the United States target you?"

What it feels like to me is the opening volley in the assassination of truth and truthful people. To be attacked as these women were attacked is a violation of common decency and an assault on the Constitution of the United States. In an earlier age, before social media gained the power to convey lies to billions of people at the speed of light, there might have been time to examine the facts and call for some accuracy. But today, lies accumulate on top of lies, and the truth goes rogue.

I was moved, deeply, when I heard Ms. Moss's note that she had faced "a lot of threats wishing death upon me." These were not idle claims; they were the promise of violence with evidence that the promise might be kept. It was the time of the COVID-19 Pandemic and I was mostly hiding from public view. But my soul bled for Ms. Moss and her mother.

Three years after the attacks on these good women, I discovered that the violence of right-wing rhetoric was closer and more frequent than I'd known. For some decades Dr. Michael ("Mike") Saag has been not only my cousin but my lead physician, a distinguished researcher and professor emeritus at the University of

Alabama at Birmingham. He's spent his lifetime saving the lives of others, including my own. But after dealing with lies spread by the White House during the pandemic, Mike wrote in 2023, "Like many infectious disease specialists, I attempted to keep the public informed of the new developments." For his efforts, he was "trolled on Twitter, received attacks on social media sites, and answered threatening phone calls including one anonymous caller who warned me to 'be careful' because he knew where my granddaughter lived."[2] Tony Fauci gathered so many credible death threats against him and his family that they needed 24-hour-a-day law enforcement protection.

Escalating Rhetoric.

The world has always entertained its share of kooks and fools. Most were not as well-armed as they may be today. Given the prevalence of lies and guns (a deadly mix), we've not previously faced the level of threatened violence we endure now. Violent outbursts from Trump are so frequent that they are being normalized. Unless they're accompanied by a mass shooting, we hardly notice that it's happened again. And the mass shootings are so frequent that they rarely make the headlines. We find them below the fold on page eight.

Some of us have inherited a legacy of being violated. Black, red and brown Americans have been hounded by whites and abused by the police. Black parents need to give their children, especially their sons, "the talk" about how to behave when dealing with the police. Immigrants and LGBTQ+ people have known cruelty and violence for generations. The Ku Klux Klan, which garnered outsized power in the 1920s and '30s, used lynchings and poll watchers as routine strategies for intimidation. Hatred was spewing from pulpits and bar stools in the days of Jim Crow and well beyond.

> *Long before Tucker Carlson's unvarnished nationalism, before Glenn Beck's conspiracy theories and Rush Limbaugh's philippics, Charles Edward Coughlin held millions of American radio listeners in his thrall, playing to their fears while also stoking their prejudices. Make that Father Coughlin, for he was a Roman Catholic cleric. Known as "the radio priest," he in many ways paved a path for today's relentless stream of talk-show bluster and televangelism.*[3]

The rhetoric of false accusations and promised paybacks is not new. What's new is the prevalence and acceptability of such language. The possibility that someone will visit terminal violence on your granddaughter because they disagree with your science or politics has become staggeringly common. We haven't learned, as a nation, how to manage the haters. When threats are distant and vague, they're a thunder rumbling safely somewhere over the horizon. But when those who practice the rhetoric of violence come across your front yard, armed and angry, we are in different territory. It's no longer hypothetical. Violence is knocking on our doors.

Historian Ruth Ben-Ghiat says that Trump uses rhetoric in rallies and on social media to "prop up his personality cult, circulate his lies, and emotionally retrain Americans to see violence as positive and even patriotic." That seems right.[4] Despite his denials and false claims, the fact is that "threats of violence and intimidating rhetoric soared after Trump lost the 2020 election and falsely claimed the vote was stolen."[5] The line between Trump's speech on January 6 (2021) and the mob that stormed Congress moments later is direct. Words can inspire violence and that day offered more proof than we ever needed.

I was left watching, listening, and pondering, frightened at what's to come, angry at what had already been taken away. When I sat with all this in the quiet of my home, I realized that I was feeling an agonizing sense of loss. I had lost my sense of confidence in America. I had lost my admiration for the presidency which I had served. I had lost my belief that, in the end, we'll be okay, that we'll come through this and my grandchildren's world will be intact. I was acutely, pervasively, and undeniably saddened at all that had been lost.

The Call to Courage.

The power of fear can be seen in the eyes of the Black child learning about his uncle's lynching or heard in the trembling voice of the college student facing her rapist in court. It isn't just fear; it's terror. It gives us lock jaw and makes us look away and say nothing while evil plays out next to us. We can be intimidated into obedience. But being intimidated isn't the same as being persuaded. It merely means that we dare not do what our troubled souls assure us needs to be done. We live in uneasy silence. We can't believe this is happening despite abundant evidence that it surely is.

As I write, the Brown shirts of the Nazi regime are being re-dressed in the American far right. There's a gospel of Christian White Nationalism that's being not only whispered but brazenly broadcast without shame or apology. When millions of Americans believe violence is a legitimate strategy for achieving political or social change, and those who love violence also love their (court-protected) guns, it isn't foolish to be terrified. It's human. Perhaps it's wise.

We know that we'll pay a steep price when we begin yielding to intimidation. But the cost we'll pay is in the distant future; the fear is now. I spoke at the march in Washington, D.C. the last time the AIDS Memorial Quilt was unfurled in its entirety on the National Mall. It was October 1996. I joined the marchers with friends and my sons, walking past the Quilt, visiting. Someone was singing up ahead. And then we began to hear shouts. As we moved forward, a pack of right-wing wolves was howling for our demise, chanting "Die! Die! Die!" A peaceful candlelight march brought out a gang of ugly, belligerent fanatics. I drew my children closer and assured them we were safe. In tribute to the discipline and courage of the marchers, the chants were ignored and the march went forward.

Years earlier, I had been introduced to the risk of violence when a security detail was assigned to our home because my father was a Jew influencing US policy toward Israel. The need to be protected by armed guards is enough to generate fear that's tangible, paralyzing.

Despite that fear, or perhaps because of it, I hear the words of Dietrich Bonhoeffer with renewed admiration: "Silence in the face of evil is itself evil…. Not to speak is to speak. Not to act is to act." When facing real threats of real violence intended to silence real objectors, the pastor's famous quotation is not merely an ideal we admire but a call to action. Our reputations may be stained in campaigns launched on social media. Our histories may be falsely revised. Our motives may be questioned. Some of us may pay with our lives. Too dramatic? It wasn't drama for Bonhoeffer in the Flossenbürg concentration camp when the hangman measured his noose to be sure Bonhoeffer's neck would snap cleanly in his execution. It takes vast courage — perhaps more than I can muster — not to wither under the lash of someone else's powerful fury.

It's important for me to remember that Bonhoeffer and others like him were men with families, careers, and dreams. Their courage was remarkable but, we don't do justice to them by making them more-than-human, as if they could do and say things we are incapable of doing or saying ourselves. They were "one of us" as certainly as they were grim witnesses to the cost of truth and justice when the ranks of the haters continue to swell.[6] They're remarkable in the same sense that Shaye Moss and Ruby Freeman are remarkable. They told the truth. They paid the cost.

I'm convinced that we are called to be witnesses against evil by embodying truth, showing decency and kindness, protecting freedom, and assuring justice not only, or first, for ourselves but for "the least of these" among us. If once this seemed like a distant but admirable ideal we now see that it is an inescapable and honest plea. We're being asked by our circumstances to live up to the ideals we've so frequently, perhaps flippantly, embraced.

Bearing Witness.

It isn't necessary or right for us to answer anger with anger. We won't defeat hatred with hatred. We need, each of us, to find a truthful and patient way to contend with the lies and threats spewed by so-called leaders.

In ways large or small, depending on the opportunities given to us, we're called not to cower in silence and fear but to stand up, speak out, and bear witness against evil. It may be across the family dinner table. Perhaps it's in our office or at the store, in my knitting circle or in your congregation. Maybe the opportunities come because we've volunteered to serve a community organization. Maybe we've had the courage to become election workers. Whatever the platform, my soul demands that I face lies with truth and threats with courage.

I know the excuses not to tangle with evil. I've tried most of them at one time or another myself.

> "Who am I anyway?" I'm no expert or national figure. I'm not qualified. I'll keep silent.
>
> "It's frightening." I have a family to protect, grandchildren to keep safe. It's reckless of me to challenge the fanatics.
>
> "I'm not worthy." No one's elected me to be a purveyor of truth. I need more experience, more credentials.

"I'm only one." One lonely voice won't matter. I can't do this alone.

"I'm unimportant." No one would take me seriously. I don't have any right to speak to these issues.

"I'm too busy." I don't have time to get hung up in these issues. There's dinner to be made.

The list of excuses is long. I know them all. They explain why, while the media reports the newest volley of lies and abuses, I live on in my uneasy silence. After all, most of our lives are intact and secure. No one has attacked me yet. My home is still safe. Why risk our comfort if we aren't being assaulted?

The Black poet and activist Nikki Giovanni recently told an audience, "I sometimes wonder what kind of slave I would have been." The audience chuckled, imagining Giovanni would never have buckled under the yoke of a master. It's impossible to even imagine her as a slave.

But the chuckling stopped when she added, "And I sometimes wonder what kind of slave owner [you'd] have been." The other white folk and I had the same response, a very uneasy silence.

Notes to Chapter Nine

1. John Morley, a British statesman prominent in the closing chapter of the 19th Century. Quite certainly the quote is properly attributed to him but the original source, whether from one of his many speeches or from his writings (he was, among other things, a newspaper editor), is unknown .

2. Michael S. Saag, MD, "Coronavirus Disease (COVID) and the Fog of War," Voices of ID, Infectious Diseases Society of America.

3. PBS Special, *Today in History: The Father Coughlin Story*; March 9, 2022.

4. Requoted by Jennifer Rubin in *The Washington Post,* January 12, 2024.

5. From a Reuters Special Report, "Politics of Violence," August 9, 2023, by Ned Parker and Peter Eisler. The authors note that much of the threatened violence is directed to election workers, a traditionally "safe" role carried out by ordinary American workers and volunteers.

6. The quote is nearly always attributed to the famed German pastor Dietrich Bonhoeffer, but its source is actually uncertain. Some scholars point to Francis McPeek's 1945 essay entitled "Not to Act is to Act." Historians and journalists have rummaged through Bonhoeffer's writings and come up empty. The tone of the message echoes that of Bonhoeffer's friend and colleague, pastor Martin Niemöller, the author of the famed "[T]hey came for the socialists, and I did not speak out — because I was not a socialist…."

We included the Niemöller quote in my 1992 speech in Houston using this version: "They came after the Jews, and I was not a Jew, so I did not protest. They came after the Trade Unionists, and I was not a Trade Unionist, so I did not protest. They came after the Roman Catholics, and I was not a Roman Catholic, so I did not protest. Then they came after me, and there was no one left to protest."

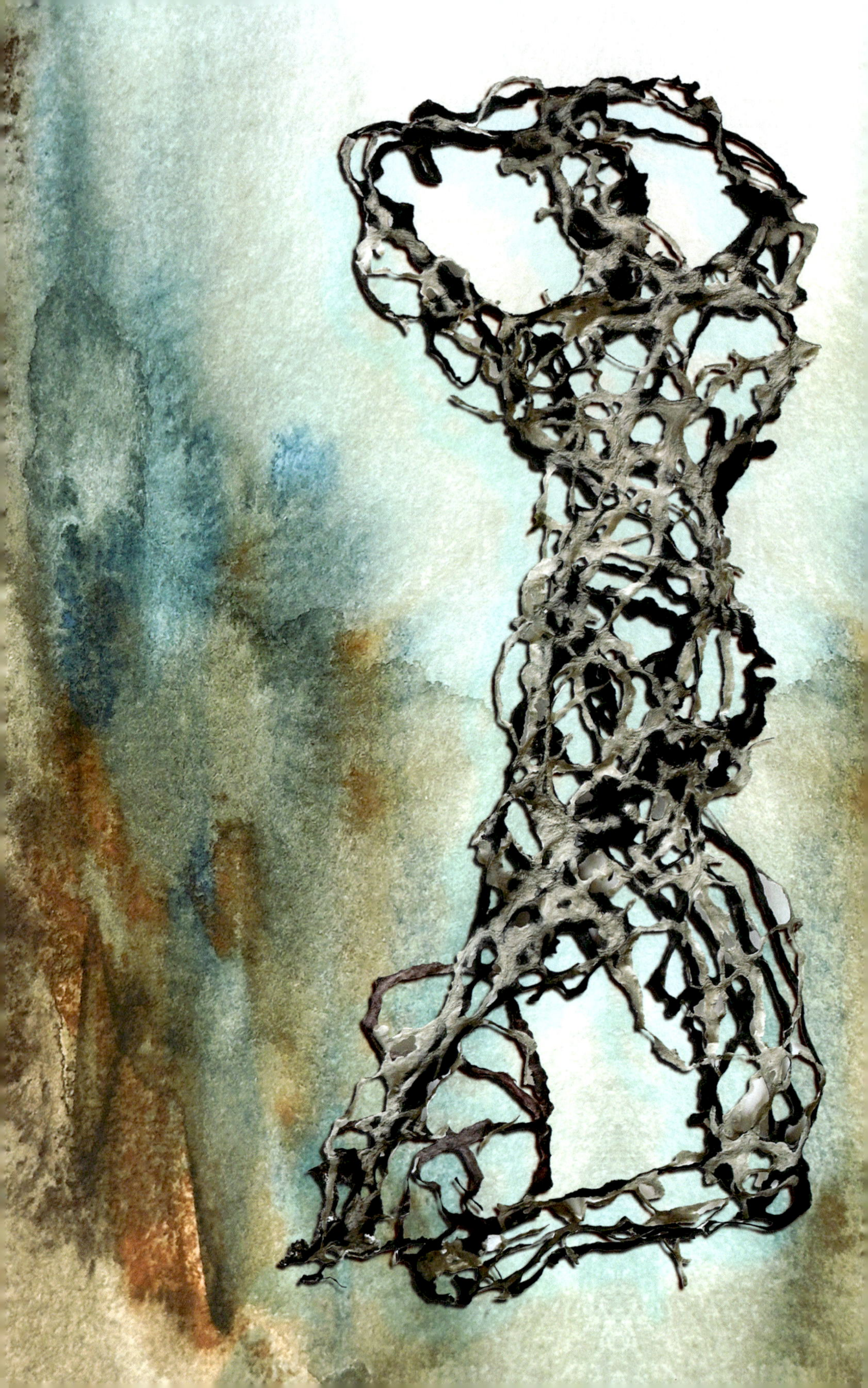

CHAPTER TEN

Not Going Quietly

Life is never made unbearable by circumstances, but only by lack of meaning and purpose.

Viktor Frankl[1]

Let me be candid: When my alarm drags me out of a sleepy morning fog, I do not sit up and think about the meaning of life. I'm thinking coffee. Then pills. Where's the dog, how did I forget the appointment that started 15 minutes ago, and is it possible to get another 15 minutes of sleep? If you really need my attention at this hour, pour a cup and give me a moment. I need coffee.

I've known other stretches of time when, in fact, I *did* wake up wondering if life had meaning. Some mornings I was disappointed to wake up, period. I was depressed, seriously. I may have felt what Senator John Fetterman, the hulking, hoodie-wearing Pennsylvanian, felt shortly after his election when he checked himself into a hospital while dealing with thoughts of suicide. His colleague, Senator Tina Smith from Minnesota, described her own depression that "drained hope away, and the promise that I'd ever feel hopeful again." I know that sense of utter hopelessness.

For more than 75 years, Viktor Frankl's landmark book, *Man's Search for Meaning*, has been a bestseller. The basic claim of

113

Frankl's book is that life can be hard, even excruciating, but it is never "unbearable" if we have a sense of meaning — if we know why we're here, what purpose our life may have.

It's a very pleasant idea, I think, until we run into real-life tragedies. What about the father who answers the midnight call to learn that a drunk driver has killed his 16-year-old daughter? Or how about the mother caressing her ten-year-old daughter's hand as she withers under the cruelty of chemo? Or, if you'll allow me, what about an ex-husband's admission that he's infected you with a terminal disease? The gruesome realities of life can make Frankl's theory seem philosophically lovely, but also useless and naïve.

What makes Frankl's claim compelling is that this man knew suffering. He was writing as a Jewish therapist in 1945, in the shadow of the Holocaust. He had narrowly survived three years in four Nazi concentration camps. His father had been shipped to the Terezin ghetto camp, where he soon died of starvation and pneumonia. Frankl's mother and brother were shoveled into the furnaces in Auschwitz. His bride, Tilly, pregnant, was a nurse caring for others until moments before she was killed in Bergen-Belsen. Against all such "circumstances," Frankl claims that the only thing that makes life "unbearable" is lack of purpose. Much of his book is an examination of suicide, a logical option if life has no purpose.

Since my adolescence, and maybe even earlier, I've swung into and out of depression. Like most people with AIDS in the early '90s, I expected death to come calling at any moment. When it didn't take me, but took so many others near me, I wondered why. I resented both their deaths and my life. Why am I still here? What actual purpose do I have that makes my life worthwhile?

Looking to Wealth, Fame, and Others.

As nearly as I can tell, one advantage of growing old is that we discover a host of things that do *not* work. We don't have all the answers when age overtakes us but we have some. Most of the so-called wisdom we accumulate is nothing more than lessons of modest success and regrettable failure.

For some of us, "wealth" means our checkbook isn't overdrawn. ("What do you mean I don't have any money; I have checks left!") Maybe wealth is having more money than I actually need to pay my bills and feed my hobbies. Maybe it's just a number: If you're one of America's 500 billionaires, you're wealthy. Agreed. At that number, you'd definitely be wealthy.

But does having wealth make me happy? Do I feel fulfilled? There's no doubt that if I'm poor, life is hard. But according to Matthew Killingsworth, a professor and researcher at the University of Pennsylvania's Wharton school, "If you're rich and miserable, more money won't help." We need enough money to feel reasonably comfortable. But once we get to that level, *more* doesn't equal *happier*.[2] Maybe that's why I never saw a Brink's truck following a hearse to the cemetery.

If money won't make me happy, how about being beautiful and famous? It sounds tolerable. A good plastic surgeon can take care of the beauty part and a gifted PR firm can conjure a little fame. I might become a social media influencer. The Kardashians seem to be doing well, bless them.

But wouldn't you know it? A landmark study a decade ago began, "If you think having loads of money, fetching looks, or the admiration of many will improve your life — think again." The research behind this wet blanket, funded by the National Institute of Mental Health, demonstrates that progress on these fronts can actually make a person less happy and less fulfilled. How is that possible? It's possible because what contributes most to human happiness, says the study's authors, isn't anything outside of ourselves like our bank account, what's parked in our garage, or the number of trophies on the shelf. Satisfaction is an inside job. We are satisfied when we feel like we are (not we have) "enough," when we love and are loved. All the things we covet outside of ourselves "fade quickly; all too soon, the salary raise is a distant memory and the rave review forgotten."[3]

If money or fame won't give me what I want, maybe I need to find belonging — say, in one of those churches with great music and plenty of promises. Give me a powerful pastor or leader, and if he (rarely she) pays attention to me, I'd be good.

It feels a little iffy to label a political leader with his or her following a "cult." But if we look at the events of January 6, 2021, when the Capitol building in Washington, D.C. was attacked by a mob of Donald Trump supporters, the word fits. Encouraged by the defeated Donald Trump, thousands of supporters showed up at his call to support his false claims of a stolen election. The Proud Boys and the Oath Keepers functioned as enforcers of the Rule of Trump.

It was predictable. More than a year earlier, cult expert Steven Hassan observed the parallels between Trump "and people like

Jim Jones, David Koresh, Ron Hubbard and Sun Myung Moon." The culture Trump hoped to instill was "like a destructive cult" in which he constantly demonstrated an abiding "need to squash alternate information and his insistence of constant ego stroking…."[4] It seems so right in retrospect.

And if a cult doesn't give me meaning, maybe *you* will. I mean, maybe a relationship with you will tell me my life's purpose. If you love me no matter what, if you make decisions that I find fulfilling, if you are the one on whom I can absolutely depend and you are mine, I'll be satisfied. Like most people I know, I've had occasion to want others — children, friends, lovers, heroes — to give my life meaning. My experience is that relationships are important, sometimes enjoyable, but I was asking the impossible when I wanted someone else to give my life meaning. Even those I hoped would succeed, who tried, just couldn't do it.

Not Feeling It.

The hard reality of life in America today is that many of us don't have a sense of purpose. We're just wandering. We're trying to get by, working long hours, maybe moving one rung up the social ladder. We're living up to Tennessee Ernie Ford's old song, "another day older and deeper in debt." We're taking the gray out of our hair and being nice to the grocery clerk and at the end of the day, we're tired but not especially satisfied. If this is what life is all about, we just aren't feeling it.

Fifty or more years ago, much of life's purpose was derived from our institutions. The military assigned ranks and roles. Corporations defined what was expected and rewarded those who achieved. Stay-at-home moms were caretakers for children and spouses. Everything from the Junior League to the Miss America contest said, "Here's where you'll find purpose and satisfaction." But the sense of meaning found in these institutions, in government engagement or community service, has eroded. Government itself is struggling to survive as an institution. Loyalty to political brands has all but disappeared.

I've known (and loved) people for whom meaning came from their faith. They found a purpose in worship and service, and that purpose translated to a life with meaning. It's still possible, although during the past twenty-five years, some 40 million Americans — mostly Christian — have left the institutions that were once their home, taking with them approximately $1.4 trillion in contributions. The institutions that once seemed permanent and reliable are proving increasingly fragile.[5]

If I can't find meaning where I used to get it, if I did, what's to be done? For some 19.7 million American adults (aged 12 and older) the answer has been sought in bottles. Some bottles held pills. Some held alcohol. All held hope that life had some kind of meaning.

I've known over reliance on drugs and alcohol in my own life. As a child and teen, when others judged me to be too anxious or too heavy, the solution was usually another prescription, a new opportunity for misuse. In my mid-30s, I was for a time a resident of the Betty Ford Center in Rancho Mirage (CA). I'd gone there originally to support my mother's recovery; I returned to pursue my own. What I learned in those California landscapes is that it's easy to swallow something that makes the pain, shame, and regret go away for a while. Unfortunately, it's hard to admit that the pharmacy and the distillery deceived me: They left me in worse shape than I was before I tried them out.

For me, the solution to alcoholism was simple: Don't drink. I'm supported in my decision by attending meetings described by author Anne Lamott as the place where "precious communities" gather — otherwise known as AA meetings. "You show up as is, hangdog, skeptical, pissy, or superior. Someone welcomes you and pats the seat next to them. Someone will get other people water, or watch the kids, or do a neighbor's laundry, or wash somebody's feet."[6]

If, for whatever reason, we just aren't sensing any purpose in life, suicide becomes a viable, even reasonable, act. Our lives need what only we can give them: meaning. Frankl was right about that. And he was also right that if our lives have no meaning, we aren't likely to stick with them. (For further data, consult the weekly obituaries of famous people dying of drugs and drinking.)

What Meaning Looks Like.

In 1997 I produced a book of photographs and narratives entitled *Angels in Our Midst*. It was a collection of stories I gathered while visiting AIDS hospices and communities in a dozen American cities. The stories were all different and all the same, because they featured the incredible work and love of caregivers who tended the sick and dying.

Not one of the caregivers I met complained about lack of meaning in their lives. "For pure human power," I said in the book's Foreword, "no set of people are as extraordinary as the caregivers who come, most of them unpaid, to help us manage our lives when life itself grows fragile and fearful."[7] They offer care, genuine care. They offer affection and hope in settings where both are beyond imagination. They absolutely model *caring*.

In city after city, I visited places where people were being loved as they died. In Boston, Pat Gibbons introduced me to the power of hospice while, across town, Kate Ryan at Rosie's Place crawled on Christyne Howard's bed to be sure her hug was fully experienced. In Grand Rapids a policeman father leaned over his AIDS-stricken son. In Atlanta, Metta Johnson explained that Haven House was more than a site of care for ten AIDS patients: "It is," said Metta, "a home of love that God built." From Rikers Island to West Palm Beach; from Kansas City to San Francisco, Los Angeles to Washington, D.C. — back and forth across the country I'd traveled, taking photographs when possible, writing notes when necessary.

Leaving Boston in November (1993), the character of the book had become clear. I needed to say that

> [D]ying is not pretty and rarely graceful. Only on Hollywood sets is it clean and odorless. If we die slowly enough to have others care for us near the end, it's a physical struggle that involves a mean betrayal of our own bodies. First we lose control, then we lose dignity, then we lose life, more or less in this order.
>
> The extraordinary power of the caregivers is in the ways they find to give back what our bodies take from us. They see to it that the person whose hours are numbered stays in charge of pain killers, of color schemes and music choices of who comes and who's barred from coming. When the coughing spells lead to spurts of vomit, when bowels and bladders empty without warning, caregivers are neither surprised nor offended. I've heard them say, with quiet grace and good cheer, "I'm so glad you got that out; you'll feel better now." Love is not sanitized in this setting. It is gritty, unquestioned, and spectacular.[8]

I wasn't really certain what I'd find when I began my tour of AIDS hospices and care centers. I imagined that the dying I'd meet would no longer have meaning in their lives. That's not what I heard. I heard nothing but gratitude from those approaching the grave. Their purpose was to sustain their caregivers, to express gratitude, to use their final breath to say "thank you."

In homes God built, caregivers proved the meaning that shaped their lives. They poured it out; they lavished the dying with hugs and wipes and gentleness. They didn't long to be elsewhere or to have more of anything except time. They knew their own meaning when they looked into the haunted eyes of those they held and comforted.

Purpose? These people had purpose, the kind of certainty about their lives' meaning that Frankl, remembering the men who walked the camps handing out their last piece of bread, described as indestructible.

Notes to Chapter Ten

1. Viktor E. Frankl, *Man's Search for Meaning* (Beacon Press, 2006), one of 39 books published by Frankl during his lifetime.

2. Matthew Killingsworth, *Penn TODAY*, March 28, 2023; Wharton School at the University of Pennsylvania research paper.

3. University of Rochester, ScienceDaily, May 19, 2009. "Achieving Fame, Wealth and Beauty Are Psychological Dead Ends, Study Says."

4. Steven Hassan, *The Cult of Trump: A Leading Cult Expert Explains How the President Uses Mind Control* (Free Press, 2019).

5. Jim Davis and Michael Graham with Ryan Burge, *The Great Dechurching: Who's Leaving, Why Are They Going, and What Will It Take to Bring Them Back*; (Zondervan, 2023). "We are currently experiencing the largest and fastest religious shift in US history. It is greater than the First and Second Great Awakening and every revival in our country combined…but in the opposite direction."

6. Anne Lamott, *Almost Everything: Notes on Hope* (Riverhead Books, 2018) p. 53.

7. Mary Fisher, *Angels in Our Midst*, p. 9.

8. *Ibid*, p. 26

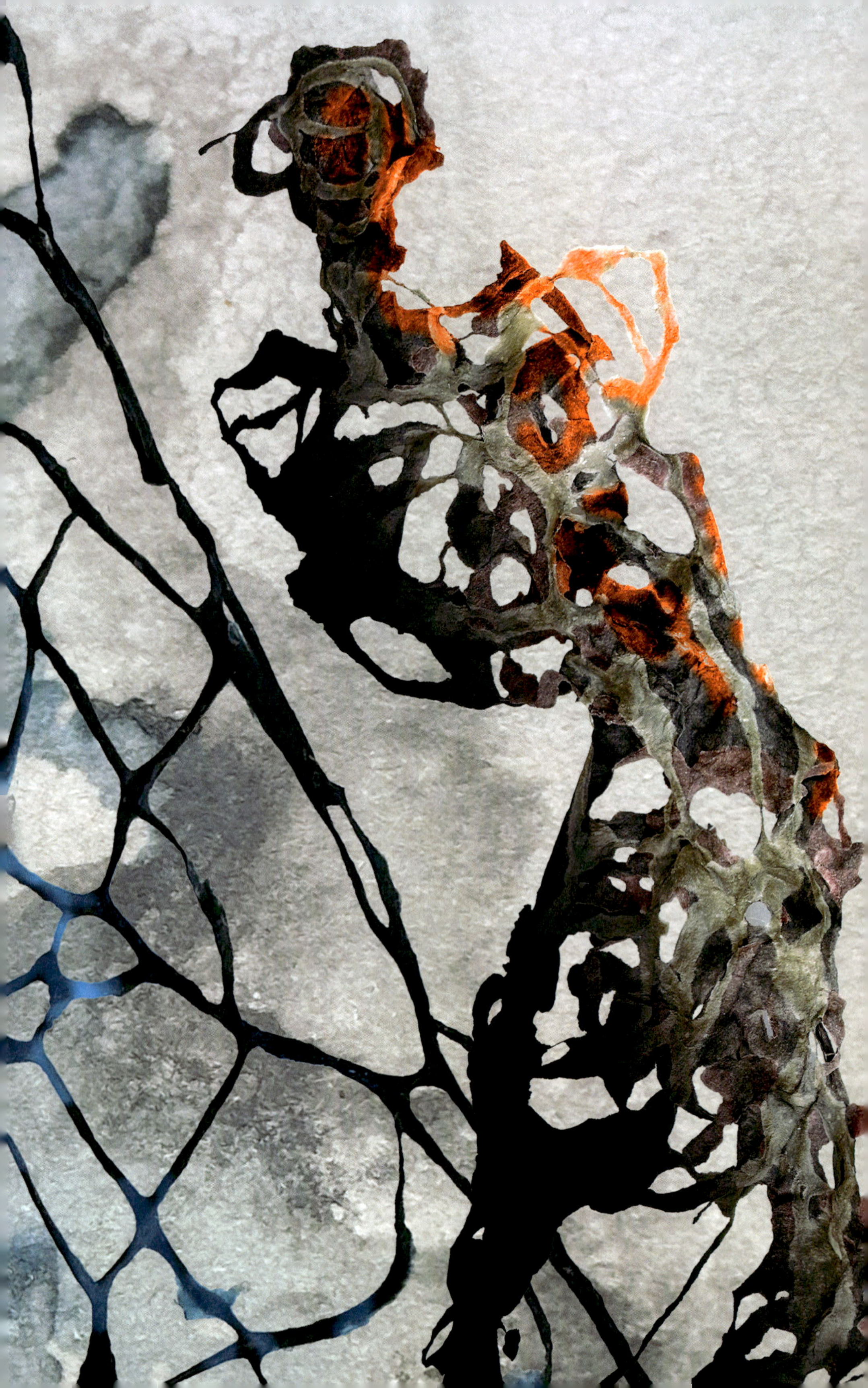

CHAPTER ELEVEN

The Measure of Love

Everything that lives must die. But while life has to end, love doesn't.

David Kessler[1]

For most of my life I've imagined that I'm "depression prone." I have certainly known moments of ecstasy and joy. But I often feel that my factory setting is mildly depressive. Maybe more than mildly.

It may have started when my (biological) father George packed up his stuff and left, never to return. I was three. He was gone. No one explained anything. And what I've carried for almost three-quarters of a century is an aching void that only my father could have filled. Perhaps I've proven Maya Angelou right: "There is no greater agony than bearing an untold story inside you."[2] Might this be why I feel best when I am telling my story in speeches, sermons, or essays?

Lately I've come to believe a different explanation for why I may feel such deep hurt and why I can't stop or fix it. Maybe I'm grieving.

I didn't arrive at this option on my own. I got here through my friend David Kessler, "the world's foremost expert on grief." David is the author or co-author of six books, including his initial writings with the famed Swiss-American psychiatrist Elisabeth

Kübler-Ross. He's a wise advisor to millions of people, a person of remarkable insight and compassion, accessible to all through *grief.com*.

I met David after he'd unexpectedly lost one of his two sons at age 21. Writing from the absolute depths of his own personal grief, David showed me (and thousands of others) that "grief is optional in this lifetime. Yes, it's true. You don't have to experience grief, but you can only avoid it by avoiding love. Love and grief are inextricably intertwined."[3]

Listening to David, and applying his insights to my own experience, I was opened to the possibility that what I have always described as "depression" has been, in fact, less depression than grief — a natural response to painful loss.

I would not have suffered my father's departure if I had not loved him. In truth, I still love the father I lost when I was three. I still see him preparing to go, ignoring my questions, driving off. I am still saddened at this loss because sadness continues as long as our love continues. And there is no calendar for grief, no reliable measure of the time it will last — except forever. And unlike depression, grief is not only a feeling, an emotion. It's a response to losses that hurt.

During the past decade, I've lost my mother. Our relationship was, as so many mother-daughter relationships are, complicated. But I loved her at a depth and with a range that I am still uncovering. Was I depressed when she died? I've said so, but now I think not. I think I've been grieving. When I let myself experience my continuing love for her, the sadness becomes focused and clear. It is not some distant or foggy depression. It is a very specific missing of mother. I am grieving her, and grieving her because I love her even in her absence.

Within months of my mother's passing, I received word that the board of our family foundation had chosen to stop funding AIDS-related causes. It was a quiet vote on how best to use funds to meet philanthropic goals. I get it. But it came as evidence that my family had given up on AIDS (read: given up on me). I was no longer worth the investment. I didn't count enough to make the foundation's list of priorities. I realize now that I loved what my family had done for those of us with AIDS. I grieved the loss of that compassionate support. I loved believing that my family would not leave me and, therefore, I still grieve.

Truth be told, among the most agonizing losses in these years was the death of my canine companion, Daisy. She had been such a comfort to me for so many years that I could not give my affection any name but love. As I think of her, my heart still breaks because I have not learned to give up love. Therefore, I grieve.[4]

I know that I am an emotional creature. I laugh easily and I cry easily. When asked to explain, I fall back on the lines of a poem I once wrote:

> Why do I care?
> My heart won't allow me not to
> My voice cracks---my tears run
> Then what?
>
> Why do I care?
> I care because I'm human and have
> a heart that loves.

I'm helped by branding my sadness as an expression of grief. Grief is not an illness; it's a healthy response to the loss of someone or something.

Bearing Witness.

When in 1991 I joined the AIDS community, I was joining a company of the sick and dying. Effective drugs were nonexistent. Nearly 100% of those infected would die within less than a decade. What drew us closer and closer to one another was the virus that was killing us. We were a community wrapped in grief over a constant stream of agonizing losses.

So where, or how, does one find comfort in our grief? We find it by finding or creating something of value as a result of our love. Candy Lightner's daughter was killed by a drunken driver who had repeatedly been an offender but was back on the roads. Candy imagined and then founded Mothers Against Drunk Drivers (MADD) which has, through advocacy and legal challenge, saved the lives of countless others. John Walsh's young son was violently killed; John founded the TV show *America's Most Wanted*, which brought meaning out of murder.

I haven't launched a campaign like MADD. I'm an advocate without a television show. But give me a platform or pulpit and you'll hear me bearing witness to the slaughter of mostly young lives in the American AIDS epidemic. Bearing witness. Telling the story. Refusing to allow the nation to forget. That's my reason to still be alive, still speak out, still keep my promise to so many who died before me.

I'll not go quietly, because I've promised that they will not be forgotten.

A Pilgrim on the Road to AIDS.

During the first decade of my journey with AIDS, those I came to love and then came to lose were countless. I'm embarrassed that I cannot easily recite all the names of such extraordinary friends and teachers. It isn't just that memory fades; it's that there were so terribly many who were ahead of me because they'd been infected earlier. They mostly died before antiretroviral medicines offered the hope of an extended life.

One gift that came into my life during these years was my friend and cousin, Dr. Michael ("Mike") Saag. He's best known to me because he not only cares for me. He loves me, as I love him. His wife, Amy, approves.

For every gained friendship there were dozens of losses. Example? Jeffrey Schmalz, a brilliant *New York Times* journalist I once described as "sophisticated, urbane, analytic." We were close, close friends for the year (1992) between his first interview of me and the week he died (November 1993). Asked to offer a eulogy at his memorial service, I noted that in his final article "he remembered hoping for a cure. 'A miracle is possible…and for a long time, I thought one would happen. But let's face it, a miracle isn't going to happen. One day soon I will simply become one of the ninety people in America to die that day of AIDS.' And so he did. And so we grieve."[5]

There it is. I loved Jeffrey, and in his death I found the urgency of telling others how his life, how he, mattered. My life had meaning so long as I could bear witness to the constant brutalities and hourly losses along the road to AIDS. By being a witness to Jeffrey's life and death, I've had a purpose to fulfill, a meaning to give another eulogy, another speech. I've promised it to Jeffrey and to hundreds of thousands of others who shared his fate. I've promised it to families suffering the losses I know too well. I've promised it to my children and grandchildren. I've promised it to myself.

When I am able to see my purpose in bearing witness, my grief does not disappear. It fuels my activism. It makes me want to say more and do more. Because I still love Jeffrey, and Arthur, and Hydeia, and Medicine, and Larry and…because I love them all, and all filled our community of grief with suffering and grace, I grieve them all.

If we're open to the possibility that our grief has a purpose beyond our suffering, we might eventually find meaning. Perhaps in the tears that followed my mother's passing I learned to wash away my own sense of loss and focus instead on creating a different relationship to my own children and grandchildren. In the loss of Daisy, I became increasingly aware of what it means to "love without expectation of being loved in return." Daisy asked nothing and gave to her last breath. She was a good teacher. And in the family foundation's rejection of AIDS as a worthy cause, my commitment to bear witness to the suffering of that plague has grown sharper and more enduring. I may be hurt but I'll not be silenced.

I have a friend who closes each day by writing a "gratitude list" of a dozen or so things that made him thankful that day. When I asked what he puts on that list, he said with a smile, "Well, there's you."

So love comes with a cost: grief. And grief can open the door to meaning that we had never imagined and now accept with gratitude. It is enough to make me — despite the horrors of war and deceits of the powerful — hopeful. If we can be grateful, then we have reason to hope that we'll find a life's purpose we did not think was possible. We know it's possible because we experience it ourselves. There's simply no better measure of our love than our grief, no better search for meaning than that which follows loss.

As David Kessler says, "Death ends a life but not our relationship, our love, or our hope." Even in the face of death, I can experience gratitude for having had a life that meant something.

Notes to Chapter Eleven

1. David Kessler, *Finding Meaning: The Sixth Stage of Grief* (Scribner, 2019); p. 64.

2. Maya Angelou, *I Know Why the Caged Bird Sings* (Random House, 1969).

3. Kessler, ibid, p. 9.

4. David Kessler says that he has "a rule on pet loss. 'If the love is real, the grief is real.' The grief that comes with loss is how we experience the depths of our love, and love takes many forms in this life" (ibid., p. 34).

5. Mary Fisher, "Love Among Strangers," *I'll Not Go Quietly* (Scribner, 1995), p. 75.

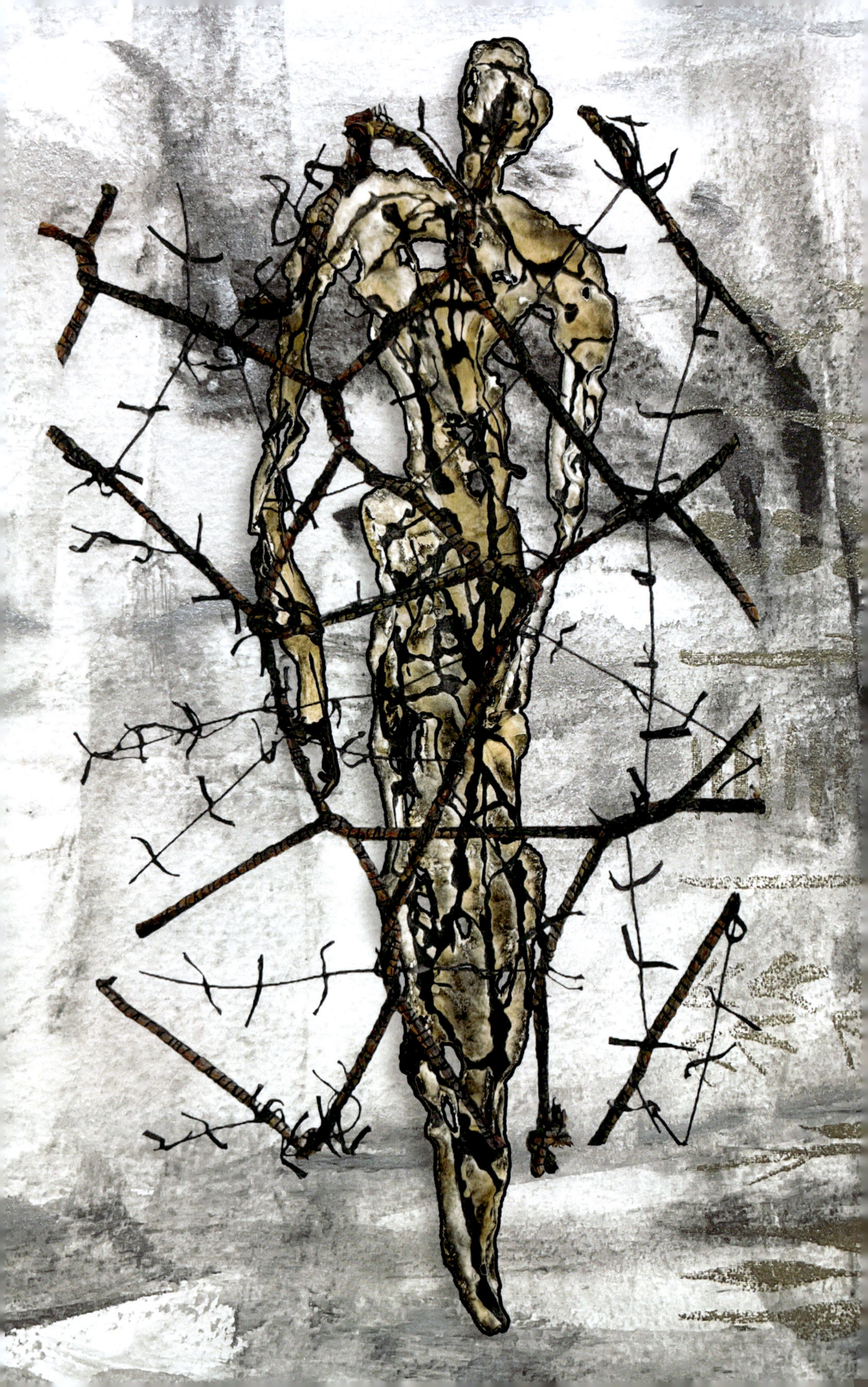

CHAPTER TWELVE

Alternative Facts

Major Media thrives on the counter-narrative, i.e., predictions of doom and gloom that seek to turn good news into bad and bad news into catastrophe.

Robert Hubbell[1]

If you're a member of my generation, this rapidly fading group of senior adults raised mostly in the years following World War II — the '50s, '60s, and early '70s — you were probably taught, as I was, to pay attention to the news.

We were expected to know what was happening in our world. The "news" was where a thoughtful person gathered facts, where opinions were confirmed or contradicted. The news reported the facts and spiced up the delivery with the gossip columnist's salacious rumor and the editorial page sermon. We could have it all for a dime on paper — driven up to twenty cents in the mid-60s — or a half-hour of TV time with Walter Cronkite (1962-81) or Chet Huntley and David Brinkley (1956-70). We were taught to know and to trust the news.

Fresh technology — cables and satellites — enabled Ted Turner to introduce CNN (Cable News Network) as global news around the clock every day, launched in 1980 just in time for Ronald

Reagan, a president who understood the power of media, to move into the White House. Whatever else we say of Reagan, he knew how to read a script.

Following CNN and its imitators came what we know today as "social media." In less than a generation, social media became a dominating source of much noise and a little news. Forty years after Turner's creation, according to a 2021 *USA Today* report, once we "tally them all, we have over 3,000 outlets that call themselves newsrooms in America. That's before we add bloggers, podcasts, talk radio and the deluge of user-generated content." I was raised on three networks and a few papers; I'm now confronted with the sound and fury of thousands of sources. Thousands. Lots and lots of noise.

If Cronkite, Huntley, and Brinkley practiced the accepted rules for journalism — be current, be respectful, and above all be truthful — social media exhibits no such loyalty to professional standards or common-sense ethics. With thousands of sites clamoring to be noticed by propagating information and disinformation, I'm sympathetic to Gary Streeter's claim that he hates social media because "it gives a voice to people who don't deserve one."

Amid the chaos and noise of social and traditional media, I'm left to sort out what's important, what's true, and what's not. So are you.

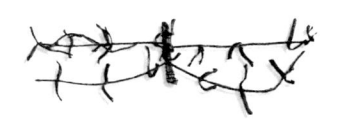

Selling the News.

So here's my bias: If I have access to Rachel Maddow, I'm in comforting hands. She offers me history, analysis, and priorities worth knowing. She's my trusted source. She teaches as she reports. Beyond Rachel, I confess I don't know what to make of much of what's pushed as "news" — although if it comes from Nicolle Wallace, I'm confident that it's truthful.

Years ago (June 7, 2011) *Psychology Today* published a definitive piece on what drives most modern media's "news." The answer? Two things: profit and fear.

About profit: "News is a money-making industry," said the researchers, thereby establishing the ground for most of our trouble. The media's drive for profit outpaces the media's interest in truth. The goal is profit, and the strategy is persuasive storytelling.[2] Truth is nice but not necessary; the news needs to make money.

And about fear: The storytelling that comes as "news" is dominated by the slogan "if it bleeds, it leads." According to the *Psychology Today* report, "fear-based news programming has two aims. The first is to grab attention. In the news media, this is called the 'teaser.' The second aim is to persuade the viewer that the solution for reducing the fear will be in the news story." Usually, there's no solution. There's just a story. If the "news" can hold my attention by keeping me afraid, that's as good as money in the bank.

When we add together the drive for profit, mostly from getting and keeping advertisers happy, plus the use of fear as a way to grab and hold an audience, we cycle back to the painful question: Who do we trust in a world where the source doesn't always make the goal to report the facts accurately?

We've been treated to years in which lies and immorality sold as well as, if not better than, honesty and honor. What I now know is that the reliability, or "factuality," of reports depends on who's controlling the reports. For many newsmakers, if lies could bring a crowd, bring on the lies.

I've worried about our global environment for years. When I hear the scientists' analyses and forecasts, I wonder if my grandchildren will have a world that can sustain human life. If any issue should make us scream for action, this is probably the one. But when University of Wisconsin professor Tim Van Deelen examined why major networks don't give most coverage to the issues most impacting human society, he found a simple explanation: "Why not maintain a focus on the most urgent work of humanity right now? It doesn't sell. Pity that."[3] Sales and profits determine our headlines. I agree. It's an incredible pity.

My professional career started in the world of public television, later producing a live network morning show in Detroit. Those were the golden days. Since then, we've been coming through a difficult storm in journalism of all sorts and we haven't reached safe territory yet. Over the past twenty years we've lost nearly 2,900 newspapers and nearly two-thirds of newspaper journalists. Losses of *papers* matter most because the majority of broadcast journalists find their stories in the day's newspapers.

And at least one media analyst has noted that "more than half of daily newspapers are owned by the ten top newspaper chains" — thus being subject to the editorial bias of a few profit-seeking owners.[4] The media landscape on which many of us were raised isn't real any longer. Profits have replaced the drive for truth. "News" has become a commodity for sale.

I love stories, and most reporting is done in the form of storytelling. Newspapers and broadcasts aren't just a recitation of facts like a shopping list. They're mostly narratives — stories — shaped to hold our interest and keep us coming for more. The problem with newsmakers' storytelling is that some facts aren't easily turned into stories. Like life, they're complicated. For example, consider reports on the rates of violent crime. The majority of American voters in 2024, especially those who said they were conservative, had a "strong" or "very strong" belief that violent crime was on the rise. They could cite stories that bolstered their belief.

In fact, however, crime analyst Jeff Asher told us at the same time "in cities big and small, from both coasts, violence has dropped." Why didn't we know this? Because, says Asher, "there's never been a news *story* that said, 'There were no robberies yesterday, nobody really shoplifted at Walgreens.'" Rachel Swan, a breaking news reporter, puts it this way: "You can put numbers in front of people all day, and numbers just don't speak to people the way narrative does." If numbers moved people, the climbing numbers of mass shootings in America would urgently move policymakers. Nope. The news that matters is "the story," and the story is shaped to make money on fear.[5]

Why It Matters.

Raised to trust the news, we're now in a world where trust needs to be earned. Ideally, the currency of trust would be truthfulness. The more truthful, the more trustworthy. No doubt about it, this is the ideal.

But the reality is that truthfulness doesn't necessarily hold an audience as much as "believability" does, and believability is often the byproduct of great storytelling. Some of what passes as a "story" would, in previous times, have been called a "yarn," a story with a great plot whether or not it has any basis in fact. It works, as a yarn, because the build-up to the punchline is believable (or at least amusing).

Sometimes the stories come from unlikely sources. Take, for example, the story based on the transcript of a radio conversation of a US naval ship with Canadian authorities off the coast of Newfoundland in October, 1995. The radio conversation was apparently released by the Chief of Naval Operations on October 10, 1995.

> Americans: *Please divert your course 15 degrees to the north to avoid a collision.*
>
> Canadians: *Recommend you divert YOUR course 15 degrees to the south to avoid a collision.*
>
> Americans: *This is the Captain of a US Navy ship. I say again, divert YOUR course.*
>
> Canadians: *No, I say again, you divert YOUR course.*

> Americans: *This is the aircraft carrier USS Lincoln, the second largest ship in the United States' Atlantic Fleet. We are accompanied by three destroyers, three cruisers and numerous support vessels. I demand that YOU change your course 15 degrees north, that's one five degrees north, or countermeasures will be undertaken to ensure the safety of this ship.*
>
> Canadians: *This is a lighthouse. Your call.*

Amusing? I laugh every time I see it. Factual? Not a bit; entirely made up. Believable? Well, yes, it has the believability that keeps us on board all the way to the lighthouse.

And here's the painful confession. If Nicolle Wallace or Rachel Maddow says something, my believability meter registers "total trust." If, say, Tucker Carlson or Sean Hannity makes an announcement, my meter spins to "total lie." For many — perhaps for you — the opposite may be true.

I worry about this believability index because we're living in a sharply divided America. My neighbors watch Fox News and root for Tucker Carlson's comeback after his dismissal. While they're taking in Fox, I'm counting the minutes to Rachel. And both of us are willing to believe what we're told based on our confidence about who we trust.

We need, as a society, to find a way to bridge the news gap between MSNBC and Fox, and between many of the thousands of voices shouting on social media. Unless we can reach across the divide, we'll never find a way to talk to one another. I'd like to think that truthfulness will be the basis of trustworthiness. But we have a long way to go. You hold your truth; I hold mine. The battle being waged in both traditional and social media is to win our loyalty that the truth is being told, whether it is or not. When nearly half of the nation's voting adults are willing to accept a torrent of lies in place of honest storytelling, we're evidently in some trouble.

Perhaps it's because I served President Gerald R. Ford, who was at once truthful and humble, that I bleed over the lies told by some so-called "leaders." I long for the moment in which every news outlet is bringing us this message:

My fellow Americans, our long national nightmare is over. Our Constitution works; our great Republic is a government of laws and not of men. Here the people rule. But there is a higher Power, by whatever name we honor Him, who ordains not only righteousness but love, not only justice but mercy....

It's a half-century since President Ford took office, and once more we're struggling to "bind up the internal wounds."[6]

To stitch us back together, we need to find a way to share a common truth, resist motives of profit and fear, and reach out to people with whom we disagree, sometimes strenuously. But my behavior shows that I'm staying home, close to friends and family whose life views are close to mine.

Reach out to strangers who stormed the Capitol? Listen to someone who votes against my priority? Try some social stitching that'd pull together our divided population? Oh…I don't know. I'm not confident it's worth the price in time and emotional energy. So I stay home, as comfortable as I can be, listening to news stories I trust.

I may be part of the problem. I need to become part of the solution. I'll definitely need your help on this.

Notes to Chapter Twelve

1. Robert B. Hubbell, *Today's Edition Newsletter*; self-published. February 14, 2024.//
2. *Psychology Today,* June 7, 2011.
3. Tim Van Deelen, *Reformed Journal*, August 17, 2023.
4. Opinion piece by the *Washington Post*'s media critic, Erik Wemple, published December 14, 2023.
5. Karen Zamora, Ari Shapiro, and Courtney Dorning for National Public Radio (NPR), broadcast first on February 12, 2024.
6. President Gerald R. Ford's "Inaugural Address to the American People," August 9, 1974.

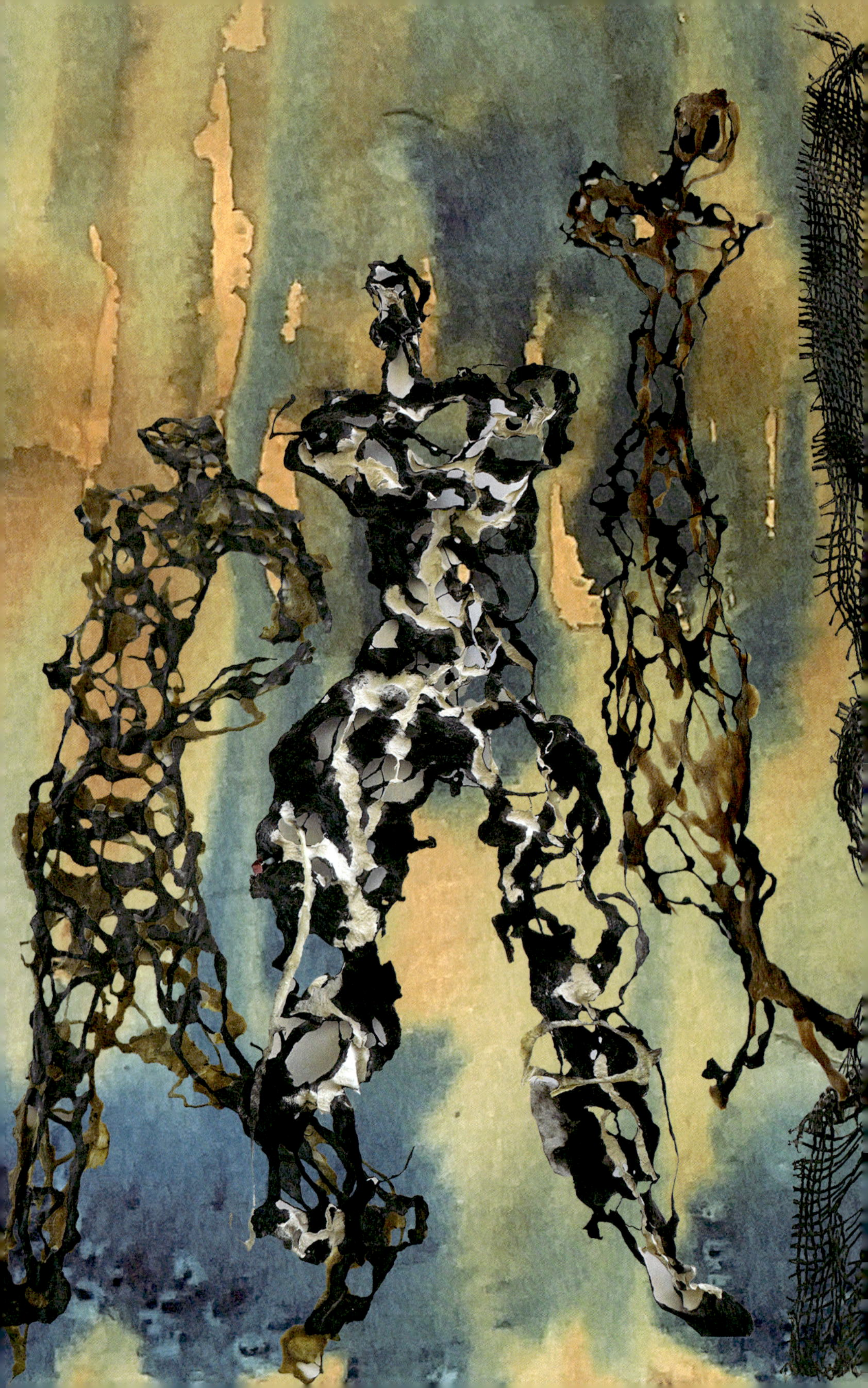

CHAPTER THIRTEEN

Poverty Next Door

This is who we are: the richest country on earth, with more poverty than any other advanced democracy.

Matthew Desmond[1]

When I think of the fault lines that divide the American populace, that separate the "me" from the "we," I tend to think first of political allegiance and the media that feeds our convictions. Never the twain shall meet between elected Republicans and Democrats, between Fox and MSNBC. Second, I think of the horrific and persistent racial divides holding us apart. Only third do I reckon with the separation of those who have enough from those who have too little.

The reality is that, while I've had ups and downs, I'm not poor. I never have been. Odds are, you aren't and haven't been either, or you'd not likely be reading this book. But here we are, you and I, making up an important segment of American society, which is divided in part by "wealth" and "poverty."

Let me introduce you to Matthew Desmond.[2] "If America's poor founded a country," he tells us in *Poverty, By America*, "that country would have a bigger population than Australia or Venezuela. Almost one in nine Americans — including one in eight children — live in poverty. There are more than 38 million people living in the

United States who cannot afford basic necessities.... More than a million of our public schoolchildren are homeless, living in motels, cars, shelters and abandoned buildings."

What we lack, according to Desmond and others who have studied poverty in America, is the courage to face up to our own ready acceptance of poverty and deprivation so long as we aren't the ones who are poor.

Charity and Justice.

Most of my life I've thought of caring for the poor as an act of charity. It belongs to Mother Teresa and others who take vows and live them out. It's all about compassion.

One of my heroes paints a different picture: "Overcoming poverty," says Nelson Mandela, "is not a task of charity. It is an act of justice. Like slavery and apartheid, poverty is not natural. It is man-made and it can be overcome and eradicated by the actions of human beings." It's about systems that create winners and losers; whole economies where profits outdistance justice. Ouch.

I play a role in keeping people poor and odds are, you do too. We own stock and want it to generate profits, even if profits come at the cost of laying off workers or replacing them with contractors to reduce cost.[3] We love cheap prices, even if they're the result of immorally low wages for some. We own property; we have good credit reports; we have wills in which we pass along resources from parents to children, giving our children a head start on gaining wealth.

For those of us educated in part by Isabel Wilkerson in her blockbuster book, *Caste: The Origins of Our Discontent*, there's a direct line in American history between the Great Migration of Black people and the poverty in which their descendants find themselves. In her earlier work, *The Warmth of Other Suns: The Epic Story of America's Great Migration*, Wilkerson shows the familiar pattern in the American housing market that greeted newly arrived folk from Mississippi, Alabama, and elsewhere: "The least-paid people were forced to pay the highest rents for the most dilapidated housing owned by absentee landlords trying to wring the most money out of a place nobody cared about."[4] It echoes the observation of James Baldwin: "Anyone who has ever struggled with poverty knows how extremely expensive it is to be poor…."

Poverty, like blue eyes and blonde hair, turns out to be multigenerational. My parents passed along some of their wealth to me because, as with most white families, they had resources. Some white families experience poverty, some Black families have wealth, but "in 2019, the median white household had a net worth of $188,200, compared with $24,100 for the median Black household." And lest we think that the difference results from educational achievement, one more note: "The average white household headed by someone with a high school diploma has more wealth than the average Black household headed by someone with a college degree."[5]

When I moved to Los Angeles a few years ago, my realtor paid attention to the kind of neighborhood I'd choose. I could afford what I thought of as reasonable costs for a place in a city where "reasonable" excludes most people. What's easy to ignore when we have adequate resources is that we have what the poor do not: choices.

Choices enable us to live independently. We do not need to stack multiple relatives in a single bedroom. We don't fear the knock on our door the day rent is due. We aren't dependent on public transportation and where it enables us to shop, worship, work, or live. We have access to healthcare. We don't have to wait until a petulant government sends us a check to buy our children's breakfast. We have choices. We can choose to care, to have compassionate hearts. Or we can choose to see poverty as an issue of justice or color or laziness. In other words, we can choose to care or not to care.

Dissolving Neighborhoods.

During the COVID-19 Pandemic (roughly 2020-2023), I withdrew from nearly everything and everyone. There's a difference between solitude and isolation. I was frightened, so I isolated.

The traditional American concept of a neighborhood has been dissolving for years. Patterns of housing and immigration changed wherever and with whomever we lived. The automobile eventually created suburbs, and suburbs were less cohesive than urban blocks. Social media became "social" only in the sense of letting us find whatever we want somewhere in the ether. We've come to live more on the internet than on the street passing our front door.

It wasn't just the Pandemic that separated me from my neighbors. Americans had already begun to leave the systems and networks that had once bound us to each other. Some of these systems had woven a so-called "safety net" under those suffering illness or needing a loan. Networks like CBS or NBC have mostly disappeared into the fog of social media. Institutions, including the synagogue and the church, no longer claim the loyalty of the masses. The collection plate no longer moves a dollar from those with resources to those without.

Among the most familiar biblical stories is the parable of the Good Samaritan. The plot is simple. A man on a journey is mugged and left for dead. First a priest walks by without stopping to help. Then comes a Levite, what today we'd think of as one who helped the poor; the Levite moves to the other side of the road to avoid touching the victim. Then comes a Samaritan — a member of the lowest caste, one of the untouchables, someone loathed by the religious elite. The Samaritans were so despised that the very idea of a "good Samaritan" was nonsense. But let Martin Luther King, Jr. finish the story:

> *So I can imagine that the first question which the Priest and the Levite asked was, "If I stop to help this man, what will happen to me?" Then the good Samaritan came by, and by the very nature of his concern reversed the question, "If I do not stop to help this man, what will happen to him?" And so the Samaritan stopped to save a stranger's life.*[6]

Perhaps our view of the past is a bit romantic or naïve. Our cities weren't all filled with happy ethnic neighborhoods. Television's

Andy Griffith Show gave us a folksy but unrealistic portrayal of small-town America. Life wasn't as perfect as we'd like to remake it.

I think columnist David Brooks was right that "we're living in brutalizing times: Scenes of mass savagery pervade the media. Americans have become vicious toward one another amid our disagreements. Everywhere I go, people are coping with an avalanche of negative emotions: shock, pain, contempt, anger, anxiety, fear...." According to Brooks, if ever there was a time when the poor and the rich need to find each other, and find their mutual dependence on one another, now is the time. But our relationships are slaughtered by a rage that "hardens into the sort of cold, amoral nihilistic attitude that we see in Donald Trump...."[7]

Honestly, we can do better. I can do better. If I work at it, I can see that the poor are not all strangers. They are brothers and sisters, children and grandparents. They are neighbors in the sense that answers the question that prompted the Good Samaritan parable, "Who is my neighbor?" We are one, as Dr. King taught us, "caught up in an inescapable network of mutuality, tied in a single garment of destiny."[8]

Matthew Desmond claims that "America's poverty is not for lack of resources. We lack something else." He spends nearly 400 pages explaining that what we lack is will. Desire. Commitment. Compassion. Justice. We just don't care.

"Simply collecting unpaid federal income taxes from the top 1 percent of households would bring in some $175 billion a year," enough to "fill the entire poverty gap in America if the richest among us simply paid all the taxes they owed."[9] Under funding the IRS has become a primary strategy of those who want to protect the rich at the expense of the poor. I need at least to whisper my concern to those we've elected to govern.

I realize that poverty is more than I can change. I laugh when I remember E. B. White's confession, "I get up every morning determined to both change the world and have a good time. This makes planning my day difficult." I laugh, but I also sympathize. I want to make change. I want to offer the poor better choices. I want not to suffer guilt for having a bank account or shame for buying a house. But planning my day is difficult, and these noble thoughts run contrary to my plans for dinner.

My friend Sarah Collins invented the Wonderbag and thereby took on world poverty. Her Wonderbag is a slow-cooking container that uses retained heat in the place of electricity, charcoal, or wood to finish cooking food. In thousands, perhaps millions of settings where girls spend up to four hours a day harvesting fuel and cooking, the Wonderbag gives back life-redeeming time, money, and fresh food at a cost approaching zero. With neither fame nor fortune, Sarah Collins has vastly reduced the impact of global poverty. For this, and for her indestructible sense of humor, she's earned my love.

But I do not need to become an inventor, a rabbi, a priest, a social worker, or a community organizer. To cite Desmond one more time: "[M]ass movements are composed of scores of people finding their own way to pitch in. Some abolitionists participated in slave revolts and sheltered runaways; others gave fiery sermons and refused to buy goods made by enslaved hands. Movements need people to march, but they also need graphic designers and cooks and marketing professionals and teachers and faith leaders and lawyers…."[10] I need to do what I can do, perhaps what I can do best. I'm not being asked to become a martyr. I might remember the immortal assessment of civil rights matriarch Rosa Parks about refusing to change seats on the bus: "All I was doing was trying to get home after work."

So, I can write an essay that shows up in Substack; maybe it will make a difference. I can say yes to invitations to speak or preach; I may change one mind. If I see poverty and wealth as issues not merely of compassion, but of compassion and justice, I will have a way of interpreting the news that goes beyond human interest stories.

For my part, I want not to run away from what makes me uncomfortable. To some extent, this has become easier with age. I know that I can survive with some tension and difference in my life. So I'll try to listen to contrary voices and be open to different views. I'll vote with my conscience but also with my mind, knowing that poverty and wealth have long histories and deep traditions.

If I cannot change everything about poverty and wealth, perhaps I can change something. I can observe our differences and see where injustice supports continued poverty. I can risk giving a misguided gift, knowing that if my little contribution doesn't change someone's life, perhaps it will change her day.

I have little to fear. Because I'm not poor, I'm largely protected from the assaults of those who wear red hats, or brown shirts, or white hoods.

Notes to Chapter Thirteen

1. Matthew Desmond, *Poverty, by America* (Random House, 2023).

2. Desmond (*Poverty, by America*) says that "to understand the causes of poverty, we must look beyond the poor. Those of us living lives of privilege and plenty must examine ourselves…which makes this a book about poverty that is not just about the poor" (p. 8).

3. Ibid. Desmond traces changes in employment patterns that once provided benefits like paid leave and health insurance. He notes that in 2020, roughly 750,000 workers around the world helped make and sell Amazon products. Only around 63,000 work directly for Apple. Most of the rest are "contractors" who receive no benefits. By this strategy, tech companies like Amazon save about $100,000 per year per person. Labor costs go down; profits go up.

4. Isabel Wilkerson, *The Warmth of Other Suns: The Epic Story of America's Great Migration* (Vintage, 2010), pp. 270-71.

5. Desmond, ibid., p. 28.

6. Dr. Martin Luther King, Jr., from a sermon draft sometime between July 1, 1962, and March 1, 1963. The sermon was entitled "On Being a Good Neighbor," based on Luke 10:29-37. Elsewhere, King (and others) have made a similar point when referencing the familiar biblical text, "The poor you will always have with you" (Mark 14:7). Originally, this was issued as a challenge: We will always need to find a way to deal with poverty. But it's become popular to turn the text around and see it as a call to doing nothing: I'll never be able to change this because the poor will always be here. We create a do-nothing strategy to leave things as they are, so long as we aren't the poor.

7. David Brooks, November 2, 2023, *The New York Times*, "How to Stay Sane in Brutalizing Times."

8. Martin Luther King, Jr. "Why We Can't Wait" (Penguin, 1964), p. 65.

9. Desmond, ibid., p. 167.

10. Ibid., p. 226.

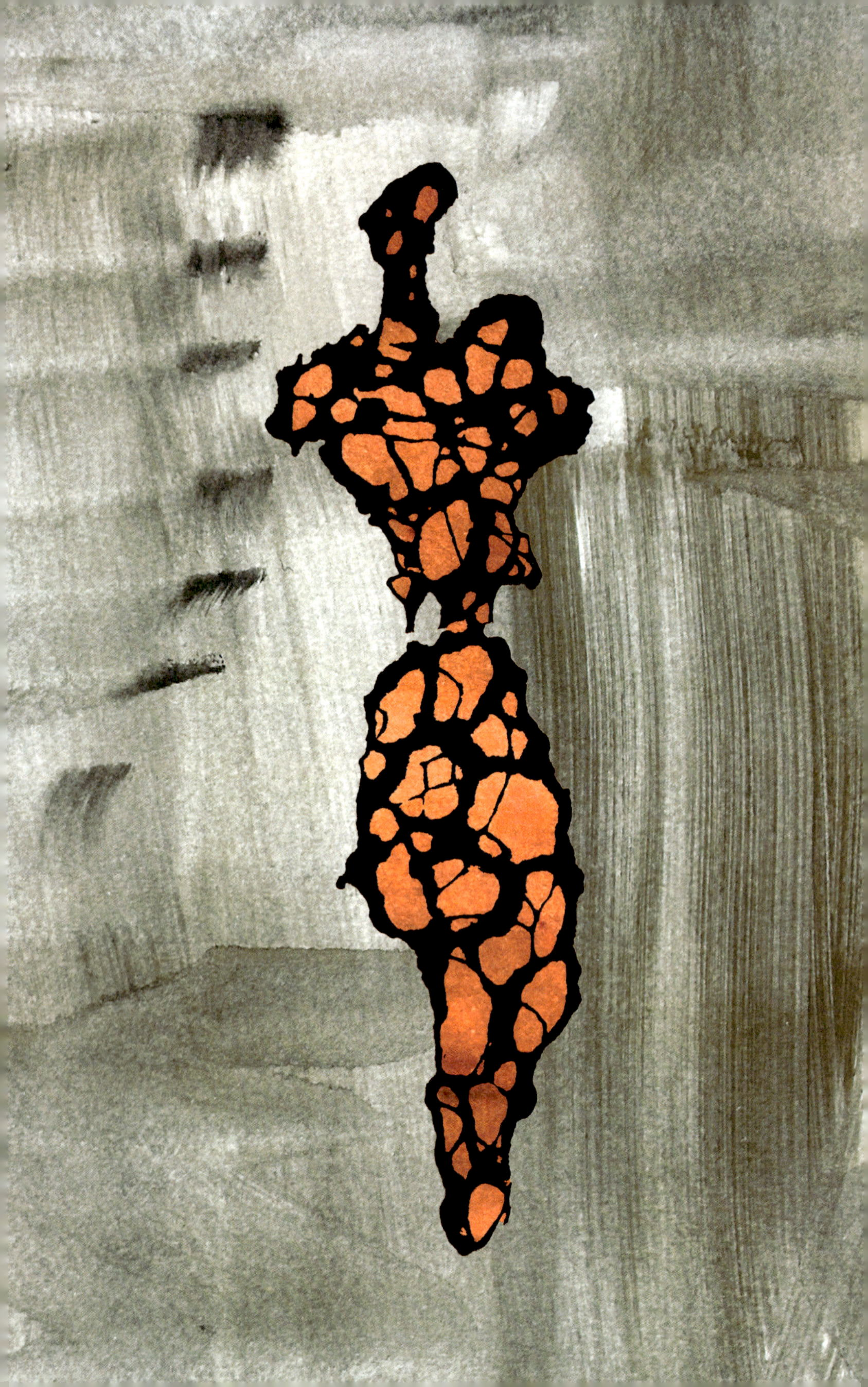

CHAPTER FOURTEEN

Harvest of Hunger

*Gandhi called poverty the harshest form of violence.
I believe hunger is the harshest form of poverty.*

Jeremy K. Everett[1]

I'm troubled by those who've forgotten the scourge of AIDS in America. I'm frustrated over lies told as truth in the media; very irritating. I'm infuriated by economic systems that promote poverty; they're unjust and show me I'm part of the problem. But if I'm riled up by AIDS, media, and poverty, nothing burns in my consciousness more than hunger.

The world is hungry. At the close of 2022, the globe held a human population of about 8.1 billion. Of these, 3.1 billion could not afford a healthy diet for themselves or for their families. Of these, 828 million were flat out hungry.

The world's hunger is reported in a variety of clinical terms ranging from "hunger," defined as an uncomfortable or painful sensation, to "malnutrition" of the sort that leads to child stunting. Midway between starvation and health is "severe food insecurity," meaning folks have run out of food; their cupboards are bare. And none of these terms will rival, for pure gut-turning agony, the reality of a child's swollen belly, the violence evoked by hunger, or the horror of the teenage Sudanese mother feeding her 2-year-old gravel and stones because they may fill the stomach and quiet her dying cries.[2]

If we were to list the nations struggling most with hunger, it would mirror the list of nations enduring conflict within or at their borders. War of all kinds produces hunger, and most of the hunger will be suffered by non-combatants. The world watched as the violence between Israel and Gaza (beginning in 2023) evolved from bombs to starvation. Years of warfare have helped Burkina Faso and Mali become the two nations that are hungriest.

According to global statistics, in 2022 "an estimated 45 million children under the age of five were suffering from wasting, the deadliest form of malnutrition, which increases children's risk of death by up to 12 times. Furthermore, 149 million children under the age of five had stunted growth and development due to a chronic lack of essential nutrients in their diets." I've cradled such children in my arms. I've tried contributions to alleviate some suffering and adoption to bring one child home with me. I've pushed for "foreign aid" no matter how unpopular the idea has become. Tackling global hunger is like bailing the Atlantic Ocean with a thimble.

Since the beginning of the global COVID-19 Pandemic, the rolls of the world's hungry have increased by about 150 million. But we don't fairly measure global hunger in numbers like "millions" or "billions," because numbers aren't hungry. Individuals are. They aren't "just statistics," even if we wish they were. Numbers like 150 million don't move us as much as one 2-year-old swallowing gravel.

American Hunger.

If global hunger is such a massive quandary we don't want to consider it, how about hunger at home? We don't need to visit Africa. We can find hunger next door. More than 44 million Americans face hunger, including one in every six children who live in a food-insecure household. When the City of New York declared a "snow day" owing to inclement weather, nearly a million children went hungry because the school wasn't open to provide their meals.[3]

Who's hungry in America? The AARP Foundation surveyed the nation and reported (March 2024) that "food insecurity among older adults has increased by a shocking 25% in just one year, now affecting nearly 11.8 million older adults. That means 1 out of every 10 seniors is at risk of going hungry." In addition to older adults, populations bearing the most hunger are "single-parent families with young children, people with disabilities, American Indians, people with family members in the prison system, immigrants, people experiencing declines in mental and physical health, and minority households." [4] I've never suffered hunger. Those near me obviously have.

Hunger has consequences beyond a growling stomach: anger, lethargy, pain, and depression strike the hungry. Parents who cannot feed their children suffer shame and embarrassment, which leads them to hide the realities from social services, and other resources. Hidden problems don't get resolved. The kids go hungry.

The actual causes of hunger in America are varied, but most are rooted in poverty. When faced with lack of funds to pay all the bills, the question becomes, what will *not* be paid?[5] Rent's necessary or we'll be homeless. Car, gas, and insurance are needed for employment. We need electricity and other utilities, and so it goes. The loser in our list of priorities is food. First we buy less. Then we buy cheaper. Then we go hungry.

Just for perspective, we want to recall that the American weight loss market grew to $75 billion in 2023. Starvation and dieting are alive and well, living in the same neighborhoods. Including mine.

Food and the Soul.

One set of twins that has grown up among us is food and hunger. They're different but inextricably linked. In a wealthy and happy setting, the former satisfies the latter. Hunger becomes a positive called "appetite." It's a measure of good health. Food is the satisfier and, if in sufficient quantity and quality, it is the most ordinary gift enjoyed by those of us who can afford it. Those of us who can't deal with hunger.[6]

As nearly as we can tell, every human culture ancient and modern has generated a unique and often tempting menu of foods. "Soul food," for example, was once scratched out of the staples fed to (or left for) slaves in the American south. The culinary assembly — from collard greens to pork chitlins — became popularized in the 1960s when "soul" was an adjective applied to most things African American, from music ("soul") to identity ("soul sister") to food.

"Particularly in rural areas, foods like fried chicken, fried fish, sweet potato pie, red drinks, black-eyed peas and others were served during Emancipation celebrations and church gatherings," according to food historian Millie Peartree.[7] The fact that the food was originally identified with the church may have given it a religious twist; hence, soul food. The diet came north as part of the 1915-1975 Great Migration of Black Americans. "They brought their culinary traditions with them and preparing these foods helped build new communities and served as a reminder of home," said Peartree.

Food and soul are connected because food (eating or fasting) is part of nearly every religion practiced in the past or the present. The Zoroastrians used eggs and pomegranate seeds to solicit wisdom and to ward off evil. The Muslim faithful observe Ramadan to recall that the Holy Qur'an was sent from heaven as a guide for men and women to be saved from filthy sin; they observe a strict daily fast from dawn to sunset. Many Christian traditions include giving up certain foods and drinks during Lent, and the high point of the Catholic mass is the eating of bread (Christ's body) and drinking of sacred wine (Christ's blood). We eat and we drink, and therefore we believe.

My own Jewish tradition's holidays are full of food, with the Passover Seder the most recognized. When we gather around the Seder table, someone is likely to cite the ritual's basic pattern: "They tried to kill us all. We survived. Let's eat."

Even modern day practices such as "saying grace" before a meal, or preserving a small bite of the day's food for blessing in homes, reflect a spiritual dimension to food. And there is something spiritually healing about those dishes we've labeled "comfort food."

When my children reached an age where they could express pleasure and rage it took no time at all to figure out who liked lima beans and who didn't. I don't recall the ancient who said something like "all species feed but only man and the gods dine." Dining is a leisure satisfaction denied the starving and taken for granted in my home.

Coming to Hunger.

I didn't set out to learn more about hunger. In some sense global hunger is like the AIDS virus: I didn't find it, it found me.

I did a bit of global travel as a young adult. I spent nearly a year in Israel, for example. And since being infected with HIV more than three decades ago, I've been privileged to travel the world identifying with and empowering women. I've committed myself to bearing witness to the ravages of AIDS. In places distant and nearby, I've pressed for AIDS relief in categories not only of health but also of social justice, gender discrimination, economic deprivation, and the desire to survive.

If we have seen AIDS up close, we've seen hunger. Those who suffer the virus eventually move into a phase known as "wasting." Robust men and elegant women are reduced to fragile skeletons on their way to the end. In many cases, it's illness and poverty that gang up on our bodies, denying nourishment and rendering us too weak to go on. On their behalf, I speak out about AIDS, which has continued to thrive in the absence of a cure. I publish articles. I offer sermons. I call my legislators. I do not blanch when I'm labeled an "AIDS activist."

In nations I've visited, two kinds of hunger are usually visible. "Extreme hunger" of the sort that threatens people with immediate starvation is rampant in some nations. Experts say that we need $23 billion annually to combat extreme hunger today. Meanwhile, "chronic hunger" that yields malnutrition, stunting of children's growth, and a stunning array of other painful symptoms requires another $14 billion to tackle hunger's causes. Put it together and we're looking at only $37 billion to end world hunger. That's just one-half of what Americans spend annually on weight loss products and dieting fads.[8] Half.

On a typical day, I eat when I'm hungry, refrigerate what I leave behind, and never give a moment's thought to where tomorrow's food will come from. I'm among the blessed. If I'm willing to look, I may see some of the 1,132,600 people who last year earned the label "food insecure" in the California county where I live. Of that million-plus, nearly a fourth are children. Many have traveled here with their migrant parents. Nearly all would qualify as invisible: We walk by them every day without seeing them.

What we noted earlier with poverty is what we see again with hunger. We have adequate knowledge to combat both chronic and extreme hunger; we know enough. We have adequate resources to replace the gravel and stones being fed to starving little ones; we have enough. But so long as it is others who suffer, we devote ourselves to studying their suffering instead of doing something about it.

The truth is painfully obvious. Any claim that we cannot solve hunger around the globe or around the corner is hypocrisy. It's a lie. As with poverty, it's a fixable problem. We could reduce, perhaps eliminate, hunger as an agony in the United States if only we wanted to. But we don't want to — not enough, not really, not now.

We allow others to suffer because we lack human compassion. We know enough and we have enough, but we simply do not care enough.

Notes to Chapter Fourteen

1. Jeremy K. Everett, *I Was Hungry: Cultivating Common Ground to End an American Crisis* (Brazos Press, 2019), pp. 8-9.

2. "The number of people affected by hunger globally rose to as many as 828 million in 2021, an increase of about 46 million since 2020 and 150 million since the outbreak of the COVID-19 pandemic, according to a United Nations report that provides fresh evidence that the world is moving further away from its goal of ending hunger, food insecurity and malnutrition in all its forms by 2030." Source: July 6, 2022, news release jointly offered by the Food and Agriculture Organization of the United Nations (FAO), the International Fund for Agricultural Development (IFAD), the United Nations Children's Fund (UNICEF), the UN World Food Programme (WFP) and the World Health Organization (WHO).

3. For a reliable summary of data on hunger in America, see www.feedingamerica.org, especially its section entitled "Hunger in America."

4. Jeremy K. Everett, *I Was Hungry: Cultivating Common Ground to End an American Crisis* (Brazos Press, 2019); pp. 44-45.

5. Katie S. Martin, *Reinventing Food Banks and Pantries: New Tools to End Hunger* (Island Press, 2021); p. 58.

6. Sabrina Medora, "The Use of Food as Religious Symbolism"; blog site, January 19, 2022.

7. Millie Peartree, *Delish*, January 26, 2021.

8. Report by Oxfam, "How much money would it take to end world hunger?", December 9, 2022.

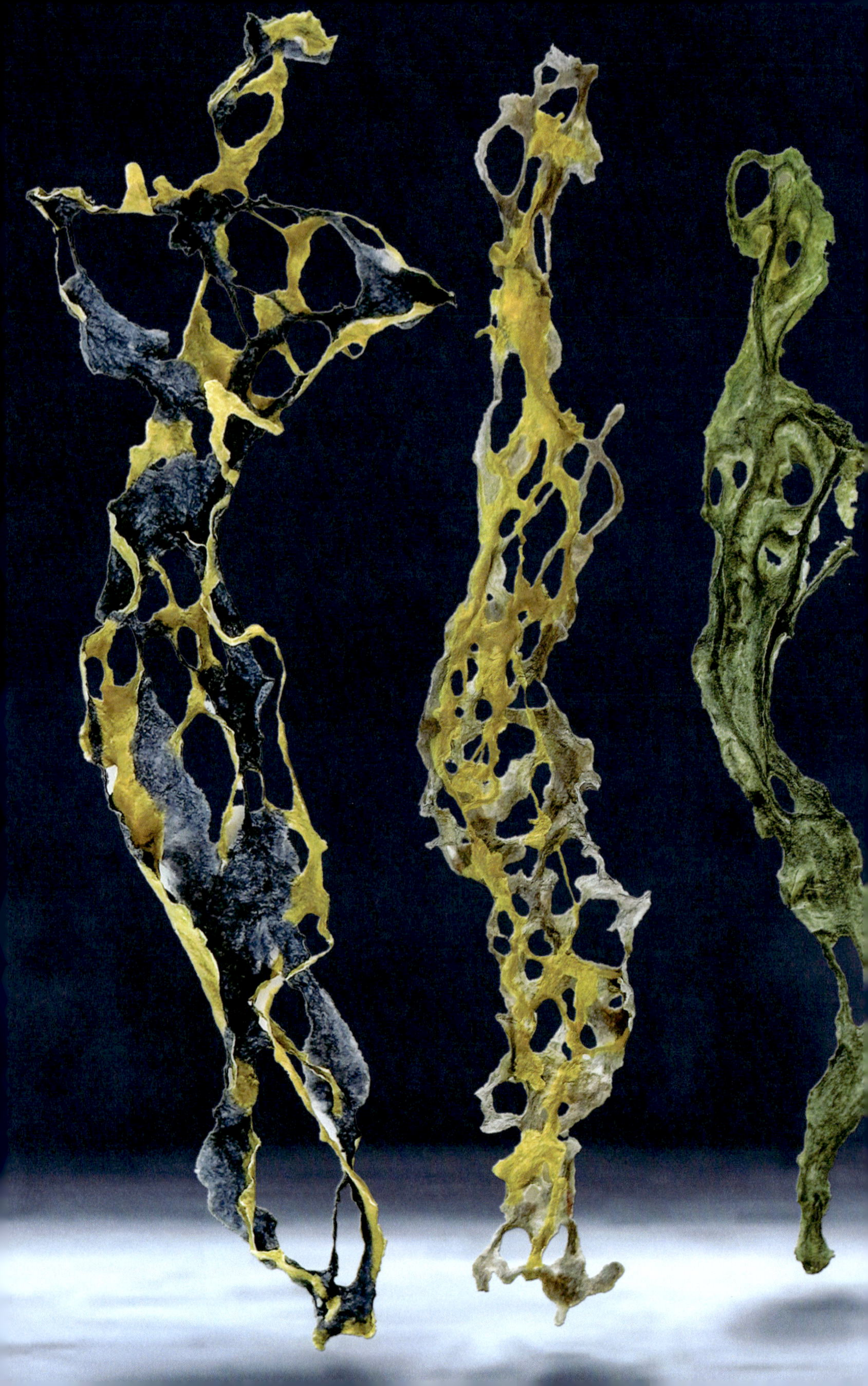

CHAPTER FIFTEEN

The Other

If we have no peace, it is because we have forgotten that we belong to each other.

Mother Teresa[1]

Of all the lessons I've learned, however imperfectly, over my surprisingly long life, none has been harder to grasp completely and hold onto consistently than this: The way to significant human change — in politics, science, education, or in healthcare, you name it — is always the way of love. It feels sticky just to say it, like the pathetic ending to a soap opera.

What's most irritating, I think, is the discovery that it's true. If I'm looking for justice, the way I'll find it is on a pathway of love.

I've explored some alternatives over the expanse of my life. There were spells when I imagined that if only I had more money, I could buy some social change. If only I had more intelligence, I could outsmart the critics and win every argument. If I had the power of the presidency, I could enforce decency and honor in place of what's indecent and dishonorable. When I was being saluted for my 1992 speech, I may have believed for a while that rhetoric was the way to persuasion, and persuasion was the way to justice. And so it has gone, looking in one corner or another for the magic potion that will set things right.

In my experience, none of these things yielded significant change. I can feel rage when I see injustice in front of me, but I can't fix the injustice by force. I can't secure justice by demanding it. I only lose when I try to force my will on others. When I've approached others with love, I've been amazed at the results. A small example: In my early days in the AIDS community, I dreaded meeting Larry Kramer. I was intimidated and frightened by him. But when I approached him gently, lovingly, he embraced me. We spent thirty years loving each other. And Brian, the man who brought me AIDS: When he was dying, we held one another. I assured him of forgiveness. I said "I love you" and heard his whispered "I love you" in return.

Frederick Buechner recounts stories of men being tortured in the dark prisons of Argentina. Some of them actually cared for those who were breaking their bones and scalding their backs. Amazing. "The world is always bewildered by its saints," he wrote. "And then there is the love for the enemy — love for the one who does not love you but mocks, threatens and inflicts pain. The tortured's love for the torturer. This is God's love. It conquers the world."[2] I can just barely imagine such love.

I never signed up to be an activist. I was drafted by a virus, conscripted by forces larger than myself. Once I learned that I was infected, and once I'd determined that I should speak out, I was surprised to learn that I was not just a mom or an artist; I was, and still am, an activist. My primary cause is justice for those impacted by AIDS and this cause spills over into all kinds of other justice-related causes: poverty, gender bias, imprisonment, violence against women, human and civil rights, and more.

What I now believe is that I'm able to win support and sometimes secure change when I come in love. Every other approach has failed.

Discovering The Other.

I suppose it's fairly common at age nineteen to be struggling with one's identity and purpose in life. My father thought, perhaps correctly, that I lacked life goals. He invited me to join him on his next trip to Israel in the late '60s. I agreed.

For seven months I devoted myself to life in Israel. I attended an *ulpan* where I was immersed in Hebrew. It was my first real experience with communal living and learning; mostly, I liked it. I also grew fond of the midwestern American family that had sold their home and moved to Israel to help build the new nation. Both the father and mother were as kind as they were committed. They, too, were being immersed in Hebrew because they intended to make their stay in Israel permanent; they'd need to know the language. But when the time came for them to find a more permanent home in the land for which they had sacrificed everything, they were rejected. Kibbutz after kibbutz denied them. They were committed but they weren't Jewish. They couldn't fit in.

I had never really grasped the system of Jewish citizenship with its biological test for worthiness until I saw that system at work. When I witnessed the non-Jewish family being denied ordinary rights, I saw how The Other could be defined and treated. I heard the whispers, "What if one of *their* children grows up and marries one of *our* children?" I was disbelieving, furious. My activist blood boiled. I called and visited every friend or official I knew.

Eventually, we found a place for the non-Jewish family — a family that was The Other in Israel. The family stayed. I'd become sick and returned to the US to think about The Other and recover from my illness.

Radical Polarization.

It's impossible to watch, hear, or read any current news accounts of life in the United States without smacking into the description of a nation divided by "radical polarization." I suppose it's a fair term, although it leans toward a bleak future with only grim options. I want to believe there are ways we can find something like common ground without a host of references to civil war. I want to claim membership in the Rodney King school of personal relations: "Can't we all just get along?"

The idea of The Other has floated around philosophies for more than a century. It's a term used to capture ways people are different from us, who we want to keep distant because they're not trustworthy, like us. Our group knows The Other doesn't belong; they're different. I, Mary, am who I am. The Other isn't like me. They're like them, not us. So I'm Mary and The Other is Not-Mary.

If we aren't careful with our ideas about The Other, we begin to draw lines of distinction that may be ridiculous. Take South Africa's not-too-distant system of apartheid, for example. It was a racially defined world that divided all human beings into one of three categories: White, Coloured, and Black. Whites had, by law and custom, all human rights. Coloureds were halfway toward justice, but never equal to Whites. Blacks had nearly nothing with which to defend themselves or rise above their assigned place at the bottom of society. Blacks were the essential Other, different from Whites in that they were less than fully human.

We don't have to go overseas to find systems built on Otherness. Look through the eyes of historian Isabel Wilkerson to the century of Jim Crow laws and customs that defined and divided life in the American south. "I remember the exact moment I discovered each insane code of the caste system," she said, "and the absurdities of Jim Crow…: the ban on checkers between Blacks & Whites, separate bibles in the courtroom. Even corpses in the morgue were segregated. It was a sickness."[3] Indeed it was.

Perhaps the most potent American version of Otherness today is found in White Christian Nationalism. Nationalists clamoring for a return to a Christian America that never existed are proof that Jim Crow is sick but not dead. They press hard for a system of Otherness which divides "good Americans" from all others. On one side are grandchildren of European immigrants, Christians — mostly white and evangelical — who want to keep America "pure"; on the other side are immigrant felons who should be denied passage into our nation.

Nationalists hope to cleanse their public schools and libraries of books telling the truth about American history (ask your Native American or Black friends). They perpetuate myths about race — Blacks have more children out of wedlock than whites, or Blacks receive more public assistance than whites — claims that are demonstrably not true. These people imagine that they can create a nation of purity and unity if only they can get rid of liberals, intellectuals, progressives, RINOs (Republicans in Name Only), and People of Color. They constitute one side of our polarized society; I live on the opposite side.

All this becomes personal and painful when I acknowledge that these are my Others. My Other is a truck-driving MAGA fan. I want my gay and lesbian friends to marry and raise their families; The Other wants them to scramble back into the closets "where they belong." I wish the Electoral College didn't exist; The Other adores the imbalance of power the Electoral College protects. The Other contributes time and money to elect school boards and admires Supreme Court justices who have been bought…. And so it goes.

My sense is that, if White Christian Nationalism wins, America loses. We do not return to some imagined Golden Age. We go back, instead, to the glory days of Jim Crow and lynchings. I admire the ideal of embracing The Other; I struggle with actually doing it.

The Wisdom of South Africa.

I once was offered a telephone visit with Nelson Mandela during his declining years. The quarter-century of breaking rocks in the Robben Island Prison off Cape Town had done nothing to dim his mind or diminish his courage. Spending time alone with him was a rare and deeply spiritual experience for me.

I was having coffee in a London airport lounge when I looked across the room and saw Desmond Tutu, sitting alone. I ventured over to thank him for his immeasurable contributions to peace and justice. He was as gracious as possible, asking about my life and work, encouraging me with his words and his smile. I was grateful just to be in his presence.

They're gone now, Mandela in 2013 and Tutu eight years later in 2021. But in the quiet of the night I can still hear their distinctive voices. Their legacies are as bright and hopeful as ever.

Desmond Tutu was frequently asked how he stopped short of hating whites when he was being stomped into the muddy injustices of apartheid. He'd always affirm a "non-racial ideal for our country's post-apartheid future." In other words, he wanted to end all divisions based on race. By holding out this non-racial possibility, he could embrace his Other.

"God's dream," he told the white Afrikaners, "is that you and I and all of us will realize that we are family, that we are made for togetherness, for goodness, and for compassion." He believed it and he preached it. When he saw the end of apartheid approaching, and the angry cries of Black and Coloured crowds demanding retribution for years of oppression, he answered their rage with his core belief: "Without forgiveness, there's no future."[4] He rejected Black superiority just as he rejected white. Neither was superior. The road to equality and justice was paved with forgiveness. Love.

Nelson Mandela spent 27 years imprisoned for his opposition to apartheid. In his imprisonment, his belief in embracing The Other was undiminished. Whether he achieved freedom or not he was certain that, to quote him, a "fundamental concern for others in our individual and community lives would go a long way in making the world the better place we so passionately dreamt of." There it is again: concern for the Other.

They're gone now, both of them. But I'm still here. In the immortal words of Monty Python's *Spamalot*, "I'm not dead yet." I'm alive, but I'm not fully comfortable with the notion of embracing the Other. I listen to a right-wing pundit call for revolution, justified by lies large and small but broadly believed. I just bristle. Then I hear Tutu's sweet alto voice calling me to forgiveness. I don't know if I have it in me.

If there is a model that we could follow to discover a way back to The Other, it may be in one remarkable broadcast of The Rachel Maddow Show (MSNBC). On the evening of Monday, December 4, 2023, Maddow spent nearly a half-hour outlining all the ways her views differ from those of her guest that evening, Congresswoman Liz Cheney.

"We disagree on…everything," said Maddow of Congresswoman Cheney and of her father, Dick Cheney. But after listing in her introduction all the areas in which they disagree deeply — the environment, women's health, voting rights, war, terrorism, guns, and more — Dr. Maddow and The Honorable Ms. Cheney spent the remainder of the program seeking common ground on one issue that let them speak to their Other: the danger of Donald Trump.

What it will take for me to embrace The Other is, I fear, a miracle not of my own making. It will require a degree of humility and courage I do not know that I have. From some unseen force, I need to receive the power to change myself before I reach out hoping to change others. But perhaps I can do this as Rachel Maddow did it: by acknowledging all the areas of profound disagreement, and then seeking common ground honestly, directly, openly, without hostility or rebuttal. If these two women could speak to The Other, why can't I?

I've never shaken the claim that Tutu has on my soul: "Peace comes when you talk to the guy you most hate," he said. And I hear him. But I want justice as I define it, and I want my justice to win against the ugliness of violent fanatics and various forms of dehumanizing prejudice.

Okay. I hear Mandela tell me I need "a fundamental concern for The Other." And Tutu promises that "God's dream is that you and I and all of us will realize that we are family, that we are made for togetherness, for goodness, and for compassion."

It's all well and good. But the uneasy silence in my soul reflects the truth that I have only a frail hold on God's dream for togetherness and a fragile embrace of The Other.

To be clear, if Frederick Douglass were The Other, all the differentness between him and me would mean nothing; it'd be an easy step to embrace this man. But if The Other were the master who whipped Douglass's back into raw meat, I would be hard-pressed to believe that forgiveness with indestructible love is the strategy I most need.

So I look for friends and advisors, wiser women and men who will bolster what I want to do and what I truly want to be. I want in my closing years to be known as one who could embrace The Other — not by erasing what divides us but in spite of all those differences.

What is it that Frederick Buechner said? Oh, yes: "This is God's love. It conquers the world."

Notes to Chapter Fifteen

1. Frequently attributed to Mother Teresa but source is actually unknown.

2. Frederick Buechner, *The Magnificent Defeat* (Harper One, 1985).

3. Isabel Wilkerson quoted in a November 12, 2021, interview regarding her book, *The Warmth of Other Suns.*

4. Farid Esack, *Global Currents,* June 8, 2023, "Desmond Tutu: A Much-Loved, Deeply Disturbed, and Offensive Prophet."

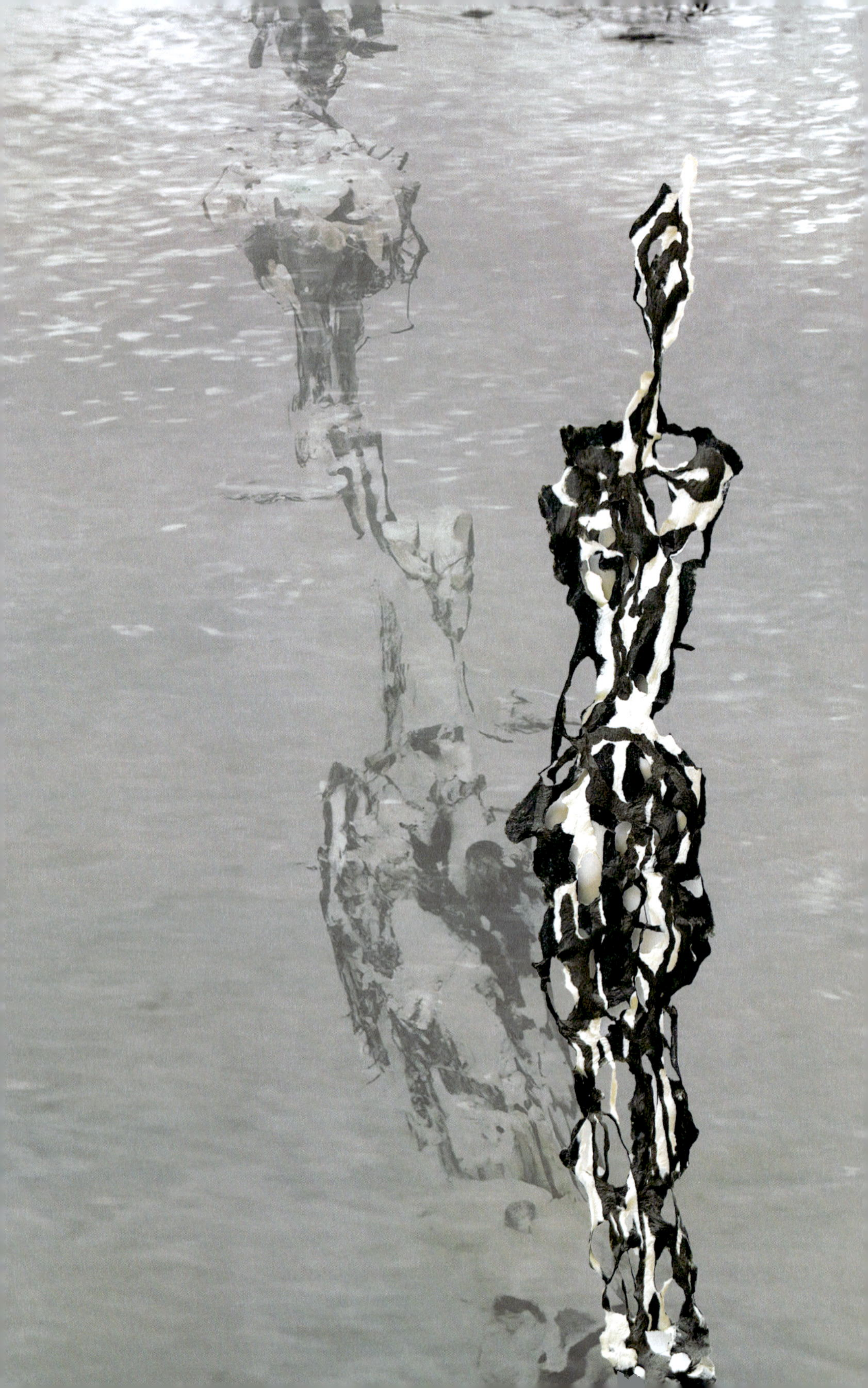

CHAPTER SIXTEEN

Family of Choice

The eternal quest of the individual human being is to shatter his loneliness.

Norman Cousins[1]

It appears from the constant patter of 24-hour news that we Americans are so divided, polarized, and angry that anything resembling a "community" has disappeared. From a social and communal point of view, we're busted.

This isn't where we began. For nearly 200 years, America was a land — as described by our earliest social critic, Alexis de Tocqueville — where we built associations and communities "of a thousand different types: religious, moral, serious, futile, very general and very limited, immensely large and very minute." We knew how to bring folk together for a common purpose, how to uncover our shared needs and how to tackle our communal problems. Together.

Over the past forty years or so, American community-building of almost every sort has gone into reverse. Where once we were adroit at friend-building, during most of my adult life we've been retreating from interactions with each other. Over twenty recent years (2003-2022), the average number of hours of face-to-face

177

socializing by American men decreased by about 30%. For unmarried Americans, the decline was 35 percent. For teenagers, more than 45 percent. We're going in reverse.

One pundit defined "community" as "where people keep showing up." That's not bad. In the mid-1980s culture critic Neil Postman said that, historically, community meant figuring out ways to get along with people who weren't like you. Communities held folk with different and even opposing interests who nonetheless lived in acceptable harmony.[2] In other words, communities were places where we embraced The Other and The Other embraced us.

When I was welcomed in as a member of the American AIDS community in the early 1990s, I was admitted to a place that held people of every stripe. It was enough that either we were dying, we loved someone who was dying, or both. We were collectively warmed by the AIDS Memorial Quilt. When Larry Kramer filled Washington, D.C.'s streets with ACT UP protestors, he spoke for a community.

I'm grateful medications mostly now keep AIDS from achieving its deadly aims for those who have access and can tolerate the medication. But when the dying slowed in the late '90s, and many of the community's elders died as well, a scattering of social programs was all that remained of a once-vibrant community.

There's good evidence that we human beings need community. "Just like hunger and thirst are signals that we need food and water," according to Dr. Stephen Braren, "loneliness signals that we need connection. And this signal is rooted deep within our brain."[3] We've evolved as a species in need of affiliating, bonding, joining, grouping, connecting. It's a basic human need that hungers to be met.

Researchers' numbers tell us communities are disappearing. At the same time, if I examine my own longings, I want to be in community.

For a year or two after I'd become a mother, before I'd become an AIDS activist, I had community in south Florida. It wasn't as ethnically or economically diverse as I might have wished, but a network of young mothers forged bonds that carried us through exhaustion, disappointment, and divorce. When I let them know that I was on the road to AIDS, things changed. A few relationships survived, but not most. There were other communities where I was being called, especially art and artist communities that overlapped with communities of AIDS.

Probably a dozen times in my life I've gone actively looking for a community, usually in groups that shared some spirituality. My trip to Israel in 1968 was inspired at least in part by a desire to find myself in a Jewish community. Nearly twenty years later I experienced community in what Alcoholics Anonymous (AA) calls "a home group." Sedona, Arizona, has been a spiritual center for Indigenous and other communities; I moved there in 2007. A decade later, in the spring of 2017, I briefly moved to rural England to be part of a community there. Between major investments and very high hopes, I regularly thought "I've found it!" only to learn that I had not. My initial enthusiasm ran into realities.

We start life in the community called family. As the daughter of an alcoholic, my childhood and early adolescent experiences at home were often troubling. Throughout my adulthood I may have grasped for community to fulfill what I've failed to find in family: reliable, got-your-back protection in a bonded group of people. Most of the closest relationships I have today are in my "family of choice" — the collection of people who've come into my life and I want never to leave. In this chosen circle of trusted women and men, I've experienced the promise, "We'll love you until you love yourself."

Leaning Toward Isolation.

Judy Sherman, my dear friend since childhood, says that "Years ago, we had it. We had community. We knew each other's names. We cared about the group, not just the individuals. We went to each other's weddings and bar mitzvahs and funerals; we visited in each other's homes; we laughed and cried together…we were a community."

Robert Putnam's classic *Bowling Alone: The Collapse and Revival of American Community* explains what changed. Putnam says we're suffering a "friendship recession," a diagnosis he offered a full two decades pre-pandemic. He notes that American community-building thrived until the 1970s and then, suddenly and without warning, began to decrease. It's been decreasing ever since, driven (according to Putnam) by differences between the generations, television, urban sprawl, and the demand for human time and money.[4]

I want to be careful not to idolize communities. The urge to organize may help create an idyllic village but it may also offer sheets to the Ku Klux Klan. American history is replete with illustrations of community gone wrong, especially for those who are not in the majority such as recent immigrants and People of Color. Isabel Wilkerson reminds us that "African-Americans were mutilated and hanged from poplars and sycamores and burned at the courthouse square, a lynching every three or four days in the first four decades of the twentieth century." The difference between a mob and a community is breathtaking.

During the '90s, as I grew less well and more exhausted, I may have retreated from some offers of community. I wearied of being The AIDS Lady. Every commitment required energy I often didn't have. I was a single mother of two young sons giving fifty to seventy-five keynotes a year. It was easier to say "I need to go home" than "I want to go out." And then, as the years rolled on, I experienced losses that brought grief: Mother died. Daisy died. Siblings withdrew.

A man I'd trusted had been dishonest. Betrayal is its own form of loss.

Then came the COVID-19 Pandemic. I'd just moved to California to be near my children (and, now, grandchildren). The Pandemic and I arrived at nearly the same hour. If the doorbell rang, masks came on. For nearly two years, I never saw a stranger's face. I viewed the outside world through my television screen. If I ventured out at all, I maintained at least the six-foot distance required by health policy. Groups didn't meet. Events were cancelled. My new and faithful daily routine included counting the dead and the dying.

Speeches (including sermons) have been important to me. They've been my primary way to bear witness to the AIDS community's suffering which gives me meaning. But pulpits and podiums also offer emotional value: They let me grieve out loud, in public, until The Pandemic stopped speeches and sermons. I'd already contracted AIDS and cancer. I had no desire to add COVID-19 to the mix. In fact, I was terrified. My best defense against the virus was simple: Hide. So I did.

Cost of Loneliness.

When I went into full-fledged retreat during the Pandemic, I was — however unwittingly — joining a vast majority of Americans who were pulling back from others into their own nests of self-preservation. By May 2023, enough of us were isolating to create "the public health crisis of loneliness, isolation, and lack of connection in our country."[5] According to Surgeon General Vivek Murthy, "Even before the onset of the COVID-19 Pandemic, approximately half of US adults reported experiencing measurable levels of loneliness." Loneliness has consequences: 29% increased risk of heart disease, 32% increased risk of stroke, 50% increased risk of developing dementia; overall, 60% risk of premature death. We need, says Dr. Murthy, to "cultivate a culture of connection."

The Surgeon General's warning was one of many. A 2020 Cigna survey warned of "depressions and suicides" as consequences of isolation. CNN noted that nearly 16 million people aged 65 and older in the US lived solo in 2022, three times as many who lived alone in that age group in the 1960s. Katie Couric reported that

"17 veterans die by suicide every day in our country, and two of the top risk factors are loneliness and isolation." Reports of teen loneliness surged from 36 to 57 percent, and "the share of girls who said they've contemplated suicide increased 50 percent" in the past decade.[6]

The litany goes on and on. What's inarguable is that isolation yields trouble. Failure to have actual, live, human interactions in something that resembles a community will come at a cost of real suffering and real death.

The Beloved Community.

The ideal of life-in-community is part of all my speeches. It litters the pages of my essays and books.

I was in Lusaka, Zambia in the spring of 2013 to dedicate The Mary Fisher Community Centre, a facility I'd helped fund on a healthcare campus where I'd worked with HIV-positive women.

"We've gathered," I said that morning, "to dedicate this Centre to some purpose greater than ourselves…in the hope of what Dr. Martin Luther King, Jr., called 'the beloved community.' It was the kind of community that Dr. King persistently urged us to pursue, in which poverty would have no place, racism would have no quarter and violence would have no purpose."

Across the United States, we now have rallies with inflammatory speeches, hatred dressed up as patriotism, flag-waving, and threats against all who differ from "real Americans." Lynchings don't feel very distant from these rallies.

By contrast, there's the vision that the late Congressman John Lewis kept alive: "When you see something that is not right," said Lewis, "you must say something. You must do something. Each of us must do our part to help build the Beloved Community."

I appreciated columnist David Brooks' recent appeal to see people "with generous eyes, offering trust to others before they trust you. That means adopting a certain posture toward the world. If you look at others with the eyes of fear and judgment, you will find flaws and menace; but if you look out with a respectful attitude, you'll often find imperfect people enmeshed in uncertainty, doing the best they can."[7] I hear this as a call to embrace The Other.

I'm a Jewish woman with AIDS and no theological degrees. But I've never been more at home in community than in Black churches. In September 1993 I stood before the congregation of Birmingham's 16th Street Baptist Church where I preached on the anniversary of the bombing thirty years earlier that had killed four Sunday School girls.

"You and I cannot call God our Father," I said then, "and deny that we are brothers and sisters, Jews and Christians, Black and white, HIV-positive and HIV-negative. When we begin our prayers together, 'Our father who art in heaven,' we will end those prayers in the arms of brothers and sisters — else it is not a prayer we offer. It is a lie."

Let us pray to experience the comfort of that Beloved Community.

Notes to Chapter Sixteen

1. I've found multiple attributions to Norman Cousins, enough to tag him with near-certain authorship. But, in fact, I could not find a citation with his (or another's) name as an original source.

2. Neil Postman, *Amusing Ourselves to Death: Public Discourse in the Age of Show Business* (Penguin Random House, 1985). Postman's book was an expose of the corrosive impact television had on politics and public dialogue, on how we find and speak to one another, and on how we don't. With television now joined by hundreds of other sources of information — the digital platforms that empty into our lives — *Amusing Ourselves to Death* is rightly described as "a twenty-first-century book published in the twentieth century."

3. Stephen Braren, PhD, *The Creature Times*, "The Evolution of Social Connection as a Basic Human Need," May 24, 2023.

4. Robert D. Putnam, *Bowling Alone: The Collapse and Revival of American Community* (Simon & Schuster, 2000).

5. Release from the Office of the US Surgeon General, May 3, 2023, "New Surgeon General Advisory Raises Alarm about the Devastating Impact of the Epidemic of Loneliness and Isolation in the United States."

6. Isolation, loneliness, and resulting or parallel clinical depression was reported in nearly all areas of the US starting in about 2020. That was the year that Cigna issued a report on the topic of growing loneliness. Other sources soon joined in: Data on CNN's *5 Things*, April 3, 2024, cited Gallop findings, and on August 5, 2023, CNN issued a discreet report on the elderly population living alone. Katie Couric's Newsletter, *Wake-Up Call*, on July 11, 2023, reported about suicides among military veterans. Derek Thompson's *Work in Progress* (a digital newsletter) featured a thoughtful February 14, 2024, analysis entitled "Why Americans Suddenly Stopped Hanging Out."

7. David Brooks, *The New York Times*, "How to Stay Sane in Brutalizing Times," November 2, 2023.

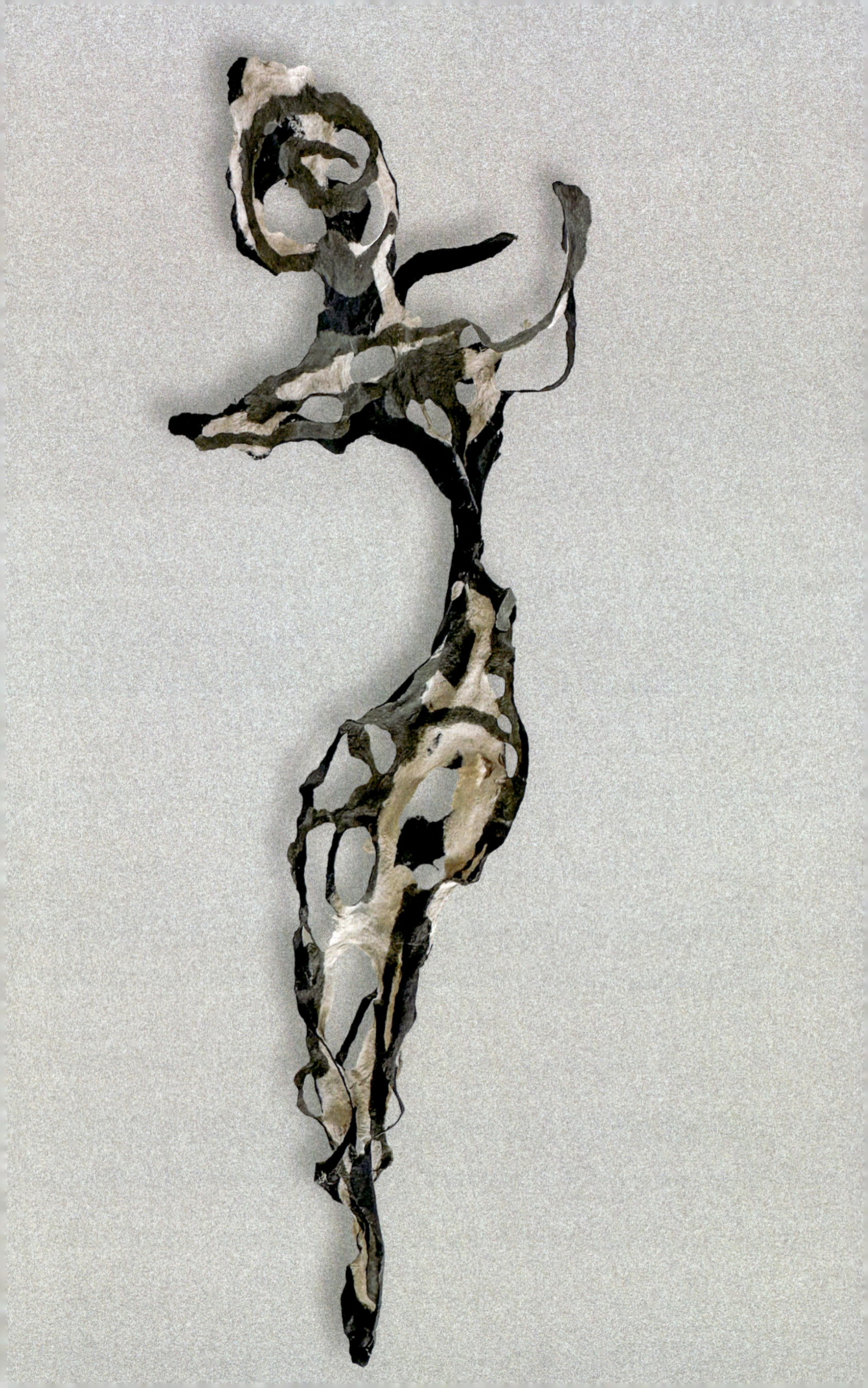

CHAPTER SEVENTEEN

Joy

Service is the rent we pay for being. It is the very purpose of life, and not something you do in your spare time.

Marian Wright Edelman[1]

The COVID-19 Pandemic came without warning, a gloomy cloud of lonesomeness rolling into every American's life.

I'd moved to California days before the Pandemic's alarms were being sounded. Twenty-five years earlier, I'd been an active citizen in the AIDS community, one among many, accepted and even valued. I was part of the informal team, the woman who was called to speak the truth to power. I had a role in the community, and I knew how to fulfill that role. I was a messenger, and I was grateful for it. Subsequently, other communities welcomed me in: an international quilting community, for example.

But as the years rolled by, age and illness took a personal toll on my social interactions. I circled the world a few more times, meeting with government leaders and women with AIDS. But calls for me to speak to a live audience or worship community slowed. I'd paid my own way when giving speeches, contributing any honoraria to charity because I could. I was grateful for every opportunity and every audience because speaking had been my primary mode of bearing witness to the devastation of the American AIDS community, my way of keeping alive those we lost and preserving the truth about brutalities we endured. When invitations to speak slowed almost to a halt, I felt diminished and my sense of purpose wilted.

Then came the Pandemic. It shut down social interactions of nearly every kind, from worship to parades, shopping to funerals. If requests for speeches had previously slowed, now they stopped. Recognizing that speeches were no longer a way to make a difference, I tried publishing essays on various online platforms, including Medium and Substack. My pieces were warmly received. But by the time 75 or 80 essays were circulating, I knew how keenly I missed face-to-face connection with a live audience.

It was 2022. By almost any measure, I did not have a bad life. I had survived COVID-19. I wasn't impoverished. I had grandchildren to wear me out. But my life wasn't satisfying. My interaction with the world was mostly as a spectator, seeing troubling events and noisy people through a television screen. I occupied the sofa. I felt old. Finished. Done.

Project Angel Food.

I'm told that there are more than 60,000 food pantries and charitable meal programs in the US. The one I've known longest and best is Project Angel Food in Los Angeles.[2]

The AIDS epidemic was in full force when I was first introduced to Project Angel Food. The Project had begun in 1989 providing food prepared in the borrowed kitchen of a community-oriented church. Founder Marianne Williamson was supported by a team including David Kessler, Ed Rada, Howard Rosenman, Freddie Weber and a myriad of other committed volunteers.

"We launched in a big church that had lots of twelve-step programs," David Kessler remembered. "We'd take over the kitchen every morning to create meals. People volunteered to clean up, break down the kitchen and put everything away."

From the beginning, food has been delivered to the homes of those too sick, too poor or too frightened to travel. Volunteers followed carefully mapped routes in every kind of weather. Whatever was promised by Project Angel Food was delivered. Always. No promise was broken, no one hungry was left behind.

The Project moved to Sunset Boulevard when it outgrew its church basement and it moved again after more growth. Clients today receive a once-a-week delivery of a week's worth of meals.

As COVID-19 crept deeper into the community, lasting longer than any had anticipated, other food-related programs in the Los Angeles community closed their doors. Project Angel Food accepted their clientele. The number of lunches prepared daily swelled from 1,500 to 2,500 despite threatened revenue short falls and the challenges of the Pandemic's rules (especially avoiding human contact).

Richard Ayoub, Project Angel Food's Chief Executive Officer, began making deliveries himself during the first week of the Pandemic's shut down. As one client accepted his food, he asked

Richard doubtfully, "Will you be back next week?" Richard says he felt a higher power at work when, without hesitation, he said, "Yes, absolutely," having no more than a Field of Dreams conviction that "if we do the work, they'll support us." Richard returned to his office, penned an urgent appeal for funds, and within days had received some 9,000 donations totaling $893,000. He remembers the amount.

Project Angel Food focuses not just on food but on nutrition, creating Medically Tailored Meals designed to the individual nutritional needs of each client. A "Healthy Mornings Program" brings nutritious and tasty breakfasts to the children of health-compromised clients receiving meals.

Project Angel Food still serves a substantial HIV/AIDS population. But it has broadened to serve, with individually designed menus, clients with congestive heart failure, kidney failure, severe diabetes, cancer and Alzheimer's. Nutritionists design the diet for each client, and staff in the Project's kitchen make sure every meal is "worthy": tasteful, colorful, even surprising.[3]

Volunteers are still at the heart of Project Angel Food, providing some 40,000 donated hours per year. In 2019 the Project delivered 650,000 meals; by 2022, they were delivering 1.2 million. Of those receiving meals, the majority are elderly and alone. For many, the visit of a Project Angel Food driver is the only social interaction they'll have each week. "Remember," Marianne Williamson told volunteers nearly 30 years ago, "we're delivering more than food. We're bringing love." This hasn't changed.

Moving into the Community.

During the press of the COVID-19 Pandemic, Project Angel Food's Director of Philanthropy, Mark McBride, visited me with a request for support. I promised to keep helping.

Weeks later, an acquaintance called to ask if I'd join her at Project Angel Food for a "Chef's Dinner." We'd tour the place, she explained, then meet a volunteer or two, listen to a staff member explain the challenges, and go home. Frankly, I was still fearful of the COVID-19 virus but I heard myself offer my caller a reluctant "okay."

On a cool December evening in 2022 I was one of perhaps a dozen guests at Project Angel Food. As promised, we toured the kitchen — immaculate! — and the offices. We heard stories from staff and volunteers. If my mind wandered it was because I was remembering food brought to me in communities that had no food to spare. I recalled meals of *nshima* with AIDS-infected women around charcoal fires in Zambia.[4] I heard David Kessler saying, "Our first act of love in this world is feeding someone, our child." I remembered other evenings around meals in other places where the gay community and the AIDS community were one, embracing me.

When I refocused on what was actually being said in that room, I offered to volunteer my time in the kitchen or wherever I could be useful. Being a donor is fine; it's also solitary. I wanted to become a member of the crew volunteering to serve. These were my people. If they'd let me in — and they have! — this is my community.

Birthdays and Everydays.

On the occasion of my 75th birthday, I invited friends from around the country to come to Los Angeles without gifts but with good shoes for working in the Project Angel Food kitchen. For one glorious afternoon, my tribe and I sliced onions and chopped carrots. We bagged celery and salads. We laughed, we sang, and we knew the simple joy of doing something good for others. It's called "serving."

I've now come to know others who work at Project Angel Food, both professional staff and volunteers. I've spent time with a man of a wrestler's size and a biker's tattoos who volunteers because "I've never been loved like they love me here." My kind of person.

John Gordon, the Executive Chef, says he can only do his job because he's been sober for the past thirty years. "I'm just so grateful for what I'm allowed to do here." Ben Martin, Associate Director of Client Services and Programs, traces his professional journey from lawyering to sobriety to supporting Project Angel Food clients. "I was just very lucky that in my darker years I was never formally unhoused or hungry." John and Ben both identify closely with their clients, working creatively to strengthen what ties this community together.

Around here, lonesomeness isn't necessary. Jeffrey O. has been a client of Project Angel Food for more than twenty years. He says his hero is his father. "He's been gone 27 years. I miss him. He was so proud of me for getting clean and sober." He stays sober, he says, "because with Project Angel Food I don't need to be alone." Kathy S.'s hero was her husband. "He died the day before Christmas. He gave me a life I never imagined I'd have. Now I'm alone. Volunteering lets me be with others. Sometimes I get a hug."[5]

A familiar theme is the impact of earlier-in-life spiritual guidance. Robert C. acknowledges that being raised Catholic developed in him "a real sense of social justice in the church." Dina M. says she volunteers because she "wants to be like the priest I had in my childhood, always fighting for justice." Says client Tony R., "When you're a child who's hungry, you have self-esteem issues. You feel worthless. You wish you could be like everyone else. I remember. But I grew up in church. I learned to be thankful for what I still had." John G. says he "grew up Baptist." Smiling, he adds, "When things get tough, I sing *Amazing Grace*."

Butterflies and Tennis Shoes.

No personal account moved me more than Laura's. She originally came to Project Angel Food working for a contracted cleaning service.

"People say I'm always working," says Laura. "But it's just my way. When my baby sister died in May, I came to work. It's how I grieve. My grieving is that I start working. I'm sad in my heart but still have my job to do. And Project Angel Food is my family. So I came here to grieve and work."

Laura does more than work. She cares. "I buy one guy breakfast at the 7-Eleven and always bring him things. I asked him one time, Do you have shoes? He said no. I had some brand-new tennis shoes at home so I got to bring those to him." She's proud to be a giver in this community, one who serves.

Laura tells of her mother's recent passing. "I thought I'd see her before she died. I was supposed to go home but it didn't work out. I'm sad because I missed her then and now I'll never see her again." She looks away and begins to tremble. "I never cried until right now." Tears are flowing.

After a deep breath, Laura finishes: "So I asked God to give me some confirmation that she knew I loved her. I needed a sign." She's smiling although her voice is breaking. "You know, my mother always loved butterflies. Just loved 'em. Me too. And just then a butterfly came in and landed on my shoulder."

I couldn't help it. I wept with her, sisters in one community.

Angels in the Details.

Given the richness people experience when we're serving others, when we're creating community with love, what keeps so many of us from making the effort to reach out and show that we care? What holds us back?

Torie Osborn, a community organizer I've known for decades, thinks that much of today's lack of person-to-person interaction has risen from our extensive use of social media. "People think they're communicating and relating to one another, but they aren't," says Torie. "They don't ever get out and actually see other people. Then Trump unleashed the worst of our instincts, making them acceptable to the gullible: divisiveness, hostility, anger, racism, sexism, homophobia."

Project Angel Food client Richard E. thinks "folk just don't know how to communicate anymore. We'd like to build community but we really don't know how to talk to each other about anything that matters. So…I guess we just stay home."

Perhaps there's selfishness at work. "People think they're so important that they can't waste their precious time on others," said one of Project Angel Food's long-term volunteers. Said another: "People don't want to be bothered; they're busy."

A close friend thinks "the Pandemic just tore us apart." I agree that's part of the answer.

The response I've heard most often is that we're afraid. Fear tells us that we aren't gifted, we can't really make a difference, no one wants us to help. And the irony is that, as Doug M. learned through volunteering at Project Angel Food, when "I came out of a hard period of my life, I found that helping others was really helping myself."

For the Project Angel Food staff, the key to success with clients isn't mysterious, as Alyssa Baldino, Associate Director of Nutrition Services, explains. "It isn't one thing or another; it's *everything* that generates stress. We need to understand how much stress accompanies poverty," she says, "what it means to be three months behind on your rent. When our driver comes with a week's worth of meals, he may be the only human being that person sees all week. Lack of community, lack of self-confidence, lack of human touch — all the little things accumulate. They build up. We need to watch and listen because 'the angels are in the details' of each person's life.[6] We need to be ready to listen and respond."

The angels were definitely in the details when Tony R., a Project Angel Food client, suffered four strokes and lived despite a diagnosis of post-stroke dementia. "It's so humbling," he says, "losing control of everything, being embarrassed all the time." After a brief pause, Tony says, "But the Project Angel Food people make you feel like you matter anyway, like I have value. I can hardly tell you what that does for a person."

These really are my people, my community. If I originally came in a bit fearful, even a little disbelieving, those uncertainties have been erased. My sense of purpose and meaning has been restored. I'm back to service, back to joy.

John Baackes has led L.A. Care Health Plan for years. He's also been an observer, a board member, trustee, and a fan of Project Angel Food. He describes his long struggle to have Medicaid pay for home-delivered food, thereby offering financial support that wasn't available until the recent approval of payment for Medically Tailored Meals. John lives in Los Angeles, in a community that includes struggles with poverty and illness. Why stay when he could afford to move elsewhere? Because, as he explains, "you have to be part of the community you're serving or otherwise your interest isn't 'community first.'"

Community-building is the aim of Food Forward, one of nearly 200 Project Angel Food community partner organizations. Rick Nahmias, Food Forward's CEO, explains how his organization harvests produce that would otherwise go to waste. Beginning with a few volunteers who "picked what we could" in 2009, his organization now "moves about 250,000 pounds of produce in a single day, about 80 million pounds a year" distributed by a staff "of around 50 and, in a normal year, about 4-5,000 volunteers."

It's impressive. When I told Rick I was in awe of what he's doing, he hesitated a moment and then railed against what he sees as "the most self-centered leadership in human civilization. One 'leader' after another says 'I'm going to screw you before you screw me.'" Rick pauses, then asks, "This is leadership?"

"We have a different model," says Rick. "We see it working every day, building the overall health of communities across Southern California. It's this simple: Put down your iPhone, take something nature has given us and move it to a place of scarcity. The volunteer in the middle finds a sense of peace and reward. The hungry are fed. The community is strengthened."

Leaders don't bark and growl. They serve.

Notes to Chapter Seventeen

1. Marian Wright Edelman, founder and president of Children's Defense Fund and life-long advocate for disadvantaged Americans.

2. Project Angel Food's mission is "to improve health outcomes and end food insecurity for critically ill men, women and children in Los Angeles by preparing and delivering Medically Tailored Meals with compassion and hope." Its motto is "For LIFE. For LOVE. For as long as it takes…" They deliver meals throughout all 4,700 square miles of L.A. County to a population that is 39% Latinx, 24% African American, 23% white, and 14% "other." See *angelfood.org*.

3. Mindy Glazer, one of Project Angel Food's development officers, reports that the combination of age and poverty are complicating the medical and nutritional responses needed while the L.A. population grows older. According to Glazer, "more than 75% of the people we serve need to choose between paying rent and buying food." Most have become poor "because of a single, sudden setback. Their car breaks down. Their part-time job is eliminated. Their partner dies. Their pharmacy closes." One day they're okay, "hanging on by a thread." Something happens. The thread breaks.

4. *Nshima* is a staple in Zambia. It's a thick, lumpy porridge made from finely ground cornmeal, called "mealie meal," eaten with your hands. To eat it, you take a handful and knead it in the palm of your hand to about the size of a golf ball. You press your thumb into the top, making an indentation sort of like a spoon, then scoop up whatever relish is served along with it. You take it in one bite. It's the core of a communal meal I've shared in many women's circles, usually accompanied by much singing, dancing, and laughter.

5. The names of Project Angel Food staff and clients are generally abbreviated to ensure our promised confidentiality.

6. The slogan, "The angels are in the details" preceded the more famous "The devil's in the details." The version offering angels is usually attributed to the French novelist Gustave Flaubert, but the original source is unknown.

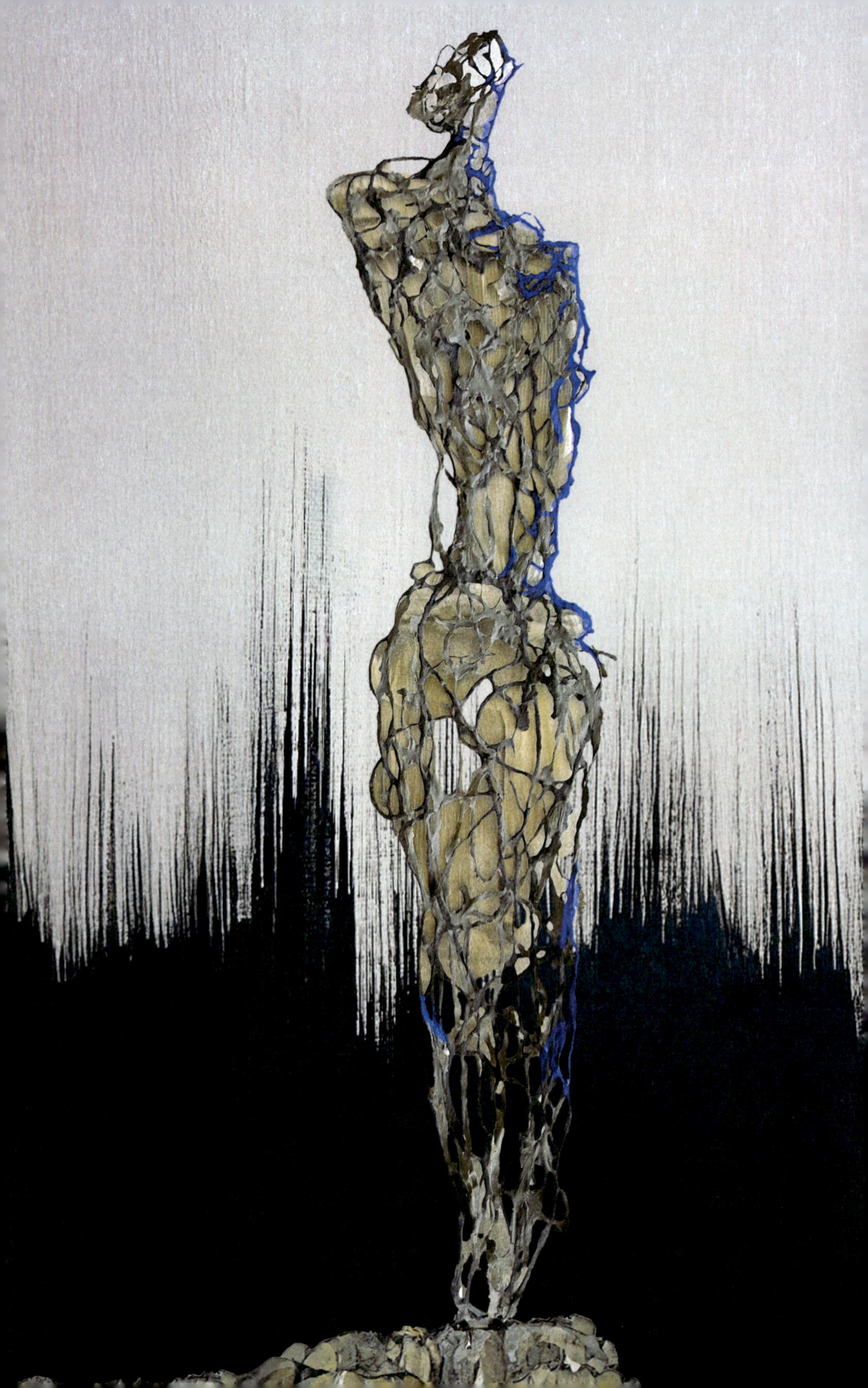

CHAPTER EIGHTEEN

Stand Up!

Develop enough courage so that you can stand up for yourself and then stand up for somebody else.

Maya Angelou[1]

It was an accident. I never intended to be an activist. I was working on being a contented artist when I was found by a tiny virus that changed my life.

When I think of activists, I think of Ida B. Wells (anti-lynching), Malala Yousafzai (girls' education), Opal Lee ("Grandmother of Juneteenth"), or Gloria Steinem (women's rights). Interestingly, none of the activists that come to mind are elected leaders. They don't have lofty titles or huge armies. What they have in common is a strong conviction that something in society needs to change, and change now.

My friend Larry Kramer released *Reports from the Holocaust: The Making of an AIDS Activist* in 1989. I didn't put his book on my reading list. But by the time we met four years later, I knew he was leading a campaign for change in how America responded to the burgeoning AIDS epidemic. I was a quiet mother from Florida who spoke softly in public. He was my screaming colleague, my model of what an activist should be.

I thought of activists as the organizers of marches, authors of diatribes, and firebrand community spokespersons. Larry fit the mold. I clearly did not. But between our first meeting in 1993 and Larry's passing in 2020, I came to see myself as engaged in my own campaign for change.

I had become an activist.

Bearing Witness.

My campaign for change centers on the truth about AIDS and how America responded, and still responds, to this disease. As best I can, I try to tell the truth without exaggeration. I prefer not to take cheap shots at those with whom I disagree, in part because I want their support. If someone is clearly opposed to the truth, I'm willing to call them out. But overall I won't achieve much by irritating those I want to convert.

The United States has never had an official policy of extermination for those hosting the AIDS virus. But the epidemic flourished in the '80s and early '90s owing in part to the intentional inaction on the part of political leadership. Those with the power of the purse strings chose to look the other way while hospices filled with dying young men. Then came Republican President George W. Bush. In his January 28, 2003 State of the Union Address he announced the launch of PEPFAR (The President's Emergency Plan for AIDS

Relief), marshaling private and public funding to slow, and eventually eradicate, HIV in Africa and elsewhere. In its first twenty years, more than $100 billion dollars have been invested in PEPFAR's goals saving no less than 25 million lives. Note: That's 25,000,000 men, women and children. It's no wonder that when I visit Rwanda or Zambia or any AIDS-battered nation, George Bush is seen as heroic and Bill Clinton is remembered for talking a good game."

Bearing witness to these truths has its own power. When Jewish survivors of Dachau bore witness, they told the truth about the cruelties and deaths that permeated the camp. They established on the record the brutality of individuals, some of whom were subsequently prosecuted for their crimes. Without the witnesses who told their own stories, conviction of evildoers would have been improbable. It was the truth, recounted by witnesses, that offered the power of justice.

A new crop of Holocaust deniers has recently sprouted, popularized in right-wing media and aimed at dismissing the truth of six million victims of fascism. Fascism isn't really that awful, they claim. Tortures weren't really severe and malnutrition comes with war. Talk of a holocaust is merely exaggeration by Jews and their sympathizers. Since the Holocaust didn't happen, then we needn't worry about the lies that resulted in the concentration camps: division of the races (Jewish and Arian in Germany, Black and White in the US), establishing that certain groups are not fully human (gypsies in Germany, Black slaves in the US), and so forth. Denying history enables us to deny the impact of the patterns we see being repeated today.

Tour the National Memorial for Peace and Justice (informally known as The Lynching Memorial) in Montgomery, Alabama. Read the narratives describing the conditions of slavery and sanctions of Jim Crow. Stare at the photographs of Black bodies that have been dragged through the streets of rural Mississippi or slashed, branded, and hung in a nearby sycamore. Come face-to-face with the realities of thousands — thousands! — of lynchings used to instill fear and assure obedience. The Memorial bears witness. Powerful, shameful, unforgettable witness.

The State of Florida recently instituted a new educational curriculum in which it is noted that "some slaves developed highly specialized trades from which they benefitted." Claiming that slaves were helped by slavery is absurd. It can only be imagined to be true if we yield to the fallacy of "balanced reporting" in which each of two sides are seen to be of equal importance, accuracy, and usefulness, whether or not they are equally true.

The media has fallen for the fallacy, and someone should quickly and consistently bear witness to the truth.

Lesson Learned.

During the winter of 1991-92 I decided to tell my story publicly because I thought others might learn from it. In me, they could see that AIDS is not a "gay disease," that women are not exempt from the virus, and that AIDS is an illness not a moral failure. I genuinely believed that ignorance was the problem, that if political leaders heard the truth (read: my story) they would no longer be willing to let others suffer.

I was naïve until a few years later when I encountered a wonderful, elderly public health nurse. I met her in Little Rock, Arkansas, in the spring of 1996 when Little Rock's favorite son, Democrat Bill Clinton, was running for re-election. I'd been invited to keynote an AIDS benefit. Before I spoke, awards were being given to various local AIDS champions — including the nurse.

Of the several hundred people in the room, I was probably the only Republican. Everyone was being very discreet. No one mentioned politics or party loyalties. No one, that is, until the nurse was granted the final tribute. She sprinted to the podium, took firm grasp of the microphone, and opened with "I've had it with them dumb Republicans." No one moved while she proceeded to make her point:

> *For fifteen years I've talked to them dumb Republicans. Over and over, I've explained there ain't but three ways you can get AIDS: swap needles or blood, have sex, or get born with it. And for fifteen years, them dumb Republicans kept askin', 'Cain't you get it from mosquitoes?'*
>
> *I'm telling y'all right now that, from now on, I'm gonna' tell 'em, 'Yep, you can get it from mosquitoes. But only in three states: Florida, Louisiana, and Arkansas. 'Cause them's the only states mosquitoes grow so big them Republicans can have sex with 'em.'*

I've learned that Republicans don't have a monopoly on ignorance; they've had more than a few Democrat bedfellows. But my belief that if policy makers *knew* better they'd *do* better, they'd *change*, was fundamentally flawed. Education may change some minds, but not all. Facts matter, even to politicians. But probably not as much as money. Or prejudice. Or flat-out meanness.

The more I recognized the array of challenges faced by the AIDS community, the more directly I took on issues like bias, cruelty, discrimination against women and gays, actual hatred, and tangible fear. I became increasingly willing to make hard points in pointed language.

Anne Lamott tells the story of her friend Father Terry Richey, who once said, "You have to learn not to have a broken heart after learning there are people all over this country who would volunteer to work for free in a death camp."[2] When I started my campaign for change in 1992, I wouldn't have believed that. Today, with the deepest possible regret, I do.

Joy in Service.

I live with an uneasy silence when I think of all the troubles that scar this world. Raped women dare not speak out; someone needs to speak for them. Why not me? Why not now? Abused children are gagged by their abusers. Political "leaders" in Texas and Arizona say they're "in prayer" for survivors of mass shootings and of migrants who were stuffed into a hellishly hot truck and died at the border. And the ghoulish list goes on. I can paralyze myself with the desire to represent every cause and cure every evil. It doesn't work.

According to my friend David Kessler, the first day we met I said to him, "I'd like you to help me die." It told the truth about how I was feeling.

I've changed. The depressive moods have lifted, in part because David helped me see that I wasn't so much "depressed" as "grieving," and that I could live with the grief while finding avenues to joy.

What I need to do is speak clearly using my story to bear witness to the truth that I know. That's all; stop. Now I need to get off the sofa and into serving others if I want to retain some semblance of a grandma's mental health. There's plenty of science that proves helping others helps us. Even without the science, my experience says it's true.

For me, my engagements with Project Angel Food were at least mood-shifting and perhaps life-changing. It's a special joy to belong in a crowd of people happily meeting the needs of others. Peeling an onion isn't saving the world but it may add savor to a meal that would otherwise be bland. Such are the hopes amid the kitchen volunteers, including me. There are tens of thousands of places where you could volunteer. Step up and join the community!

One of my important heroes is Mother Pollard, whose life of service was famous. "For untold decades she had cared for the sick and raised the orphans, Black and white alike," wrote historian Taylor Branch. Like Mother Pollard, my feet are often weary but my soul is rested.[3] Martin Luther King, Jr., two months before he was assassinated, said that he hoped to be remembered as one who "tried to give his life serving others."[4] One by one the people I admire have given testimony not only to the power of service but also to the satisfaction that serving others brings us.

I've long lived with gratitude for my sons, serving them as a mother does. Now I live with the staggering joy of grandchildren, a gift I never imagined I would live to enjoy. They call me to report their important preschool projects. They explain why they're afraid, or why they're ecstatic, using tears and giggles to express it all. They bring light to the darkest day, joy to the hardest moments. They're noisy, busy, and bundles of love.

I feel no sorrow at the recognition that, by the time my grandchildren read this book (if ever), I will likely have transitioned to another world. I hope those I love will miss me but not too severely. I trust that one of you will take up the role of bearing witness for justice. Another might say that I learned joy through service. I hope you'll be willing to speak for those who are unheard in our society because "when you don't have a voice you can't stand up for yourself."[5]

My hope is that we will, all of us, grandchildren and grandmother included, stand up courageously because

> *a man dies when he refuses to stand up for that which is right. A man dies when he refuses to stand up for justice. A man dies when he refuses to take a stand for that which is true.*[6]

Take my hand, let me pull. I want to stand up.

Notes to Chapter Eighteen

1. Maya Angelou, *I Know Why the Caged Bird Sings*

2. Anne Lamott, *Somehow: Thoughts on Love*, Riverhead Books, New York, 2024, pp 183-184

3. Taylor Branch tells this story in his history of the civil rights movement, *Parting the Waters: America in the King Years 1954-1963*:

   Early in 1956, the Alabama bus boycott was failing. No laws had changed; no buses had been integrated. No one was suffering except those who walked.

   Then came a little-known hero from Montgomery's African-American community, Mother Pollard. For untold decades she had cared for the sick and raised the orphans, Black and white alike. Now, in her waning years, Mother Pollard joined the boycott and walked. As the days stretched to weeks, and then months, she walked. When the winter weather worsened, and she began to slip and fall, against the advice of King and others, she would pick herself up, time after time, and walk.

   A meeting was called to consider ending the boycott and finding another means of protest. The crowd was divided between speeches and arguments until Mother Pollard rose to speak.

   'I would rather crawl on my knees than ride on a bus,' she told the hushed and now embarrassed crowd. She spoke of years of humiliation, of self-hatred, of injustice and shame. She noted that the outcome would have little to do with her life, but much to do with the lives of her many children. And then she gave the entire civil rights movement one of its classic refrains when she concluded, 'My feets is tired, but my soul is rested.'

4. From a sermon by King entitled "Drum Major Instinct" at Ebenezer Baptist Church in Atlanta, GA, February 4, 1968

5. Arti Manani, *Seven Sins*, Elephanda Publishing 2020

6. Martin Luther King, Jr., in a sermon the day after "Bloody Sunday" (March 8, 1965) when civil rights protestors were beaten on the Edmund Pettus Bridge

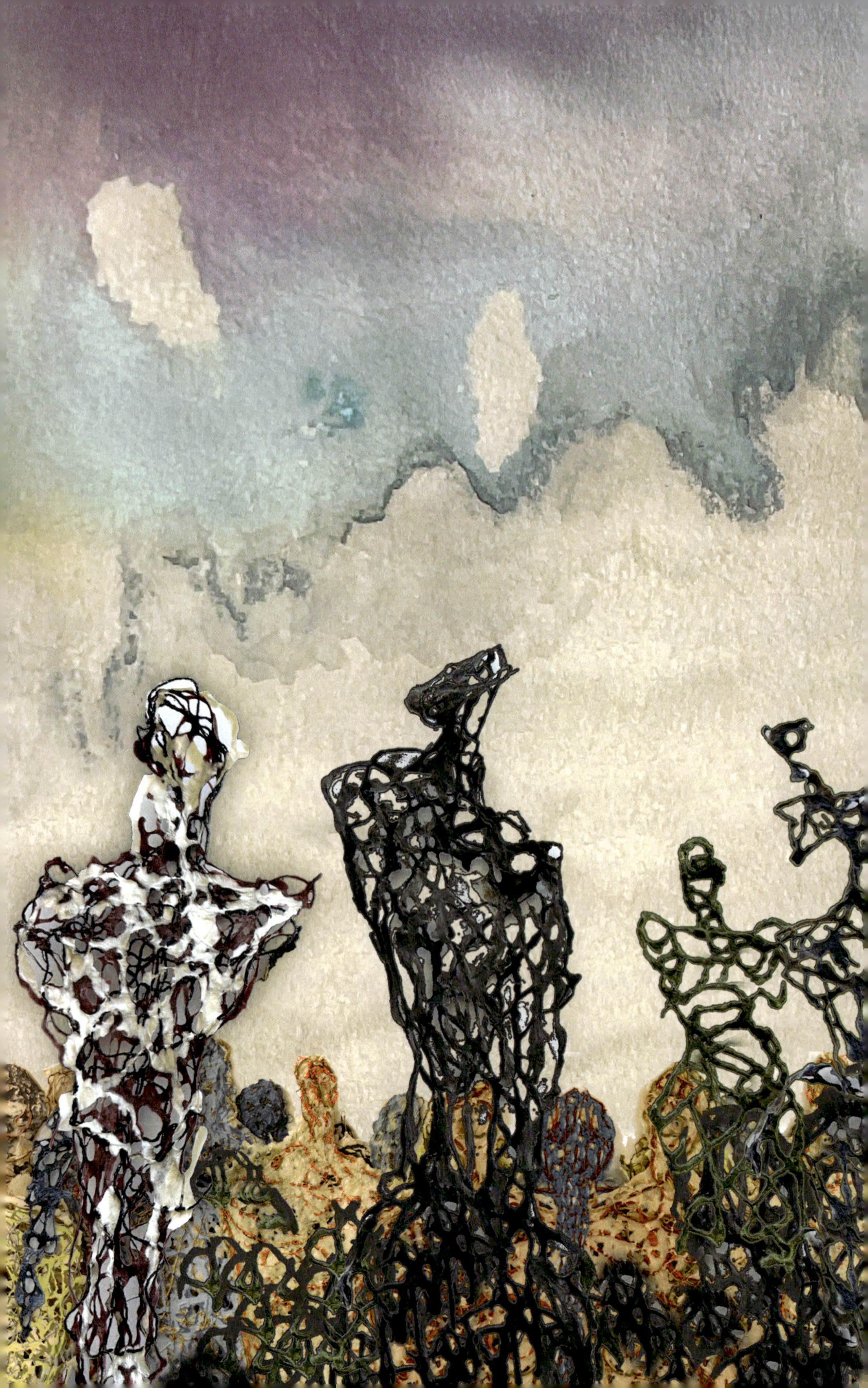

AFTERWORD

The final chapter of this book was put to bed some time ago but I've not yet let it go to print. We're in an election season and it seemed important to know what the voters have to say before I air my ideas. Why? Maybe I've thought that election results will change some of what I've said here. Maybe I'm just nervous about saying in public stuff that's private until I say "Go!"

About elections: I've always cared, always voted, always had strong opinions about local and national leadership. Having served President Gerald Ford as the nation's first woman "advanceman" when he occupied the Oval Office, I care profoundly about that office and who sits there. I genuinely care. Oh, how I care!

But caring about elections doesn't require withholding publication of this book. If I wait for elections to clear out before I make my case in public, I'll never publish. We're nearly always in one election season or another. Decisions made by voters migrate by the day, maybe by the hour. And my thoughts are as valid (or not) the day before an election as they are the day after.

A good deal of thought poured into this book has to do not just with what I want to say but also with what our culture is telling us. Overwhelmingly, the messages I hear being emptied into the American culture is "we don't know." Will inflation erode our savings accounts so severely that we can't win admission to a nursing home? We don't know. Can we trust most institutions? We don't know. With good reason, we doubt the validity of "news" as delivered in social media. We're uncertain about our collective values and divided on what is and isn't "the truth." And so it goes. The times are unstable. Futures are unpredictable. We're living with unprecedented, unsettling, zany cultural chaos.

Just for the record, I'm not running for office. (Not that anyone suggested I should.) Seriously, I busy myself bearing witness to the truth and speaking that truth to leaders who hold power. I don't need your vote. All I need is the courage to stand up for what I believe despite the chaos, and to offer my core beliefs that can't and won't change with the winds of politics.

I was supposed to die in my forties. That didn't work out, as you can plainly see. But I never anticipated that I would grow so old and still be capable of thought. At times, I doubted that I could really make a difference. But more than half-way through my eighth decade I discover that I'm more committed to advocacy for justice and compassion than ever. Given the opportunity, I'm a more fierce advocate today than I was when younger. If I've irritated some power brokers, tough. What are they going to do to an old woman?

I began work on this book because I wanted one more good shot at inviting others to join me. The communities I know are starved for individuals who will bear witness to the truth whether it is popular or unpopular, who will offer leadership whether it's rewarding or taxing. In the words of Maya Angelou that open the book's final chapter, we're called to develop enough courage to stand up for ourselves and then stand up for somebody else.

I'm convinced that Angelou is right: It's all about somebody else. Life is full of meaning when we focus not on ourselves but on others. He or she is not the enemy, no matter what political ads may tell us. Differences in belief or practice are only that; differences. They aren't felonies. Especially when we consider the struggle of immigrants we need to proclaim, loudly, that they are not unAmerican. On the contrary, there's hardly anything more American than an immigrant seeking refuge in the Nation of Dreams: America, built by immigrants.

I long for the day when we experience our differences as gifts contributed to the whole of us. All that's needed is a strategy for coming together to resolve problems as deep as poverty and as old as hunger. We need to care enough to get the work done.

I believe that the first step toward change is the conviction that each of us matters. If we do nothing, we're wasting our life's purpose. Knowing we matter, we can yawn at every sunrise, grateful that we're equipped to make a difference, small or large. Tiredness and illness slow us down. Age has its challenges. But no excuse justifies failing to treat the stranger as my neighbor. No matter what, so long as I am alive I want to stand up for those unable to stand for themselves, to bear witness to the courage of all who demonstrate their integrity through service to others — no matter our histories of uneasy silence.

It's enough. Join me in a commitment to build communities rich in justice and compassion. There's great joy to be found in meeting a neighbor's needs and serving a righteous cause together. Over the moans of those who suffer and the noisy promises of slick politicians, despite all the chaos, there's laughter to be shared and satisfaction to be enjoyed.

That's enough. It's time. Let's go!

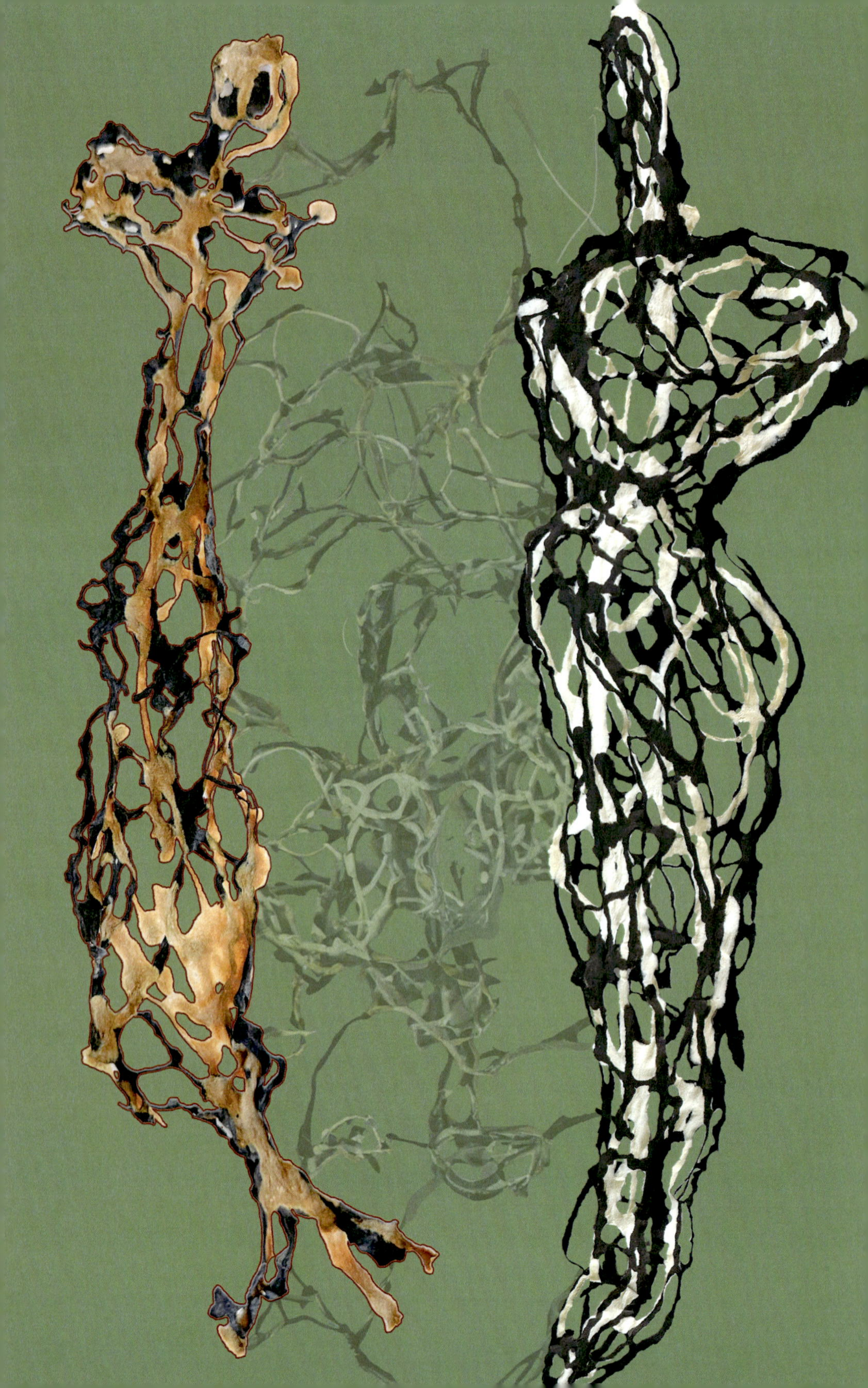

Acknowledgments

The people named in my stories are mostly alive. I hope they'll forgive any trouble I cause by naming them here. To protect promised confidentiality, a few are cited using only their first names or initials. But mostly I've named names. And I owe a public acknowledgement to several friends without whom my life narrative would have almost certainly ended earlier and differently.

To all who have generously spoken and written about this book, including many who are unnamed, my immense gratitude.

To Jennifer Reddington, who has with patience, wisdom, and grace, made this book — and so much more in my life — possible.

To David Kessler, Scott Beinner and Stacey Beck, three people who've brought insight and joy to my life in remarkable ways, and whose wisdom I've scattered throughout these pages without giving them credit, my most profound thanks. Together with Judith Light, Anne Emerson, Joy Anderson, Kathleen Glynn, Joy Prouty, Torie Osborn, Jan Silverman, and Chris Kocielski, they have coaxed me into laughter in the hardest times and lifted me with kindness and grace when I was down for the count.

To Patrick Fallon, Holly Ward Bimba, Patricia Abt, Jan Beaney, Jean Littlejohn, Jane Dunnewold, and Raashan Ahmad, my thanks for demonstrating that art can carry us through the most arduous journey.

To Judy Sherman and Stuart White, both of whom have been faithful friends since we were school mates sixty years ago, thanks for sticking with me.

To Jacqueline Miller, Bethany Goldberg, Scott Mahoney and the leaders of Project Angel Food (Richard Ayoub, Mark McBride, Brad Bessey, my fellow board members, and the amazing volunteers), my thanks for reminding me that life finds its meaning through service.

To those elected public servants who've visited with me, my thanks for the private modesty and the public courage with which you serve a sometimes hostile nation.

To doctors Michael ("Mike") Saag and Raphael ("Raphy") Landovitz, my hope you've heard my appreciation for keeping me physically and emotionally alive while comforting me with your brilliance and your tenderness.

To Sally Fisher, who I doubted when she told me decades ago that the world was waiting for me, and to Willa Shalit and Jim Heynen who helped shape every page of this book — my thanks.

Beyond all else, thanks to my sons Zachary and Max, to my daughter-in-law Natasha and to my grandchildren. Thank you for making me what I never imagined I could be: a grateful mother and a doting, loving grandmother. You are my greatest joys and my greatest teachers.

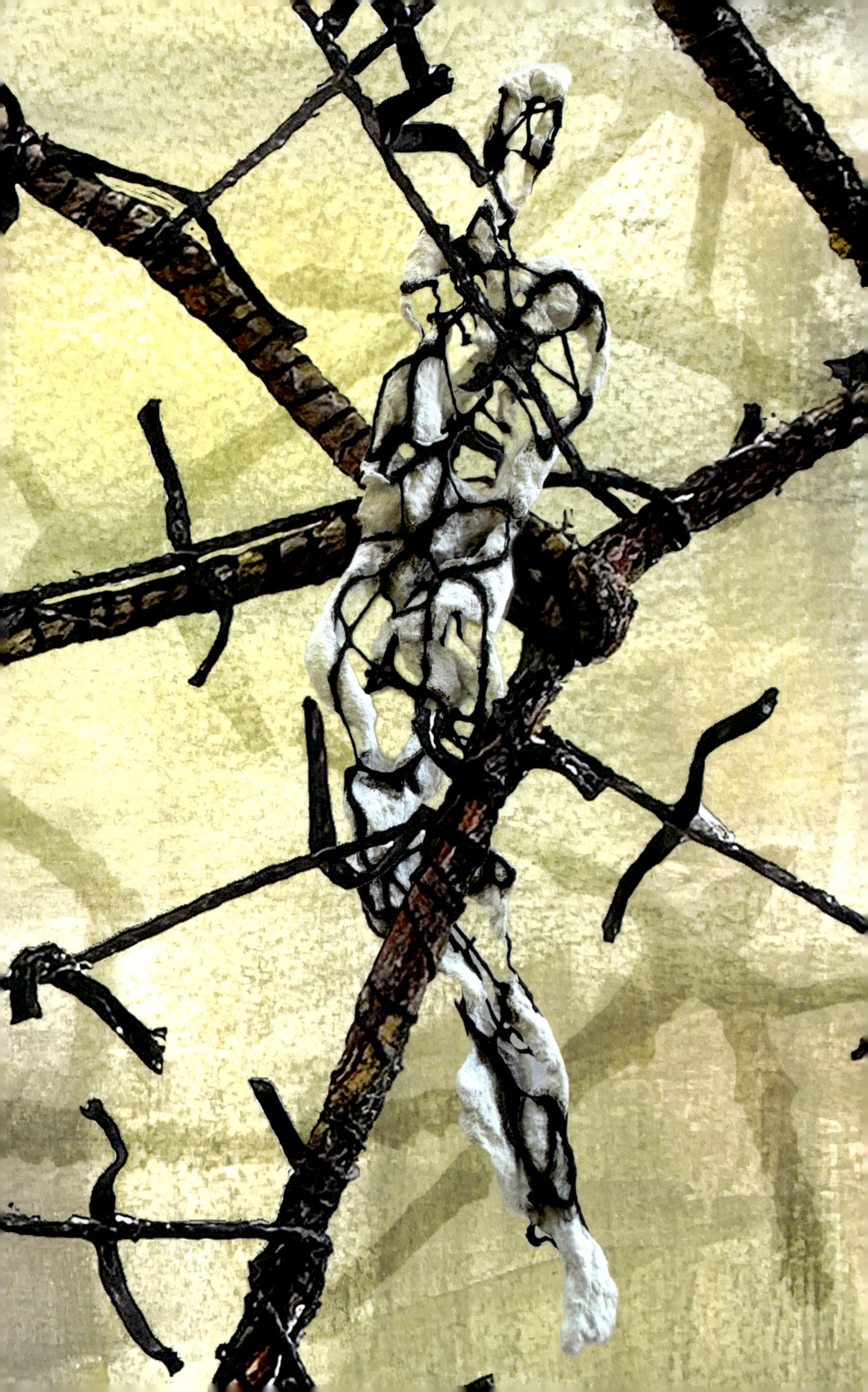

Bibliography

Maya Angelou, *I Know Why the Caged Bird Sings*, Random House, New York, 1969

Kenny Ausuble, *Dreaming the Future: Reimagining Civilization in the Age of Nature*, Chelsea Green Publishing, White River Junction, VT, 2012

Robert N. Bellah, ed. *Habits of the Heart: Individualism and Commitment in American Life*, University of California, Oakland, 1986

David W. Blight, *Frederick Douglass: Property of Freedom*, Simon & Schuster, New York, 2018

Taylor Branch, *Parting the Waters: America in the King Years 1954-63*, Simon & Schuster, New York, 1992

Also, *Pillar of Fire: America in the King Years, 1963-65*, Simon & Schuster, New York, 1998

David Brooks, "How to Stay Sane in Brutalizing Times," The New York Times, November 2, 2023

Patrick J. Buchanan, *American Rhetoric: On-Line Speech Bank*, www.americanrhetoric.com, Address to the Republican National Convention delivered August 17, 1992

Frederick Buechner, *The Magnificent Defeat*, Seabury Press, New York and Cambridge UK, 1966

Jim David, ed., *The Great Dechurching: Who's Leaving, Why Are They Going, and What Will It Take to Bring Them Back*, Zondervan, US, 2023

Max De Pree, *Leading without Power: Finding Hope in Serving Community,* Jossey-Bass, San Francisco, 1997

Matthew Desmond, *Poverty, by America,* Random House, New York, 2023 Also, *Evicted: Poverty and Profit in the American City,* Crown Publishers, New York, 2016

Frederick Douglass, *Narrative of the Life of Frederick Douglass* (1845 Edition), Printed by Amazon

Vijay Eswaran, "Don't Underestimate the Power of Silence," *Harvard Business Review,* July 22, 2021

Jeremy K. Everett, *I Was Hungry: Cultivating Common Ground to End an American Crisis,* Brazos Press, US, 2019

Viktor E. Frankl, *Man's Search for Meaning,* Beacon Press, Boston, 1959 Also, *Yes to Life: In Spite of Everything,* Beacon Press, Boston, 2019

Amanda Gorman, "The Hill We Climb," written for and read by Ms. Gorman at the Inauguration of President Joe Biden, January 2021 Also, *Call Us What We Carry,* Viking Press, New York, 2021

Steven Hassan, *The Cult of Trump: A Leading Cult Expert Explains How the President Uses Mind Control,* Free Press, New York, 2019

Robert B. Hubbell, *Today's Edition Newsletter,* Self-Published, February 14, 2024

Ibram X. Kendi, *How to Be an Antiracist,* One World Random House, New York, 2019

David Kessler, *Finding Meaning: The Sixth Stage of Grief Workbook,* Bridge City Books, 2024
Also, *Finding Meaning: The Sixth Stage of Grief,* Scribner, 2019
Also, *You Can Heal Your Heart: Finding Peace After a Breakup, Divorce, or Death with Louise Hay,* Hay House, 2015
Also, *Visions, Trips and Crowded Rooms,* Hay House, 2010
Also, *On Grief & Grieving: Finding the Meaning of Grief through the Five Stages of Loss with* Elisabeth Kübler-Ross, Simon & Schuster 2005

Also, Life Lessons: Two Experts on Death and Dying Teach us about the Mysteries of Also, Life and Living with Elisabeth Kübler-Ross, Simon & Schuster 2001
Also, The Needs of the Dying: A Guide for Bringing Hope, Comfort, and Love to Life's Final Chapter, HarperCollins 1997 and 2007

Matthew Killingsworth, *Penn Today*, Wharton School at the University of Pennsylvania, 2023
Martin Luther King, Jr., *Transcript of an Evolving Sermon* entitled "On Being a Good Neighbor," preached sometime between July 1, 1962, and March 1, 1963
Also, *Why We Can't Wait,* Penguin, New York, 1964
Also, *Transcript of a March 8, 1965 Sermon* delivered in Selma, Alabama the day after "Bloody Sunday" on the Edmund Pettus Bridge.
Also, *Transcript of a February 4, 1968 Sermon* entitled "Drum Major Instinct," delivered at Ebenezer Baptist Church in Atlanta, Georgia

Transcript of a March 8, 1965, Sermon delivered in Selma, Alabama the day after "Bloody Sunday" on the Edmund Pettus Bridge.
Also, *Transcript of a November 1967 Sermon*, "The Trumpet of Conscience," delivered in Montgomery, Alabama
Also, *Transcript of an Evolving Sermon* entitled "On Being a Good Neighbor," preached sometime between July 1, 1962, and March 1, 1963
Also, *Why We Can't Wait,* Penguin, New York, 1964
Also, *Transcript of a February 4, 1968, Sermon* "Drum Major Instinct," delivered at Ebenezer Baptist Church in Atlanta, Georgia

Elisabeth Kubler-Ross, *On Death and Dying*, Collier Books/Macmillan Publishing Co, New York, 1969

Anne Lamott, *Almost Everything: Notes on Hope*, Penguin Random House, New York, 2018

Also, *Somehow: Thoughts on Love*, Riverhead Books, New York, 2024

John Lewis, *Across that Bridge: A Vision for Change and the Future of America*, Grand Central Publishing, New York, 2017

Elise Loehnen, *On Our Best Behavior: The Seven Deadly Sins and the Price Women Pay to Be Good*, Bench Road LLC, 2023

Stephen E. Lucas and Martin J. Medhurst, eds, *Words of a Century: The Top 100 American Speeches, 1900-1999*, Oxford University Press, New York, 2009

Katie S. Martin, *Reinventing Food Banks and Pantries: New Tools to End Hunger*, Island Press, 2021

Heather McGhee, *The Sum of Us: What Racism Costs Everyone and How We Can Prosper Together,* One World, Penguin Random House, New York, 2021

Jon Meacham, *His Truth Is Marching On: John Lewis and the Power of Hope*, Random House, New York, 2020

Sabrina Medora, "The Use of Food as Religious Symbolism," blog, www.feedthemalik.com, January 19, 2022

Neil Postman, *Amusing Ourselves to Death*, Penguin Random House, New York, 1985

Robert D, Putnam, *Bowling Alone: The Collapse and Revival of American Community*, Simon & Schuster, New York, 2000

Sarah L. Quinn, *American Bonds: How Credit Shaped a Nation*, Princeton University Press, New Jersey, 2019

Arundhati Roy, *The God of Small Things,* Random House, New York, 1997

Quentin Schultze, "Communicating for Life," *Reformed Journal*, December 20, 2023

David Treuer, *The Heartbeat of Wounded Knee: Native America from 1890 to the Present*, Riverhead Books, New York, 2019

Sheldon Vanauken, *A Severe Mercy*, Harper, San Francisco, 1977

Brian J. Walsh, ed. *An Ethos of Compassion and the Integrity of Creation*, University Press of America, New York, 1995

Elie Wiesel, *The Night Trilogy: Night, Dawn, The Accident,* Hill and Wang, New York, 2008

Isabel Wilkerson, *Caste: The Origins of Our Discontents*, Random House, New York, 2020

Also, *The Warmth of Other Suns: The Epic Story of American's Great Migration*, Vintage Books, New York, 2011

Interviews

Richard Ayoub, July 2023
John Baackes, August 2023
Alyssa Baldino, June 2023
Mindy Glazer, July 2023
John Gordon, June 2023
David Kessler, July 2023
Elise Loehnen, July 2023
Doug M., July 2023
Robert Cliff-Malagon, June 2023
Ben Martin, June 2023
Dina M., July 2023
Laura Martin-Marsh, June 2023
Rick Nahmias, August 2023
Torie Osborn, July 2023
Sarisa R., July 2023
Kathy S., July 2023
Judy Sherman, July 2023
Tim Troester, June 2023

Confidential interviews with Project Angel Food Contacts
Jean B., July 2023
Richard E., July 2023
John G., July 2023
Jeffrey O., July 2023
Tony R., July 2023
Gregg S., July 2023

www.ingramcontent.com/pod-product-compliance
Lightning Source LLC
Jackson TN
JSRC080725240325
81203JS00024B/5